THE TROUBLE WITH TINSEL

a novel

JULIET GIGLIO & KEITH GIGLIO

sourcebooks
casablanca

Copyright © 2023 by Juliet Giglio and Keith Giglio
Cover and internal design © 2023 by Sourcebooks
Cover illustrations by Guev

Sourcebooks and the colophon are registered trademarks of Sourcebooks.

Published by Sourcebooks Casablanca, an imprint of Sourcebooks
P.O. Box 4410, Naperville, Illinois 60567-4410
(630) 961-3900
sourcebooks.com

Cataloging-in-Publication data is on file with the Library of Congress.

Printed and bound in the United States of America.
VP 10 9 8 7 6 5 4 3 2

To Ginny,
who loved stories,
and lived an amazing one.

CHAPTER 1

November 26

KERRI WRAPPED HER CHILLY ARMS in the airplane-issued first-class cashmere blanket and snuggled into seat 2B. *To be or not to be,* she thought to herself. Her eighth graders were studying Hamlet, the most indecisive character in the history of literature, and someone to whom Kerri related deeply. But she must have made one good decision, because why else would she be lounging in first class, where everything was superior—from the selection of current movies that were still in the theaters to the delectable fresh food, to the endless hard alcohol drinks served in crystal glassware. *Enjoy it,* she thought, *because this won't happen again.*

She nodded hello to the guy next to her. He looked like he was in "the business" as they called it in Los Angeles. He was Hollywood handsome with a script on his lap and a phone to his ear.

"I'm halfway through the script. I love it. I'll call you when I'm done," the guy said. Kerri surmised he had no intention of finishing the script and watched him wave to the flight attendant, who rushed over.

"What can I get you, sir?"

"A Bloody Mary. And can you toss this in the trash? It's stinking up the plane," he said, handing her the script. She took it and disappeared behind a curtain, along with the script he lied about loving. Yep, that was the LA she remembered, and it was personified by the handsome hunk sitting right next to her in first class. He gave her a sparkling grin.

"Looks like we're plane buddies," he said. "Drew Fox. Nice to meet you."

"Kerri."

"Visiting family?"

"Working."

"Are you in the business? Are you an actress?"

"High school teacher."

"You sure you're not an actress? You look like you could be an actress." He smiled.

Kerri suppressed the urge to roll her eyes. She would need a couple of those little bottles of liquor to deal with this guy next to her, and what was waiting ahead. She flagged down the flight attendant and asked for a screwdriver. *An actress!* She chuckled to herself and thought about film school, when she had played a small part in a friend's student film. She had not been able to remember her lines and had ruined every shot. Happily, that was the extent of her thespian experience. Her phone vibrated, and she noticed it was a call from Beau. She still thought it funny that her beau was named Beau. She answered.

"Hey, I just boarded." She didn't want to mention how much she was enjoying first class. Beau had an issue with anything that was first class. He liked to think of himself as a member of the proletariat, when in fact his parents were quite wealthy. But that was wealth that hadn't been shared with Beau ever since he'd rejected their offer of joining the family investment firm in favor of an architectural firm where he was a rising architect.

"Just want to say have a great week. Good luck with *him.*"

Him was Jon. Her old boyfriend and writing partner.

As much as Kerri had wanted to shield Beau from her past life in LA, she felt inclined to tell him, given that they were now engaged. She fiddled with the stunning engagement ring Beau had given to her five days ago. Kerri knew that Beau wasn't even remotely jealous about Jon. In fact, he was thrilled that Jon and Kerri were working together again, because the movie money would give them enough cash for a down payment on a condo in Williamsburg. He was proud of his successful fiancée.

Kerri settled into her seat and turned toward the window, determined to ignore Drew Fox sitting next to her. She had decided she was going to enjoy this week, rewrite the script she and Jon had written that was now inching toward production, head back to Brooklyn, and direct her students in their holiday show. She knew she didn't want to go back to her old life. Especially not with Jon. She nodded off.

"Hey," Drew said while flying somewhere over Indiana. "This is you."

Kerri opened her eyes and struggled to get her bearings. Then she saw Jon. On the tablet Drew was holding up. She took the tablet from his hands to see the headline of *Variety*, the Hollywood newspaper. There it was: AMARI TO STAR IN FIRE AND ICE above an article about the script and how it was going into production. Below that was a large picture of Amari, and below that a smaller picture of the writers. They must have gotten it from Jon. It was the picture they had used for their first Christmas card.

Kerri and Jon wore matching Christmas sweaters while clutching hands and smiling happily at each other. Kerri rolled her eyes at the photo.

"This is cool. I guess Christmas came early for you this year," Drew said.

"Thank you," Kerri said, returning the device as fast as she could.

"Or maybe it didn't."

"What do you mean?"

"You can't tell anyone I said this, but I produced a movie that starred Amari. Just a warning: she can be kind of intense on a set. It kind of killed a relationship I was in. Good luck with her," Drew offered.

"Thanks."

Kerri ordered more vodka and OJ. She was going to need a lot of cocktails to get through the next week. She took the script out of her travel bag and was determined to read it again, for the first time since she and Jon had written it several years ago.

There on the title page: FIRE AND ICE BY KERRI WILLIAMS AND JON ROMANO. It was a comedy about a Beverly Hills celebrity who is rescued by a working-class San Fernando Valley firefighter. People from two different worlds fall in love. She and Jon had poured everything they had into that script. Via their agent, they had hired an actor dressed as a firefighter to deliver the script to producers, and it had worked. The buzz had been incredible, and everyone wanted to meet them so that they could gush over how good the writing was. Kerri remembered her heart swelling each time that a producer praised them, but ultimately no one bought it. The experience had crushed Kerri so much that it became the last script she had ever written—period—with Jon or by herself. A few months later, their personal relationship was also kaput. Now, the script that had broken them apart was bringing them back together. The pilot announced the plane was on schedule to arrive in Los Angeles. Their final destination. *Los Angeles is not my final destination,* she thought. It was once. But things change. *I've changed.* The idea of leaving getting-colder-each-day Brooklyn and going back to getting-sunnier-by-the-minute Los Angeles did not fill her with cheer. Maybe it once did. But now, three years after returning to New York, she had forgotten how to be a Los Angeleno. Not that she ever was one. Brooklyn was her home and always would be. Hollywood Hills? Ha. A sad sequel. No, her plan was simple: to get in, do the job, and get out before they sucked her back in. *Just when I was out, they pulled me back in,* Kerri thought. Her movie mind was now activated. Like a Sleeping Beauty kiss, her screenwriting career had been awakened. Not by Prince Charming, but by Jon.

Kerri had been stunned by the circumstances that led her to fly first class to LA. It started a few months ago with an email from Jon. Then another email. From Jon. And then a phone call. She remembered thinking: *Who calls anyone these days, anyway? People text to communicate. People email to provide appointment details. People only call with bad news.* But the call she got from Jon wasn't really bad news. At one time in her life, she would have been sipping champagne with friends celebrating the really good news Jon had told her.

"It's happening. I need you to come back to LA," her old life and old love had said on the phone a few weeks before Thanksgiving.

"I'm kind of busy back here. I have a job. One that pays money," Kerri had told him. She did. She was teaching drama to eighth graders at Williamsburg Prep. She loved her job. She felt horrible that she had to leave them just as rehearsals were about to start for the holiday show. She loved her "now" life.

"This job will pay a lot more. Come on, Kerri, this is what we worked so hard for. This is what we dreamed of."

"I don't know," she said to Jon.

"I can't do it without you. They want us both for the production rewrite. If you don't do it, the deal is dead."

Now on the plane, Kerri took a deep breath and told herself that she could do this. She realized she was dealing with a first class problem most of her film school friends would kill for, and she knew she was being ridiculous. Then she did what she always did when she felt stressed, and started to meditate. She closed her eyes and imagined everything going smoothly with the movie, with Amari, with Jon. Meditation and vodka were always a good combo.

That was when the plane hit the worst turbulence ever (according to the producer next to her). Kerri's drink flew into the air, spilling all over her pants and her script. First class service was temporarily closed.

CHAPTER 2

November 26

JON LOOKED AT HIS PHONE and groaned because his Uber rating was sinking. When he sold the *Fire and Ice* script two months ago, he had removed his blue Uber placard from his windshield, thinking his days as an Uber driver were over. Feeling triumphant about his new movie deal, he ripped up the placard and threw it away. He had absolutely no doubt that he'd ever need it again. But then the check for *Fire and Ice* didn't come that first week. When he called his agent the second week, his hands sweaty and his heart pounding while he looked at his bank account online, his agent calmly told him that the money wouldn't arrive until the first day of production, which in truth, was only five weeks away, but it wasn't soon enough for Jon. He had used the upfront option money to pay his monthly student loan payment, his overdue rent, and his credit card bill. He sadly realized that he was going to have to get back in the Uber driving business. He had sighed deeply as he positioned a new Uber placard to his windshield. This was going to be his Uber job 2.0.

The first time around, he'd embraced the life as an Uber driver and had made it fun. He had relished giving out water and little snacks and creating different playlists, which included hip-hop for young adults, classic rock for anybody over thirty, and for anyone over sixty, his fail-safe had been a classical playlist filled with Mozart and Bach. All those extra touches had served him well, and he had bragged about his perfect Uber score to all his friends. But now that he'd returned to driving, he had stopped caring. As far as he was concerned, it didn't matter how thirsty his customers were, and he looked the other way if someone was wearing a freshly pressed suit in his car that was no longer immaculately clean. Now he drove around listening to the news, so there were also no more specialized playlists. As a result, he had watched his Uber score plummet.

Jon arrived at LAX, passing the colorful lit-up columns and towering palm trees. He was hoping to intercept the budget-conscious Kerri and surprise her. He figured she'd be thrilled to get a free ride and not have to splurge for a cab, so he parked his old blue Mazda convertible and hustled into the airport. He'd made several homemade signs struggling to decide between WELCOME BACK and WELCOME HOME. He thought *home* might present the wrong connotations, as if he wanted her to move back to LA and be with him. He settled for WELCOME BACK. He wiped his sweaty palms on his pants and checked his breath while he shifted his weight back and forth. The limo driver next to him noticed. She was short, with blonde hair, dressed in a suit and sharp as a knife. Her name tag said PAULA.

"You're waiting for someone on the flight from New York?" Paula asked, knowing the answer.

Jon nodded.

"You can relax, the plane's landed."

That only made Jon more nervous. He smelled his armpits. Paula looked at him oddly. Jon explained, "It's not just someone; it's someone I thought I might never see again. Someone who never wanted to see me again."

"Were you married?"

"Worse. We were writing partners."

LAX was its usual crowded mess. Passengers streamed out. He knew they were from the NYC flight because everyone was dressed in black from head to toe. Lots of black Canada Goose down coats. Black leather boots. Black laptop cases. The crowds parted, and Kerri appeared in the way that the sun does when it breaks through a cloudy day. Jon didn't realize how much he missed her until he saw her for the first time in three years. She looked radiant—but he tried not to admit that to himself. She was laughing and talking with someone, a good-looking blond guy that he thought he recognized. It might have been a producer he'd met a few years ago back when his sci-fi script had a flickering moment of potential success. Kerri still hadn't seen him. Then she waved. He grinned broadly, relieved that she wasn't angry with him for coming to the airport. He took a step toward her, but she was already rushing toward the limo driver Jon had been talking to. Paula held up a sign which also had Kerri's name!

Jon suddenly felt foolish with his sign. He quickly folded it and thought about slinking away, hoping that she hadn't noticed him. Too late.

"Jon? What are you doing here?" Kerri was no longer smiling.

"I came to pick you up," he stumbled.

"The studio sent me a limo." Kerri was firm and maybe a little annoyed. She felt her stomach flutter, and she wondered if it was nerves at seeing her ex for the first time in three years or just the early morning vodka she'd consumed on the plane. Either way, she was annoyed with herself for feeling less than 100 percent now that she was back in the land of the perfect people. She scrutinized Jon and realized he hadn't changed.

"I'll go grab your luggage. What does your luggage look like?" Paula asked.

"Blue hardcase with a purple ribbon on it," Jon said. Instantly regretting he had said it. He remembered it was a suitcase they shared, but that Kerri had used it to walk away.

Kerri nodded to Paula that Jon was right. She also realized that Jon was wearing the same shirt from three years ago. It was the blue Hawaiian one—the one worn by all the waiters at Duke's Restaurant in Malibu, and she wondered if he was working at Duke's. She softened, thinking he was now waiting tables.

"So hey," Kerri said.

"Good to see you," he said.

"Kind of stunned to be here," she admitted.

"Should we hug?" Jon suggested, leaning in just enough for Kerri to pivot away.

"I don't think so."

"Right. It's a work trip," he acknowledged.

"What are you doing here?"

"I texted you."

Kerri took out her phone. She realized that she'd forgotten to turn her phone back on. She flipped the power switch. Her phone suddenly burst into multiple dings. *DING! DING! DING! DING! DING!* Kerri read the texts. All from Jon.

Amari. Malibu. Three o'clock.

"You texted me five times," Kerri said as she looked at him oddly.

"Yeah, it's important. Amari Rivers wants us to meet her in an hour. At her beach house. In Malibu," Jon said.

"Oh, wow. That's cool." Kerri smiled for the first time since encountering Jon again.

"I was kind of hoping we could ride together. I can drive you. Maybe we catch up and, you know, talk about things."

"Nothing to talk about. At least not until we get the notes on the script. I'm only here until Sunday. I'll take the limo. A perk of living out of town." Jon could practically feel the icicles around her—she was that frosty. They saw Paula grab her suitcase from the revolving carousel and wheel it over to them. Kerri turned back to Jon and asked, "So what's Amari's address?"

Kerri settled into the cool air-conditioned limo. It felt so hot outside. Eighty degrees in late November just wasn't right. A tinsel garland decorated the back seat. Christmas music played on the radio, but Kerri didn't notice. Paula turned to her, eager to please. "Welcome to Los Angeles. City of Angels."

"City of Devils," Kerri said with a grin.

The limo driver didn't hear her. She continued, "I'm going to take Century to the 405 to the PCH."

Kerri suddenly leaned forward, eager to stop her. "No, no, take Sepulveda to Lincoln to Admiralty Way through the Marina, past Venice, and then you can take the PCH."

"You sound like you know what you're doing," Paula said as she punched the address into her GPS. Then she laughed. "Ah, ah, the map agrees with you! Very good. Thank you!"

The limo pulled out of LAX and began the journey to Malibu Colony where Amari Rivers lived. Kerri leaned back and closed her eyes. Her shoulders slumped as her body relaxed. She was suddenly exhausted from the early morning flight and seeing Jon again. *Why did he come to pick me up at the airport? It was so unnecessary. But it was sweet,* she thought. He was trying so hard. But she knew she needed to set the boundaries because she was engaged to Beau. She would rewrite the script with Jon and go back to her real life. She hoped Jon didn't have any other expectations.

"So how long did you live here?"

"Too long."

"You're so funny. I love it here. No better place to be for Christmas. So warm!"

"I'm only here for a few days." And then Kerri said the thing she'd always wanted to say. The thing that she had stopped dreaming would ever be possible to say. She smiled as she opened her mouth. "I'm here because I have a movie that's going to start filming."

"Wow," Paula exclaimed. "Are you in it?"

"No. I'm the writer."

"Cool. Hey, I have a screenplay. Maybe you could read it?"

Kerri just shook her head and smiled. Only in LA does the limo driver have a screenplay.

"Sorry. But after this movie I'm out of the business." Paula nodded in understanding.

Kerri looked out the window as they whizzed past streets decorated for the holidays. She could see that LA was getting in the Christmas spirit. Festive lights wrapped the towering palm trees and encircled the storefront windows. Oversized bows and wreaths graced the entrances, while blow-up Santas flapped next to Salvation Army collection plates. They drove onto the Pacific Coast Highway. And there it was…the sparkling waters of the Pacific Ocean. It had never disappointed. Not before, and not today. She looked at the crashing waves and smiled for the second time since arriving in LA.

Paula noticed. "Ah, now you like LA…"

Kerri laughed. Then she saw Santa skateboarding on the bike path and felt her body relax at the silliness.

Paula broke her reverie when she suddenly exclaimed, "Look! There's Santa surfing! Only in LA."

"Only in LA," Kerri agreed.

Paula took this as an opening to have a conversation. "So where do you live now?"

"Brooklyn. I love it there. It's so great."

"I'm sure it is." The sun streaked through the window and reflected brightly off Kerri's engagement ring. She admired it, turning her hand, appreciating it from different angles. It caught the light and reflected into the rearview mirror.

"Wow, that's bright. Congratulations. On the movie and your engagement."

"How did you know?"

"The ring blinded me."

"Sorry," she said, lowering her hand. "We just got engaged. Five days ago." Kerri smiled, and her heart swelled as she remembered the proposal.

"You been together long?" Paula asked.

Kerri shrugged. "Not really. Just eleven months."

Paula nodded her head. "Did you get one of those big proposals? With the photographer jumping out of a corner and snapping photos?"

"No."

"That's okay."

"It was a total surprise. I had no idea he wanted to get engaged so quickly. I just met his mother at Thanksgiving. He is older. Thirty-five. I know he wants kids." Kerri stopped, with no idea why she was gushing her life story to the limo driver.

"Sounds like a winner."

"He's a good guy." As she said that, Kerri realized that she hadn't said *she loved Beau*. But of course, she did. Why else would she have accepted his ring?!

Kerri looked out the window. She'd never gone to a movie star's house. Before she left LA, she'd met (aka "seen") a few stars but always on a studio lot or in a restaurant. She wondered what Amari Rivers was going to be like. She and Beau had watched Amari's movie *The Christmas Couple* a few days before. Kerri thought Amari had elevated the material, but Beau had fallen asleep. Kerri hadn't found much about Amari, other than a few puff pieces on the internet that her publicist had sent over and what that producer Drew Fox had told her on the plane during his drunken rant. She looked at her watch and realized they were about ten minutes away. She suddenly felt a little nervous. And it wasn't because she was going to meet a star. It was because of Jon.

"That guy, your writing partner that I met at the airport, is following us," Paula said.

"I know. We're going to the same place."

CHAPTER 3

November 26

AMARI RIVERS WATCHED AS A team of workers put up the last-minute touches on her Christmas decorations at the front of her Malibu home. Every window was outlined with lights. There were brightly lit reindeer in the tiny patch of grass. The front door was wrapped with a giant red bow. It was over-the-top, and Amari loved it. A decorator rushed over to Amari, pleased with himself. He pointed out how every single one of her fourteen palm trees was wrapped with Christmas lights. Two wooden nutcrackers flanked the doors.

Amari frowned at the decorator. "I didn't ask for Christmas. I asked for CHRISTMAS. Like the ones I had when I grew up in Milwaukee. I want to feel like skating and twirling on the ice when I see these decorations! I want to wish I could go sledding and sip hot cocoa! I want a winter wonderland by the sea." The decorator had no idea what that meant except that she wanted more. He retreated to his truck and dragged out a blow-up Santa and a sleigh. He looked up at the roof, and Amari followed his gaze. "Yes! Santa on the roof," Amari squealed.

And so it was that Amari's decorator was in a precarious position on top of the roof when Kerri's limo pulled up, followed by Jon's Mazda convertible. Kerri got out of the limo, and a stunning young woman rushed over to her. Her skin was flawless, and her shiny hair was perfectly in place. Kerri realized that it was Amari. And suddenly the gorgeous movie star was hugging her. Jon stepped out of his car, and Amari rushed over to greet him. Kerri noticed that Jon didn't hesitate to hug her back. Classic guy, she thought.

"It's just so great to meet you both. I love your script," Amari gushed.

"Thank you," Kerri and Jon said in unison.

"Come on in, I've got lunch." Amari disappeared into the house.

"I wish you had driven with me," Jon said to Kerri, wanting to get it off his chest. "It would have given us time to prepare for this meeting."

"I read the script on the plane. I'm prepared. Are you?"

"Waited my whole life for this. I was born prepared." They walked through the open door at the same time.

Inside the house, everything was oversized, from the twenty-foot ceilings to the large tapestries to the white couches to the long marble kitchen countertops. The biggest of all was an enormous twenty-foot Christmas tree that was so tall it brushed against the ceiling. It looked like it had been professionally decorated. Sand dollars were sprayed silver and gold and were perfectly placed along with gilded seahorses. Kerri looked up at the top of the tree where a mermaid was perched.

"I love the mermaid. I've never seen one on top of a tree before."

"Christmas is my favorite holiday, and since I live in Malibu, I wanted it to be a winter wonderland by the sea," Amari gushed. "Come on over. Sit." Kerri and Jon sat down awkwardly. Amari walked over with a large wooden salad bowl. Kerri realized that, even though Amari was a movie star on the rise, she seemed very down to earth. Not at all what she expected. Amari served them a brightly colored salad filled with grilled chicken, red peppers, romaine, and banana peppers. Then she grated fresh pepper on top. "Dig in."

"Aren't you going to join us?" Kerri asked.

"Oh no. I'm just doing one meal a day now that the movie shoot is so close. It's a cliché, but the camera really does add ten pounds."

"Thank you. This is delicious," Jon said as he munched on the salad.

"I love this dressing," Kerri added. She didn't want Jon to be the only one saying something nice to the movie star. "I'd love to get the recipe."

"It's from Gelson's." Amari sat down with them and settled in. "I'm really glad we're meeting in person before production starts. I know the director and the exec have script notes that they expect you to make, but I wanted you to know how much I already like the script. It's funny and it has heart. The couple seems to know each other's faults." Kerri and Jon nodded and continued eating. "I've never worked with a writing team before. Especially a couple." Kerri choked on her salad.

Jon turned to Kerri. "You okay, Kerri?"

"See, I can tell that you care for each other. You're so in love.

That's why the script feels so authentic. It's like you two are the firefighter and the diamond heiress."

Kerri wanted to laugh but wasn't sure if it was appropriate. She quickly covered her mouth with her left hand. And then the sun caught the light on her diamond ring, and it sparkled, riveting Amari's attention. Amari's eyes went wide, and so did Jon's. Amari shrieked, and both Kerri and Jon jumped.

"OMG is that an engagement ring?!" Amari exclaimed.

Because Kerri was terrible at lying, she blurted out, "Yes!" and immediately regretted it. She could have just said that she was wearing her dead grandma's ring. But no, she had to be honest.

"Where are my manners? Let me get some champagne! We need to celebrate!" Amari rushed off to the immaculate kitchen and opened a gigantic Sub-Zero refrigerator.

Jon was stunned. He had no idea that Kerri had gotten engaged. Kerri nudged him. "You okay?"

"When were you going to tell me, you're engaged?" he hissed.

"Why would I? You and I are not a couple anymore," Kerri whispered back.

"I know that. But she doesn't."

Kerri nodded. "And now she thinks we're engaged."

"Yup. Let me take another look at the ring that I bought you." Jon looked at Kerri's diamond ring. "Nice. Two karats at least. Looks like you found an eighty-year-old sugar daddy."

"Beau is not a sugar daddy. And he's not old. The ring belonged to his great-grandma," Kerri blurted out.

"Oh, old money. And Beau? Your boyfriend's name is Beau? You've got to be kidding me." Jon laughed. "He sounds like a real Bellamy." Kerri glared at him. She knew that Bellamy was a shorthand expression in rom-com movies for the wrong guy.

"Beau is an honorable guy. Something that you might not understand. I'm just going to tell Amari the truth so that we can clear things up."

Jon's mind was racing. He could let Kerri tell Amari the truth that he and Kerri were once a couple when they first wrote the script but had since broken up. But what would that get them? Amari was known to be mercurial. He was worried about the star leaving the movie—but the real reason, which he didn't want to admit to himself, was that if he and Kerri pretended to be a couple, maybe, just maybe, Kerri would fall back in love with him. It wasn't his most noble plan, but he found himself saying, "No. Don't tell her we're not a couple. She's crazy. She might not do the project if she thinks the writers hate each other."

"I never said I hated you."

"Sometimes you act like it."

"It's not my fault that you read into things."

"Fine, you don't hate me." Jon gave her a fake smile.

Kerri fake-smiled back. "I don't like to admit this, but you're right. And I promised Beau that we could use the script money for a down payment on a condo in Brooklyn."

"That's very nice of Beau to spend your money that way."

Kerri ignored his comment and continued, "There's just one problem with this fake engagement between us. I'm terrible at lying."

Jon nodded his head. He remembered that she had that problem. "So, we've got to sell the fact that we're a couple getting married. I think I have a solution. But I need your consent." Jon whispered in Kerri's ear. She paused and then nodded her head in agreement. At that moment, Amari traipsed out in a bikini. She carried a silver tray with champagne and three glasses. Kerri looked at Jon and nodded, and then Jon leaned in and pretended to kiss Kerri. Of course, from Amari's vantage point, it looked like they were making out.

"Aww, you two really are lovebirds," Amari said. Jon and Kerri pulled apart. Jon was grinning, but Kerri was red-faced. "Come on, it's time for a celebration and script meeting in the jacuzzi."

"Good thing I brought my suit," Kerri said quickly as she tried to take control of her emotions. It was supposed to be a pretend kiss, but Jon's lips had brushed hers, which caught her off guard. *Had she wanted him to actually kiss her?* Of course not, she thought. But why did her cheeks feel so hot?

"Uh, I don't have a suit unless you want me to strip down to my boxers," Jon said. He was enjoying the situation. He liked that Kerri was flushed.

"Not to worry, I keep extra suits in that bathroom. Just in case a pool party breaks out," Amari said.

Five minutes later, they were all in the hot tub, soaking and clinking champagne flutes. Amari smiled wistfully at them both, envious of their perfect relationship. Little did she know that it was all a charade.

"We got engaged a few weeks ago. We went back east and surprised Kerri's parents."

"Where did you ask her, Jon?" Amari wondered.

"Do you want to tell her, or should I?" Jon asked Kerri.

"You tell that story much better than I do. Go ahead," Kerri prompted, thinking maybe, if Jon messed up, the truth would come out and they would all have a laugh. But Jon was too good a storyteller to screw up.

"A lot of people get engaged on top of the Empire State

Building, or on a rooftop overlooking the park. Me, I had a buddy who worked at the Delacorte Theater in Central Park. We were walking through the park. It was snowing, right, Kerri?"

"It was cold as hell," Kerri sneered.

"We passed the theater, and a door was open. We snuck onto the empty stage. We saw a play there once."

Kerri remembered that. The play was *As You Like It*, the Shakespeare comedy. It was the last year of film school. Jon had waited all day to get them tickets.

"I got down on my knees and asked her as the snow fell," Jon said.

Amari marveled at the story. Kerri did think it was romantic as heck. And whenever Amari would ask about their relationship and their plans for the future, Jon was quick to answer. "We're holding off on the wedding until after production is finished. We might do a small intimate ceremony in Iceland."

Kerri smiled, but inside her mind was enraged. Iceland! Jon was the one who wanted to go to Iceland. She'd wanted to go to Thailand on their honeymoon. She was about to argue against the Iceland idea when she remembered: fake marriages don't have real honeymoons.

CHAPTER 4

November 26

JON PRACTICALLY SKIPPED OUT OF Amari's Malibu beach house emotionally energized. He was living his childhood dream of movies, Malibu, and money. (First day of production, here's looking at you!) He had promised his dad that he would never give up on the dream. An afternoon of soaking in a jacuzzi with a bikini-clad starlet talking story had turned that dream into a reality.

Amari had clutched Jon and Kerri as they were leaving. The long goodbye was filled with—*"Thanks, we had a great time," "Can't wait to make this movie with you," "See you at the studio notes meeting"*—gratitude.

Jon noted that Kerri was all smiles until the front door closed. Then she clammed up and turned away from him. The only sound was the waves of the Pacific and the traffic of the Pacific Coast Highway. He remembered how Kerri looked when she was angry. Her small, cute nose would somehow recede into her face. Right now, she looked like she was trying out for the lead in a remake of *The Shining*. He was frightened and not sure what to say, so he went for the positive. "That was fantastic," he said.

"Are you kidding me?"

"Kerri, I don't know what you're reacting to. Amari loves the script. She had great ideas for the rewrite. And more importantly, she loves us."

"Jon, she thinks we're a couple."

"We are a couple. A screenwriting couple."

"She thinks we're getting married! In Iceland!" Kerri lost it, emoting a little too loud.

"Keep it down. We'll talk about it in the car," he said, opening the door for her.

"I'm not getting in that car with you. I'll call an Uber." Amari had sent the limo home sometime during the second bottle of champagne. Jon waited as Kerri punched in the address. Jon's phone dinged.

"Looks like I got a passenger," Jon smiled.

"You've got to be kidding me. You're an Uber driver?"

"Today's my last day. You might be my last ride. I expect a high rating."

Kerri reluctantly stepped into the Mazda. Jon inched onto the PCH. Kerri didn't move a muscle and sat like a cement statue. Unmoving just like the traffic in front of them.

One of them finally spoke. It was the angry one: Kerri.

"We have a problem."

"I don't think so. We can handle the notes. Remember what Professor Hodes told us: *Writers who argue live in little houses.*"

"Stop changing the subject, Jon! It's what you always do when you're backed into a corner. Why did you jump into the engagement story?"

"Not my fault. You're the one who brought the baseball-sized diamond, which could be seen from the moon, into the meeting."

Kerri was flummoxed. "I brought the engagement ring into the meeting because it was on my finger."

"And Amari saw it. And she loved the idea that we were engaged. She loved the idea of us as a married writing team. It was going so well. She was laughing at our jokes. She loved us as a couple and was excited by the script. Did you want to buzzkill the movie? I didn't. I got scared."

"Scared of what?"

"If Amari knew we weren't together, she might cancel the movie or kick us off the project."

"Drew Fox said she could be volatile," Kerri stated.

"The guy who produced *Captain Midnight*? The big sci-fi flick?" Jon said, intrigued. He was and would always be an out-of-the-closet sci-fi, fantasy, and horror geek.

"Yes. That Drew Fox. He worked with Amari on a different movie. And he said Amari was a little offbeat. Out of control."

"You had a meeting with Drew Fox? Without me? When?"

"I didn't have a meeting. We sat next to each other on the plane."

"Really. Did you talk about us? Maybe we can get a meeting with him when you're out here? I have some big sci-fi ideas."

"I have a fiancé, Jon. We need to tell Amari the truth."

"No."

"Fine, I'll have Charlotte fix it," Kerri said.

Jon cringed. "You know she dumped me a few years ago. I gave her *iFear*, my VR horror script."

Of course, you did, Kerri thought. Jon was always fantasizing about selling a million-dollar script, getting a movie made, and appearing in Hall H of Comic-Con.

"But when *Fire and Ice* sold, she was suddenly my best friend again," Jon said.

Kerri dialed. Suddenly the ringing was coming out of the car speakers. Jon had the same car. Kerri had the same phone. The Bluetooth was still working. She went to stop the call when the car hit a pothole and the phone fell out of Kerri's hand, landing somewhere under the seat. She was reaching for it when the young, sharp assistant answered.

"Charlotte Adams's office."

"Hi, Naomi, it's Kerri Williams. Hoping to speak—"

"Putting you through now."

Both Jon and Kerri were surprised. They knew the unofficial hierarchy of calling your agent. If you call your agent, and they take your call, you are making money for the agency. If you call your agent, you are asked to leave a message, and they call you back the next day, they still believe in you. If you call them and they ghost you, you are a nonclient. Jon had remembered when he sent Charlotte *iFear* and he never heard back. Eventually, he got an email saying he was writing unsellable material and that he should find new representation. That hurt.

"Kerri, how was the meeting?"

"The meeting went good and not so good," Kerri answered.

"It went great," Jon shouted.

"Who is that?" Charlotte wanted to know.

"It's Jon," Kerri explained.

"Who's Jon?" Charlotte wondered.

"The other name on the *Fire and Ice* script, Charlotte," Jon said firmly. "The guy who got interest from the studio." It was true: Jon was the one who had given it to an old studio contact at Warner Brothers.

"Jon, of course, how are you? I believe I owe you a call."

Three years ago, Jon thought. But he kept that inside. He took over the conversation: "Listen, the meeting went great. Her notes were solid. We can knock them off in a few days."

"Yes, but there was one hitch," Kerri added. "Amari thinks Jon and I are engaged. And I don't feel right lying to her. I want to tell her the truth, that Jon and I are no longer a couple, we're never going to be a couple again, and I have a fiancé waiting for me back in Brooklyn."

"I understand your concern…" Charlotte said thoughtfully.

"Thank you," Kerri said, relaxing a bit. She smirked at Jon with an "I told you so" look.

"I want you to listen to what I say. I know how you can handle this," Charlotte said calmly. Then she blew her stack. "If Amari Rivers says you're a couple, you're a couple! If she says you're married, mazel tov! I'll send you an air fryer. But get this straight…you two are a friggin' couple, deeply in love, writing *Fire and Ice*!" She paused. The aggressive reply was followed by a calm: "Do you understand me?"

Shaken, Kerri nodded her head and muttered, "Yes." Two days in LA. She could make this work for two days. Collect a check. Go back home to her real life as soon as production begins, leaving the old exactly where she left it.

Jon pulled up at the Christmas-decorated Roosevelt Hotel.

"You can afford this on a schoolteacher's salary?"

"It's another Writers Guild perk of having to come to LA." Kerri sensed Jon was a little jealous so naturally she rubbed it in. "And I get a per diem." Kerri was certain that Jon knew when a writer who lived out of town had to fly to LA or any location, they were given first class tickets, accommodations, and a per diem for food and expenses.

"We should split that. My name's on the script too."

"I'm not splitting my per diem," Kerri laughed.

"How about you buy me a coffee with that? I love the Roosevelt around Christmas. We can talk about the script." Kerri was gathering her stuff and didn't acknowledge him. Jon continued, "Remember when we tried to spend a night here without paying for it?" Jon's lips curled up at the memory. "We snuck into a room, but they found us like ten minutes later."

Kerri opened the car door and turned to Jon. "And they banned us from the hotel. Great memory, Jon," she said with a tinge of sarcasm. "I'm exhausted. And you're even more tiring. I am going to go to my free room where I will take a nap, order room service, and reread the script. So good night."

CHAPTER 5

November 26

JON SMILED AS HE HUNCHED under the bright Christmas lights at the infamous El Coyote restaurant bar. It was the struggling writer, actor, musician, model watering hole where you could get chips and salsa and tasty margaritas surrounded by festive Christmas decor. The walls were filled with signed celebrity photos of Oscar winners who probably made up their Oscar speeches while drunk on El Coyote margaritas when they were first starting out in the business. Jon remembered Kerri debating who would get to speak first if they ever won an Oscar. Kerri was concerned that Jon would talk too much and she wouldn't get to say anything before the music ushered them off the stage. Jon would always be the "talk first and thank me later" guy. Kerri was the opposite: "think first, talk later." That fake Oscar speech that they'd crafted had been written a long time ago, but not so long ago that it had been forgotten.

"You're pretty happy with yourself, aren't you Jon?" said Ira, their old film school friend and the only person Jon had bothered to stayed in touch with. Ira graduated from NYU knowing he wanted no part of New York. He had moved to LA and worked in development, giving writer notes on scripts for various companies.

"I am," Jon said. "I have a movie about to shoot, and I'm engaged to Kerri."

"Fake engaged. And you think, during this fake engagement, she'll fall back in love with you."

"A boy can dream," Jon admitted.

Ira rolled his eyes.

"Laugh all you want. You know how this movie got set up, Ira? I was Ubering and picked up a fare. Turned out to be an executive Kerri and I used to meet with: Evan Byrnes."

"That must have been awful, Jon."

"It was humiliating. Evan was the first studio exec who believed in us. He would champion everything we wrote. But nothing got sold, and now I was driving him to his office at Warner Brothers because his car was in the shop. I knew it was him right away. I pulled down my Mets cap and hoped he didn't recognize me. But he did." Jon remembered that day vividly.

The traffic had been its usual LA shit show. Jon had told Evan that he was going to take Moorpark instead of Ventura.

"That sounds good, Jon," Evan had said, clearly recognizing that this was awkward for both of them. Evan was a short guy with a big heart.

"Hey, Evan, funny meeting you here. In all the Ubers in all the world…"

"How's it going?"

It wasn't going. *I'm driving an Uber. Driving the only studio executive who ever believed in me to Warner Brothers where I used to go to have meetings with him.* But he didn't tell that to Evan. Instead, he said, "Hey, I heard you're running the place now." Jon knew that because each morning he would still read the trades.

"I'm running the streaming division. Movies in the ten million dollar and below range. Doing everything. Horror. Thriller. Action. The studio mandate is big international action CGI movies for the theatrical side, but I have more control with the streaming content. Always looking for a good low-budget, high-concept comedy," Evan said.

"You were the comedy guy," Jon added.

"That's how we met. Your agent sent me that script, *Fire and Ice*," Evan said.

Jon was thrilled Evan would remember him and his script (well, the first script he wrote with Kerri). "We had that meeting at your office, and that night, we ran into each other at some party."

"That's right. Jodie something. I don't remember whose party that was, but I remember *Fire and Ice*. Great script."

Jon went into pitch mode as soon as Evan had said he remembered that script. How could he not?

"It's available. *Fire and Ice*. I heard you have a deal here with Amari Rivers. She would be perfect for it." Jon arrived at the Hollywood Way gate. He turned around to face Evan as he stopped the car.

Evan sat there, one foot out of the car. Thinking. Pausing. Jon waited nervously…

"I have a meeting with Amari and her team today. She just fell out of a movie she was supposed to do for Paramount. She has a window. Send me the script."

Jon reached into his backpack. "Here you go." He always carried a script with him, just in case.

Evan cracked up. "That's the Jon I remember. Always prepared." Evan took the script and walked into the studio gate.

That was six months ago. Now back at the bar, Jon drank his margarita on the rocks with salt. He turned to Ira. "He called me a week later and said he had given the script to Amari. It took her a while to read, but she loved it. The movie was a go."

"So, the story has a happy ending,"

"The story's just getting started, Ira. Today was Act One, Scene One. The return of Kerri. You know that—you work in development."

The hostess came over. Their table was ready. El Coyote was packed with friends, families, coworkers having their office parties, exchanging gifts. There was even a mariachi band playing Christmas songs. Jon and Ira squished into the booth right next to the band as they were finishing up the song. That was why Jon did not see Kerri sitting in the booth right next to him.

Jon ordered his dinner, turned off his phone, and relaxed. "I have a feeling that once we start rewriting the script, things will go back to the way they were. It's the script that matters," he said to Ira.

"Where is she tonight?"

"She said she was tired and jet-lagged. She's at her hotel reading the script."

In the booth next to them, Kerri was having dinner with her old film school friends. Their waitress arrived with margaritas. They all raised their salt-rimmed glasses filled with the delicious concoction. "Welcome home, Kerri!" they cheered.

Jon's skin prickled at the sound of Kerri's name. His shoulders tensed as he swiveled in his booth, surprised to see Kerri.

"Hi, Kerri."

Kerri did a spit take with her margarita. She looked like teenager getting caught past her curfew.

"I thought you said you were too tired to go out," Jon said, wondering why he felt so defensive.

By then, Kerri's friends had seen Ira and called him over. Everyone hugged gleefully at the impromptu reunion. Kerri and her friends pushed in closer, allowing Ira to slide in at one end of the large circular booth, and forcing Jon to squeeze in next to Kerri.

Jon and Kerri's faces were blank, unsure what to say. But their friend Rebecca quickly raised her glass, and everyone followed suit. "To Jon and Kerri. We always knew you two would be the first to get something made," Rebecca said. "And how many Ubers did you have to drive to afford that engagement ring!" Everyone toasted their favorite couple who were not a couple anymore. The dramatic irony was not lost on either of them, but a few more margaritas made the night slightly more manageable.

Kerri whispered to Jon, "Did you tell them?"

"No, I think it was mentioned on social media. I'll tell everyone the truth."

"No," Kerri said, "I'm in. I don't want this to fall apart. You believed in us and the script, and you never gave up on it. I appreciate that. I have a great job back in Brooklyn. I have a great fiancé. I have stability in my life. And I like those things. Also, there's a town house in Brooklyn Heights that is no longer out of my price range. I would love to surprise Beau and buy it for us for Christmas."

"Making movies was your dream too," Jon said, forever stuck in the past.

"It was once. Not anymore. When I left LA, I stopped dreaming and started living, I found out that I liked living more than dreaming. So once this rewrite is done, and the film is completed—the fake engagement is off. Okay?"

"Ok," Jon agreed.

"Now let's do some engagement shots with our friends. And remember, Jon, this isn't a movie; we are not going to fall back in love again."

CHAPTER 6

November 27

THE NEXT MORNING, KERRI HAD butterflies in her stomach
as they approached the Warner Brothers studio lot gate, which
was decorated with garlands and red bows. A large wreath on
the side of the small guard building did nothing to cheer her up.
Last night, after the El Coyote dinner, Kerri had a Zoom call with
Beau. He was at home, tired and stressed, working remotely on
a new building project in India. He wanted to prove himself and
was working overtime, causing him to sport a three-day beard
that was already speckled gray. Also, the Indian food he'd been
eating with the clients was not agreeing with him. Beau asked
about Jon and the rewrite she was doing, and Kerri told him it
was all good. Beau was not jealous at all. What was troubling
Kerri was something she said or, rather, did not say: Kerri left out
everything about the fake engagement. Beau was under enough
pressure, she rationalized. She was prepared to do the rewrite and
get out of the broken-dream factory and get home.

Kerri was also filled with dread. Hollywood was a land of no.

She had been on this lot pitching with Jon one too many times. Each meeting always ended with a smile. The "no" would come through their agent, or they would be ghosted by the studio.

Kerri tried to remind herself that she already had the job, that the studio had already green lighted her script. Of course, it didn't help that she was riding in the passenger seat next to Jon in the same car that they'd always driven. They had typically taken just one car to the studio, which used to be fun when they'd pull up to the gates and say, "Kerri Williams and Jon Romano for Evan Byrnes." Moments later, the guard would hand them printed car passes with their names. It had been a thrill at the beginning, and Kerri had scrapbooked those little slips of paper, dreaming of the day when an executive would say those magic words: *We love it! We want to buy your script.*

But this time was going to be different. They pulled up to the gate, and the guard scrutinized them seriously until the corners of his lips broke into a huge smile. "Jon and Kerri!" he exclaimed. "So good to see you again!"

Wow. Kerri felt like the guard had just given her a big hug of happiness. She was shocked that he remembered them. Her face lit up with a smile. "You too, Bob!" And then she went to the recesses of her mind to pull up a personal tidbit about Bob. *Aha!* She found it! "How are your daughters? Your baby is probably not such a baby anymore," Kerri said.

Jon nodded at Bob with a forced smile and then turned to Kerri with an even bigger grin. He wondered how the heck she had been able to remember the guard's name, much less his progeny. He had never been great at remembering what to call people, and while he dated Kerri, his facility for names had deteriorated further, because she always took care of that which allowed him time to come up with a joke. And that's what he was doing at that moment, racking his brain for something funny to say.

"Rosa and Sofia are doing great! Thanks for asking," the guard said.

"I bet they're driving by now," Jon offered, going for a joke that didn't seem so funny the moment he uttered it. Even Kerri gave him an odd look. Jon glanced at his watch. "Sorry, but we'd better get going. The meeting starts in ten minutes." Jon hated to be late. It was something that often infuriated Kerri, but she also respected it. Jon's attitude was always *If you're late, you're arrogant, because it means you think your time is worth more than mine*. Kerri had traditionally been late or right on time, but she'd learned how to be early, thanks to her partnership with Jon. As much as she hated to admit it, Jon had been right about being on time, as her new punctuality had helped her in her current job. Jon and Kerri waved goodbye to the guard and drove past the gates onto the executive numbered parking lot.

"Wow—they used to make us park across the street in the general lot. This is so cool to be in the exec lot," Kerri gushed.

"Maybe our luck is changing," Jon said.

They parked and got out of the car. Christmas Muzak played through outdoor speakers. Kerri proudly toted her new pink Kate Spade briefcase and turned to Jon. "You ready?"

"I've been ready for years."

"I forgot how corny you can be," Kerri said as her face warmed up with a smile. Then she noticed that his collar was up. "Here, let me fix your collar." She smoothed it down. "Better. You're still rocking that LA style. I see you're still overspending on shoes. Nice Allbirds."

"Thanks. You look good, by the way. I like your New York style."

"Thanks. You should come visit us in Brooklyn after the wedding when things calm down a bit."

Jon's face tightened as he tried to keep his lips upturned in a smile, but it was hard to do after Kerri said the word *wedding*. "Trust me, you don't want me at your wedding."

"I know. That's why I'm marrying someone else." They stepped into the building and showed their passes to a guard. Then they signed in and walked toward the elevator banks.

––––––––––––

Jon and Kerri watched the numbers tick up as they rode the elevator to the executive floor. "I wonder what their notes are going to be," Jon said, breaking the silence.

"Be prepared for the worst, expect something better," Kerri said. The elevator dinged, and Jon stepped back so that Kerri could get out first. They walked down the hallway, which was decorated for the holidays. A large tree trimmed with silver and gold balls stood in the corner with a large menorah next to it.

Waiting at the end of the long hallway was Evan. He called out, "Kerri! Jon!" He walked toward them and gave them both a big bear hug. "So great to see you both again." Evan was too nice to be studio executive. "Kerri, I see that New York is treating you right. You look great."

"Thanks, you do too. Looks like Susan is taking good care of you."

"She is. I love married life. Come on in."

They walked into his office. Posters from his latest movies hung on the wall. A large desk dominated the corner of the room, and on the other side was a seating area with two leather couches and a chair. "Nice digs," Jon said. "You've come up in the world."

"Yeah. Been a while since I was your first fan."

"You were our only fan," Jon quipped.

Evan clapped his hands together. "So, I've always loved *Fire and Ice*. I am so happy we get to make it together."

"We're ready," Kerri said excitedly as she took out a pad of paper. "Just tell us your notes, and we'll get to work right away."

"About the production rewrite: I don't have any major notes. I love the script the way it is. But of course, you'll need to make some adjustments based on the cast. The director hasn't said anything, so I'm guessing he's happy. We'll get his notes later." Kerri's body sunk into the chair, relaxing. This was going to be easier than she thought. Maybe she would even get back to Beau sooner than she'd dared to hope.

"Should we be worried about the director?" Jon asked.

"No, it should just be pro forma. Amari's already signed off on the script." Evan's phone rang. He looked at the caller ID. "Sorry. I gotta take this. Why don't you both walk down to the conference room? I'll meet you there."

Jon and Kerri settled into the conference room. In the middle of the table was a selection of Christmas cookies on a festive tray and a bowl of fruit. Hot cocoa and coffee were on a side table. Jon helped himself to the snacks, but Kerri held back. "I could get used to this," Jon said as he munched on an iced gingerbread man.

"Enjoy it while it lasts," Kerri said.

"Why are you so cynical?"

"Because I know how this business works. We're lucky to

get this one movie made, but that's going to be it. This is all just make-believe, and I've got a real job to get back to in New York."

"Wow. New York has hardened you."

"No. It's just made me realistic, Jon." Kerri bit into an iced sugar cookie. "But this is very tasty." She smiled.

While they waited, Kerri took out her phone and texted Beau. Be back soon, honey. I miss you. She waited for him to text back. Nothing. Kerri looked at her diamond ring and twisted it around. She texted again. Hope you're feeling better. Let's make brunch reservations for next Sunday. Share the good news with our friends. Kerri looked at her phone. Waited again. Still no word from Beau. She sighed.

Then there was a commotion in the hall as they heard, "Amari! You look amazing!" Both Kerri and Jon jumped up from their seats. Amari walked in, looking even more glamorous than the day before at her house. She wore slim black satin pants with a cropped black suit jacket that emphasized her figure. Tortoiseshell glasses framed her face and gave her a more studious air. Kerri wondered if Amari needed glasses or if it was all part of the effect to make everyone take her more seriously. If that was the intention, it was working because Amari looked like a badass producer as much as she looked like a superstar actress. Amari was flanked by her assistant and her agent, Richard Bryant. She gave air-kisses to Kerri and Jon. "Hey, kids," she called out to them. "Say hi to my agent, Richard." Before Kerri or Jon could say anything, Evan rushed into the room.

"Amari! So good to see you again. You look fabulous."

Amari smiled. "Evan! So good to see you again. You remember my agent, Richard?"

"Of course. We were in the mail room together. Richard was the first one to get out onto someone's desk," Evan said.

"And congrats on your promotion." Richard did a quick bow to Evan. Richard was dressed in a Hugo Boss suit, good-looking in a nerdy way.

"Ha-ha. You're the superstar agent. Every time I pick up the trades, I read about you," Evan said as he offered them all a seat. "Help yourself."

Kerri noticed that Richard pulled out Amari's seat. He seemed sweet and not at all like the killer agent that Evan made him out to be. She wondered if he was single. She still had friends in LA who were looking. Was Richard boyfriend material? But, ever so slightly, she noticed how Richard softened when he glanced at Amari, and in an instant, Kerri knew. Richard was in love with Amari. *Well, pick a number*, she thought. Everyone wanted Amari. And she could see by the look of attentiveness on Richard's face, so did he. *Let the games begin*, Kerri thought. *Tonight I am back on a plane to New York.*

CHAPTER 7

November 27

THE HUGGING AND AIR-KISSES ENDED, and everyone sat down. There was nothing left to say as they were all just waiting for the director to arrive. They checked their phones, read emails, and texted. They responded to emails and texts as if they were making presidential decisions that affected the global economy. Kerri checked her watch and noticed that the director was already five minutes late. She glanced at Jon and expected to see steam rising out of his ears in frustration, because he hated it when people were late. But he seemed surprisingly calm, which she thought odd. And then she realized it was because Amari was sitting next to him, and they were making small talk. Not sure what else to do with herself, Kerri checked into her flight for the red-eye that night back to JFK and saw that it was still on time. That's what was nice about flying out of LAX: she never had to worry about a flight being delayed because of deicing or a polar vortex. She checked her text to Beau and suddenly saw that he had returned it. Miss you. Can't wait for you to return.

I made reservations at our favorite place. Kerri smiled. She texted back, Thank you. Even though the truth was that she was a little bored by their "favorite" place, which was more like his favorite place and not hers. She craved more excitement, but her Beau was always dependable, which was also what she liked about him. They balanced each other, providing stability.

"Hello! Sorry I'm late!" Lukas, the director, burst into the room, and everyone dropped what they were doing as if the CEO had arrived, which in fact was what he was on a movie set, the head of the company. Lukas dripped sex appeal and self-confidence, and was dressed like a model who'd stepped right out of the Gucci ad pages in *Vogue*, and Kerri felt herself flushing at the sight of him. She felt like a giddy teenager at a Harry Styles concert and tried to remember that they were in a business meeting discussing their script. She knew he was an up-and-coming director of music videos, one of which starred Amari, but she couldn't remember which one. She racked her brain.

Evan reached out his hand to Lukas. "So good to meet you, man. Loved the latest Adele video."

Adele, that was it! Kerri finally remembered.

Lukas nodded his head, but he wasn't looking at Evan. He was gazing at Amari.

"Lukas," she squealed. "It's been a minute."

"Too long, Amari." Lukas stepped over to Amari and leaned in to give her a real kiss. Not one of those silly air-kisses. Kerri noticed that Richard stiffened when Lukas pressed his lips against Amari's. Kerri felt as if she was catching Richard in a private moment and suddenly felt sorry for him. Would he ever have a chance with Amari? She wasn't sure.

Sparks flew as Lukas and Amari continued their lovefest.

"Remember when we rushed to get that final sunset shot? Everybody said we couldn't do it, but we did. You looked magnificent, glistening from the whipped cream as you stepped out of the bathtub overlooking the ocean." Kerri wondered if they'd been shooting a porno flick.

Amari giggled. "That was fun. That's why—"

"And then that music video got nominated for an MTV award," Lukas interrupted her, completely caught up with himself. Kerri looked at Jon and saw that he was making the face he always made when he didn't like someone as he raised his eyebrows and widened his eyes. She had to agree with him, as she also had a bad feeling about Lukas. She tried to shake off the negative thought. He was a good director. She didn't have to like him. All that mattered was that he was making their movie.

"Should we get started? I've got another meeting in an hour," Evan interjected.

"Good idea. I've got to get back to the agency in an hour," Richard added, clearly bothered by Amari's crush on Lukas.

"Amari, do you want to lead?" Evan asked.

"Yes. Thanks. First, I want to say thank you to everyone for coming to this meeting today. I'm so excited about producing this movie. My first. No movie is good without a good script. Actors need good lines. And so, before we start this meeting, I want to acknowledge Kerri and Jon for writing this brilliant script. From the moment that Evan gave me the script for *Fire and Ice*, I knew it was something special."

Kerri and Jon murmured, "Thank you," simultaneously and inside, Kerri was doing cartwheels and backflips, like the ones she'd done as a young girl on her parents' diving board.

Wow. She'd never heard such praise. *Maybe this is going to be a good project.*

"But...I have some notes." Amari took out a script filled with yellow Post-it notes. It looked more like a sunflower than a script, there were that many notes.

Kerri sighed. So much for Amari having no notes. She knew it had been too good to be true and took out her pad, prepared to write down whatever Amari said. Jon already had his book open.

Amari opened her script and looked at her handwritten notes. "I have lots of notes. But this is my big overall note. Maybe he doesn't save her; maybe he's the one who gets trapped and he's yelling for her to run but she doesn't. They save each other. We've seen this 'fuck me, save me' thing a lot. Why don't they save each other?"

Suddenly everyone at the table was nodding in agreement as if it was the cure for cancer. Kerri was frantically scribbling notes on an 8.5-by-11-inch lined yellow pad. Jon was writing in his leatherbound journal.

The director nodded his head in agreement. "Great idea, Amari. And along those lines, I think we can completely cut the scene when she takes the firefighter on her yacht, because we don't need to see that."

Suddenly Kerri shot bolt upright. *What? We can't lose that scene,* she thought. That was a necessary, very much earned scene. It was a trailer scene, but she wasn't sure how to navigate these waters, as she didn't want to annoy the director. Jon, however, wasn't so timid.

"With all due respect, Lukas, you can't cut that scene," Jon insisted, speaking slowly, punctuating each sentence. "She lets him into her world. They hide away on the yacht. It's the midpoint. And a trailer scene."

Then it was Richard's turn to nod in agreement, and Kerri

wondered if he was really against the idea of cutting the scene or if he was only against any idea that Lukas the director had.

"What is this midpoint? I have no idea what you're talking about. What does that matter?" Lukas hissed as he glared at Jon.

"Structurally, the midpoint is very important," Jon said patiently. "It hints at the ending."

"Well, I don't care. I want to cut it."

"It's an earned scene, and without it, the audience doesn't have the same satisfaction. We don't want them to turn off the movie halfway through," Kerri said, pleased with herself for finally speaking up.

"Turn off the movie? What do you think I'm doing? Making this for television?"

"It's a streaming movie," Amari said.

"You are all thinking too small. I see this as an art picture. For Cannes. Maybe Sundance too. I want people to have to watch this movie in the front row where they can see the grain of the film," Lukas insisted.

"Wait, we're shooting this on film?" Evan asked, looking concerned. "That's not in the budget!"

"No, you wouldn't let me," Lukas said.

"Good. And it's not 2010. Now you get more eyeballs on a streaming movie," Evan added.

At that moment, Evan's assistant poked her head into the conference room. "Carr's on line one. You asked me to get you when he called."

Evan nodded his head and got up from the table. "So sorry guys, but I've got to take this call. Why don't we take a break for five minutes? I'll be finished then."

"Good idea," Richard said.

Chairs pushed back as everybody got up. Kerri and Jon left for the bathrooms. Richard stepped outside to make a call. Amari and Lukas were left alone in the conference room. Lukas turned to Amari, his face reddening and looking betrayed.

"You hired me, Amari. You've got to trust me," Lukas insisted.

"I know. And I do trust you. You're a great director."

"I have a vision... You're a vision. The camera loves you. You must trust me."

Amari nodded. Maybe it was his good looks, or maybe it was the flattering words, but she gave in. "I'll do anything you want. I am putty in your hands. Mold me."

"Thank you."

Richard listened outside the room to Amari as she caved in to Lukas. He sighed while he covered his face with his hands.

———

Kerri found Jon sitting on the steps to a trailer outside a sound-stage. She approached him. He was quiet, and Kerri knew that when Jon shut down, he was unhappy.

"Well, that didn't go as well as we hoped."

"You see those Post-its. If they love the script, why are there so many Post-its?"

"That's the business, Jon," Kerri reminded him, "No one knows what they want."

Jon looked at her. He always loved how calm she could be. He knew exactly what he wanted. "Can you stay longer?"

"Can't. I'm directing the school holiday play. A teenage version of *A Christmas Carol* set in Brooklyn."

"We should pitch that. If you stay, I'm sure we can get some meetings."

"I wasn't sure how I would feel about being back here. But after that meeting, I just want to go home. It's the Christmas season. And I don't want to spend it with sycophants who can't make up their minds on a script that they supposedly love. Why did the movie gods pick on us?"

Jon silently agreed with Kerri. Why did the movie gods bring them back together in the first place?

CHAPTER 8

November 30

AT THAT VERY MOMENT, NOTHING was working for Kerri as she struggled to print out her boarding pass at the business center in the Roosevelt lobby for her red-eye home that night. As usual, she was in a fight with technology and was losing. She would enter the confirmation number, and it'd come back incorrect. She didn't realize she was entering the wrong confirmation number in the wrong place. Jon did, who was surprisingly behind her holding two Christmas lagers. "Need some help?" Jon offered.

"I'll take the beer, for sure," Kerri said, taking it from his hand, not surprised to see Jon. He had said he was going to come and say goodbye.

"I think you need to enter the reservation number over there," Jon said, pointing at the computer screen.

"That's what I've been doing," Kerri said, instantly irritated.

"You could just get the pass on your phone." Kerri ignored Jon, determined to print out the pass.

"You've been entering the flight number where the confirmation number goes."

Damn it. He was right. She hated when Jon was right. That was okay; he hated when she was right. Scripts needed conflict. They had a lot of it to spare. But when they were writing, conflict was good. It made their scripts better. When they used to make the rounds in Hollywood, every exec would say that when they had the chance to hire them, they would. People loved them in a room together.

The printer behind Jon shot out her boarding pass. He handed it to her: "You're all set. Red-eye. Leaving at 11:59 p.m. tonight. Gets you back to New York at an ungodly hour."

Kerri folded the pass and put it in her bag. "There is no ungodly hour in New York. Maybe you forgot it's the city that never sleeps."

"Hey, I was the one who was born there. Not under a car in Michigan," Jon replied.

Kerri chuckled, surprised Jon had remembered that story. When she was in kindergarten, living in a new city, she told her teacher and classmates that she was born under a car. This was something that the concerned teacher told Kerri's parents at back-to-school night. They laughed it off, explaining that Kerri had been born in Michigan and that there was a map in their house that displayed Michigan with a car. Hence, she was born under a car.

"Tomorrow's the first day of production. Are you sure you don't want to stay another day?" Jon asked, breaking through Kerri's thoughts.

"I can't. I promised my principal I would get back in time to rehearse the students for the holiday show." They had spent the afternoon rewriting the script, following the notes that Amari and the production team had given them.

Now, beers in hand, they sat down at a small table under Christmas lights and red ribbon. Kerri admired the decor. "Boy, the Roosevelt still knows how to decorate for Christmas."

"Probably an unemployed set decorator. Do you like the beer? It's local. 8one8 Brewing's Krampus Winter Ale. Made in the Valley."

"Hence the eight-one-eight."

"Valley's gotten kind of hip since you left," Jon commented.

"I doubt that," Kerri said. Jon, the Brooklyn boy, always liked the Valley. Kerri was now the Brooklyn girl whose go-to was the Brooklyn Brewery a few blocks from Beau's apartment. *Beau?* she thought. That was the first time she'd thought about him all day. Los Angeles was like that. It was a bubble that was hard to escape, like a Blumhouse horror flick. Kerri had gotten out, and she'd told herself she was never going back. And yet here she was, in LA again. This place had broken her heart. She didn't want it broken again—not by Hollywood. And not by Jon. She admitted to herself that the notes meeting that day had brought back a lot of good memories of her and Jon working together.

"Thank you, Jon. You never gave up on that script. You always believed in us."

"I still do..." Jon said. Jon admitted to himself that, although the notes meeting didn't go as well as he wanted, Kerri was there with him. And it brought back some of his old memories. All good. "If this comes out well, I think we should talk about what's next..."

Kerri was worried Jon would want more. She cut off that path right away. "Next? I don't want this anymore, Jon. I like being back east, close to my family," she added, not mentioning Beau. Kerri finished her beer and got up from the Roosevelt bar, ready to check out of the hotel. Jon walked with her, wheeling her luggage. As they waited, he asked, "How do you think the movie is going to turn out?"

"Great," Kerri said. Jon knew she was lying.

"How do you think the movie will turn out?" Kerri asked.

"Great," Jon mimicked. They sat there staring at each other. "That director is scaring the hell out of me."

"You always worry too much, Jon."

"I'll write up the notes for the other scenes we have to do, and you can jump in on them in the morning. We'll be a twenty-four-hour bicoastal writing team, and we can always jump on Zoom together. We'll knock out the rewrite in a day or so."

Kerri nodded and finished checking out. She folded up her hotel receipt. She turned to Jon. "It was nice to see you again, Jon." She held out her hand.

"I thought we were engaged. Maybe we should do more than shake hands."

Kerri's face bubbled up with laughter.

"Seriously, what if Amari has a guy following us? We should at least hug." As he laughed, Kerri remembered that Jon hid a lot of his real emotions behind his sarcasm and snide remarks. Before she could consider it, both their phones chimed, indicating a text.

"It's Richard, Amari's agent," Jon said, reading the text as Kerri was still looking for her phone deep in her purse. "He wants us to meet him and Amari in Downtown LA for a drink. At 7:00 p.m."

"I have a plane to catch."

"Your plane leaves at midnight. Plenty of time."

———

They quickly headed downtown in Jon's car. "We're being fired," Jon worried. "They're bringing in someone to rewrite us."

"Why do you always go to a dark place?"

"Because it's Hollywood. It is a dark place. *'Down these mean streets, a man must go!'*" Jon said, recalling the famous crime writer Raymond Chandler.

The streets of Los Angeles were indeed darker in Downtown LA. DTLA (as the brand managers called it) was empty except for when the Lakers played. It was when they drove down Santa Fe that they both saw the lights. Not just any lights. Christmas lights around a small restaurant/bar called the Here and Now. A sign above the door said: LET'S GET BLITZENED. A giant blow-up snowman stood by the doorman, who was handling the throng of people waiting to get in.

Kerri wondered aloud: "What is this place? It's so Christmassy." From inside, they could hear a rocking Christmas band singing songs. A sign announced TONIGHT IN CONCERT: THE SUGARPLUMS.

Kerri said, "I'll look for Richard on the line."

"We have a go movie, Kerri. We don't wait in lines." Jon took her hand and led her to the front door. When the doorman/bouncer stopped them, Kerri let go. That eight seconds of holding his hand quivered through her body. She remembered the first time they had held hands. It was in New York at a revival cinema that was playing the Hitchcock classic *Notorious*.

The doorman tried to stop Jon, but he could be a bull when he wanted and needed to be. "We're meeting Amari Rivers and her agent, Richard."

Jon had said the magic words, and the doorman let them in. The inside was Christmas LA style, as if the director James Cameron was filming in this place. Tinsel. Lights. Every booth had garlands. The waiters were dressed as elves. The menu displayed some fun Christmas drinks: *Yule Shoot Your Rye Out!*, *Hallelujah! Holy Shit! Where's the Tylenol?*

The hostess brought them to Richard, who was sitting in the back booth. They sat down. Jon skipped the usual pleasantries of *Hello* and *How are you.*

"What's going on, Richard?"

"I think it's better if Amari tells you."

"Tell us what?" Kerri asked.

"I don't like that director," Richard said quietly.

"I'm not arguing with you about that," Jon shot back.

Richard revealed a little more. "I spoke to some other people. By the end of his last movie, *Gabrielle*, the actors hated him. I don't know why Amari hired him."

"That movie won at Slamdance," Kerri said. "Then at South by Southwest. And the guy is hot. Not just career hot. He's an Adonis."

Jon and Richard stared at her. She was right. She'd said it. They didn't want to think about that, especially Richard, who carried a lot of subtext with him. This time he didn't hold back. He blurted out, "I hate him."

"What does this have to do with us?" Jon asked.

Suddenly, there was a big commotion. A wave of excitement surged through the restaurant. On the small stage at the front of the bar, The Sugarplums finished their number, and Amari jumped on stage and wished everyone a Merry Christmas, yelling out, "And the next round is on me!"

Richard smiled and cheered, caught up in Amari's vortex with no plans to get out. He had secretly crushed on her for years. Amari arrived at the table as camera phones clicked away.

"There's my favorite couple!" Amari leaned over kissing both Kerri and Jon on the cheek—but nothing for Richard. "Don't you love this place! I wanted to come here because it's off the beaten track, and we can have our privacy."

"You just jumped on stage and wished everyone a Merry Christmas," Kerri reminded her, confused.

"I know. That was fun. Richard, where are the drinks?" And then, a tray of Christmas appetizers and specialty cocktails arrived. "I wanted them to arrive when you did," Richard told her.

"That's what I love about Richard. He's always thinking of everything. Best. Agent. Ever." Amari picked up a drink. "To my favorite writing couple." They all toasted. "Are you excited about tomorrow? First day of filming."

"I have to go back to New York tonight..."

"Why?" Amari asked.

Kerri hadn't thought it through.

"It's her mom's birthday, and her family is big on birthdays. Kerri and I will work, if needed, by Zoom," Jon said. Kerri was stunned because it was *her* mom's birthday. How had Jon remembered?

"She can celebrate it out here. My treat."

"What?"

"You two are not going anywhere. Richard called your agent. I'm giving you a producer credit. I want to see you on the set every day. Your romance, the love you two have, is the foundation of this story. You two are my fire and ice. I need you here."

Kerri downed her *Hallelujah! Holy Shit! Where's the Tylenol?* If they were her fire and ice, Kerri knew which one she was: fire. Burning with anger. Jon was playing it cool. Iceman cool.

"Anything you need, we're here for you Amari," Jon said.

Anything you need. Anything you need!!! Those words echoed in her mind for the rest of the dinner. What about what Kerri needed? She thought about herself as a character who was being taken somewhere against her will. *I have a fiancé back home! I have students rehearsing a holiday show I was supposed to be directing!* But she kept her feelings to herself and nodded agreeably.

Two hours later, she and Jon were back at the hotel. Jon watched her check back in, or rather try and check back in.

"I'm sorry, Miss Williams, you checked out. That room is no longer available. The hotel is all sold out. It's the holiday season. Sorry."

Her phone dinged to let her know that her flight was boarding, but she was going nowhere. And now she had no place to stay. Kerri pushed back the urge to tear up because she didn't want Jon to see her cry.

"You okay, Kerri? Don't worry; I'm sure we can find another hotel room for you."

"We can't do that, Jon. If she finds out we're not a couple, she might walk off the movie," she sniffed. Kerri knew how temperamental stars could be, and she didn't want to be the one to upset Amari and then mess up the movie.

"What do you want to do?"

Kerri looked in her purse. She took out a giant I LOVE NY key chain holding lots of keys and quickly found a purple key.

"Does this one still work?"

"Work where?"

CHAPTER 9

November 30

KERRI'S ANXIETY WAS AT A ten out of ten, but she tried to appear calm. How was it possible that she was going to stay at Jon's place? It was insanely stupid, but she didn't know where else to go. None of her LA friends had room for her. *And if they did, what would she say?* And she couldn't ask production for a hotel room, because then Amari would know that they were not a couple. Now she was in the passenger seat of his car, driving toward his apartment as if no time had passed. It was all too surreal. She looked around the darkened roads lit by occasional streetlights and didn't recognize them. "Did you move?"

"You'll see," he smiled.

"Seriously, where do you live these days?"

"It's nice. You'll see."

"Stop saying, 'You'll see.'" But Kerri wasn't angry. She chuckled, her anxiety lowering to an eight.

They turned down a street, and it started to look familiar to Kerri. She looked wistfully at all the apartment windows that were outlined by Christmas lights, many of which also had a lit tree. She was so busy looking at all the decorations that she didn't realize that the car had just pulled up to a Spanish-style apartment complex. Her heart beat faster, and her palms got a little sweaty. She clutched her pink purse tighter, and her eyes grew wide.

"Wait, this is our place."

"My place."

"So, you never moved?"

"Why move if you don't have to?"

"You never did like change."

"Maybe," Jon said as they both got out of the car.

"I remember when your mom told me the story about you freaking out when your parents would trim their trees," she said.

"Ha ha ha. Surprised you remembered that."

They walked into the apartment, and Kerri noticed that it was tastefully furnished. Then she realized it was because he hadn't changed the furniture or the rugs or the curtains. Even the knickknacks were in the exact same spot. Her designer friend Margaret had helped them to decorate, and when they broke up, Kerri hadn't been able to take anything with her back to Brooklyn because it would have been too expensive to move.

"I know, I know. It's like a time capsule." Jon looked a bit embarrassed.

"It still looks nice. You've kept it clean too," Kerri said. But she thought: *He never got rid of things. He's still holding on to the past. The same car. The same place.*

"Thanks."

Kerri looked at the futon couch and sat down. "Still as uncomfortable as ever," she laughed.

"Once we get paid, I'm getting rid of it and buying—"

"Don't tell me you're going to get those movie recliner seats!"

"You know me so well."

"How could I forget? It's all you ever talked about!"

"They're going to look great in this room, and I'm going to install a projector and state-of-the-art sound system." The atmosphere was suddenly light and happy.

"Wow. Going all out. I bet you're going to have Friday movie nights and invite all your friends over."

"Of course. We always said we'd do that one day." They gazed at each other wistfully, caught in the moment of what they'd lost.

Then Kerri's phone dinged with a message. She had missed a call. She checked her phone and stood up.

"Uh, I need to make a phone call."

"To Beau," Jon stated.

"Yeah."

"You can use the bedroom for privacy."

Kerri appreciated his thoughtfulness and stepped into the bedroom, which she noticed looked the same but neater. She knew that she'd been the messy one in their relationship but hadn't realized just how much of a slob she'd been until she saw how clean the apartment looked now. As she sat down on the bed, she remembered the fights and the tears but also all the fun times they'd had on that mattress. Sex with Jon had always been great, which was why it didn't feel right to call her fiancé while sitting on the bed of her old lover. She stood up and walked to the window and looked out at the Christmas lights on the block.

The phone rang just once.

"Hello?" Beau said groggily.

"Did I wake you up?"

"No. Just about to fall asleep."

Kerri looked at her watch. It was midnight. "Oh, sorry—I forgot that it's late there."

"Kerri, are you at the airport?"

"No."

"Oh." He seemed to be waking up. "Isn't your plane leaving soon?"

"Yes."

"But it's leaving without you."

"Yes. The day went in a slightly different direction."

"At least you won't miss me here. I've got to go to Mohali, India. Tomorrow."

"India? Why?"

"Construction on the new Mohali Business School campus is behind schedule. Foundations were poured in the wrong place."

"That sounds like a disaster."

"It is. The local architect is failing to ensure the project is being constructed per the original design, and both the client and the New York City design lead are furious. Now my boss wants me to fly over and redesign to account for the foundation screwup."

"Why isn't he going?"

"He's leaving on an early Christmas vacation with his family to Disney World."

"Nice."

"I shouldn't be there more than a week. So, when are you coming home?"

"I don't know. I'm hoping in a few more days." But Kerri didn't sound so sure.

"What happened?"

"It's the producer, who is also the star. She wants me on the set."

"And Jon too?"

"Yes. I'm not happy about it either, but they're paying me a lot of money, and I need to do whatever they want."

"At least you're staying at a nice hotel. I looked online and found that the Roosevelt Hotel is fancy."

"Oh. That." Kerri hesitated. She was terrible at lying. "I checked out of my room before I knew that I couldn't leave. So, now I'm staying with an old friend from film school." Kerri held her breath, wondering if Beau would put two and two together.

"Ok. Sounds good. I'll miss you."

"You too. Have a safe trip to India. Love you, Beau."

"Love you too."

Kerri hung up the phone and felt a little guilty about not being completely honest. But she wasn't lying when she said that she was staying with a film school pal, because she and Jon had gone to NYU grad together.

Kerri walked out of the bedroom, and Jon noticed she looked more relaxed.

"How's Beau?"

"Off to India."

"I got your favorite. Sam Adams's Holiday White Ale." He handed her a cold bottle.

"Thanks. You always did like festive holiday drinks."

"I guess we'll be spending the holiday season together," Jon said with a smile.

"I realized that, too."

"If all goes to schedule, production wraps on December 23rd."

"In time for me to get back to New York for Christmas."

"Just like the last time."

"I only left on Christmas because the flights were so much cheaper. And we'd broken up."

"Yeah, but it was still Christmas. You could have waited a few more days."

"Does it help that I cried like a baby on the plane?"

"A little. Until then, here's to Christmas in LA." They clinked their eggnog glasses.

Kerri looked around the apartment. "Where's your tree?"

"I've been busy."

"But it's almost December. I mean tomorrow is December first!"

"Hey, not all of us go nuts at Christmas."

Kerri smiled. "True. I do go a little overboard." Kerri wandered over to the hall closet and opened the doors to find it was stuffed with boxes. She moved away some hanging coats, and there in the back corner, she found what she was looking for, a box labeled CHRISTMAS. She recognized the neat handwriting because it was hers. And next to it, a tall thin box. She dragged them both out. Jon watched her ruefully.

"I didn't think you'd save our Christmas stuff. You threatened to throw it all out when we broke up."

"Maybe I thought you'd come back," Jon said and disappeared into the kitchen before he could see Kerri's reaction. And to himself he said, "I hoped you'd come back."

Kerri opened the long thin box and pulled out an artificial tree. "Come on, help me out here." Jon returned from the kitchen carrying two fresh drinks. He grinned as he assisted her in unfolding the branches, remembering when they'd purchased the tree over at the now-defunct Kmart at a going-out-of-business sale. They'd had so little money that year, but it was just enough for the small fake tree. Kerri plugged in the tree, and the built-in white lights popped on.

"Merry Christmas!" Jon said happily.

"Too soon!" Kerri laughed. "This tree doesn't look half bad. I'm surprised at how well it's held up."

"Kind of like us," Jon quipped looking hopefully at Kerri, but she brushed him off.

She was like a kid in a candy shop as she opened a box of decorations to discover they were all there: the nutcrackers, the Santas in all shapes and sizes, the decorative pillows with Christmas sayings, and the artificial wreaths and garlands. Her lips curled into a big smile as she lifted out the heavy snow globe.

"Maybe we should start addressing the script notes," Jon said, suddenly turning serious.

"I can't work in an undecorated apartment." Kerri joked. "I remember when we got this snow globe at the Nordstrom store at The Grove. It cost a fortune, but I wanted it to remind me of New York. I missed the snow." Kerri shook the globe and watched as the white particles drifted down inside the globe.

Jon looked in the box of ornaments. "I hated to get rid of this stuff."

Kerri smiled. "Why don't we talk about the notes while I decorate your place?"

"Works for me," Jon said as he took out his laptop and opened the script.

———

Later, the apartment sparkled with Christmas decorations, and over in the corner, the lit tree was the beacon that had called Kerri home, even if it was only for a few weeks.

"Wow. It all looks amazing. Thanks," Jon said.

"You're welcome. Consider it payment for letting me stay in your place." Kerri yawned. "Toss me the sheets, and I'll set up the futon bed."

"No, I'll sleep out here. You take the bedroom."

THE TROUBLE WITH TINSEL 63

"I can't let you do that."

"I insist." Jon picked up her suitcase like a hotel porter and carried it to the bedroom. Kerri followed him.

And so it was that Kerri found herself in her pajamas, under the covers in her old queen bed. It was surreal, almost as if no time had passed since she'd left Los Angeles. The only difference was that Jon wasn't lying in bed next to her. He was out on the uncomfortable futon couch bed. Kerri clutched the pillow, and before she knew it, she had nodded off.

It was still dark when Kerri woke up with a start. Someone was climbing into bed next to her. Was it Jon? What was he thinking? And then "he" snuggled up next to her. Kerri touched the person and noticed all she could feel was skin. *Did Jon take off his clothes? That was ballsy.*

"Jon," the person murmured. It was a female voice.

Kerri jerked up. "What?!"

"Ahhh!" the female shrieked.

Kerri leaned over and switched on the bedside lamp. Lying in bed next to her was a naked woman who seemed to be very comfortable until she realized that Kerri wasn't Jon. She looked a few years younger than Kerri.

"Ahhh!" Kerri screamed.

Suddenly Jon was at the door to the bedroom, flicking on the overhead lights.

Both women turned to him.

"Jon!" they said in unison.

"Madison, what are you doing here?"

"I told you I was coming over tonight. And who is she?"

CHAPTER 10

December 1

THE WEATHER WAS LA BEAUTIFUL: smoggy with a chance of fame. *Fire and Ice* was about to start shooting. But in the back seat of the Uber, and the back of Jon's mind, he was replaying the night he and Kerri had just shared in his (their old) apartment. They had addressed the script notes, making sure they argued about each one.

They'd also dealt with Madison, Jon's neighbor with benefits. Jon had tried to explain that it wasn't a real relationship, but Kerri wasn't convinced. She'd even suggested Jon might be more comfortable sleeping at Madison's instead of on the couch they had bought from IKEA.

"Jon, please, it's not like we're married," Kerri had told him.

"But we're engaged according to Amari."

"Well, feel free to cheat on me with your friend. Is she named after the character in *Splash*?"

Madison had never heard of the movie *Splash*. If it wasn't on TikTok, she didn't know it. Besides, Jon told Kerri he didn't want to cheat on her, even if she was a pretend fiancée. Madison had suggested the same idea of Jon sleeping at her place, but Jon had made some excuse that he and Kerri would be working all night on the script. Part of that was the truth—but the other truth, which Jon told only to himself, was that it would seem weird not to stay in the apartment with Kerri. Madison didn't like that answer, but she was okay once Jon promised her a part in the movie.

The next morning, as they drove in an Uber to the set, Kerri fumed silently about the fact that Madison was going to be in her movie, even if it was only as a background actress, but then she saw a paper sign taped to a street lamp that completely changed her mood. "Look, Jon! Look at the parking sign!"

Jon saw it. It was a film production parking sign that told the crew where to park when at a location. This one said FIRE AND ICE PARKING with an arrow. They followed the arrow to another arrow, getting closer to their destination, the Perch Hotel.

Kerri rushed out of the Uber, filled with excitement and glee, surprising Jon, who never expected her to be so upbeat and joyous. He raced to join her. They stood in front of the Perch Hotel on South Hill Street looking up fifteen stories to the rooftop where their movie would soon start filming. Fire trucks were in place, acting both as props and as safety features. The trailers for the stars and the equipment trucks had already taken over the street.

They walked into the hotel and saw different signs everywhere guiding the crew and cast to different conference rooms: FIRE AND ICE. DRESSING ROOM. PROPS. EXTRAS HOLDING. CRAFT SERVICES.

There were also complaining tourists from Budapest who had overpaid for the Perch because of its large and expensive rooftop pool, bar, space. But today it was closed because of the filming.

Evan Byrnes was working his studio exec magic, calming down the situation by placing the tourists in the movie as featured extras.

"Hey, guys, congrats," Evan said, as he saw Kerri and Jon. "I'll meet you on the roof."

Kerri and Jon took the elevator up to the roof where the doors opened up to reveal their dreams coming true. The Perch had one of the larger rooftop pool bars in Los Angeles. There were cameras and lights and scrims. There was Cage Riley, the football-player-turned-actor, who was playing the firefighter hero, taking pictures with the real firefighters. There was so much to take in. The excitement surged through them. Kerri found herself reaching out to squeeze Jon's hand.

"We did this, Jon. We did it."

"We did."

They quickly broke off their handhold when a twenty-something production assistant informed them: "We have your chairs set up in video village." Video village was where the director, producer, script supervisor, and stars would sit and watch the video playback of the scene that was just shot. Usually, if writers were "invited" to the set of the movie they wrote, they might as well bring their own fold-up beach chairs.

But there they were: two chairs. One for each of them. Each embroidered with the words WRITER/CONSULTING PRODUCER. For the first time since their reunion, they were in emotional sync. They had arrived in the land of Oz.

"We have chairs," Kerri said, joyful.

"And our names are on them," Jon said.

They sat in their chairs, loving being on the set. They realized the production assistant was staring at them. They got him to take a picture of them. But first Kerri reframed his shot, making sure it was angled perfectly, adhering to the cinematographer's rule of thirds. She'd learned this in film school and always made sure to place her subject in the left or right third of an image, leaving the other two-thirds more open. Kerri was sending all the photos back to her students. Jon put his arm around Kerri. "For Amari." Kerri smiled, remembering his touch. They kindly asked the assistant for coffee.

"Remember when we first moved to LA? I was an assistant for that crazy rich woman in Beverly Hills. The wannabe producer?" Kerri said.

"I remember the weekend she was away. We used the guesthouse to write and the pool to skinny dip," Jon said, smiling at the memory. Before Kerri could react, the assistant returned with their coffees.

It was the coffee that didn't help their relationship with the director. Kerri, drink in hand, got up quickly to talk with Evan and never saw the director, Lukas Wright, striding in, looking everywhere through his director's viewfinder.

The coffee went flying, staining Lukas's white shirt, and Kerri wasn't sure what was hotter: the coffee or Lukas Wright's anger.

"I'm so sorry," Kerri quickly apologized for something that was not fully her fault.

"Who the hell are you? What are you doing on my set? It doesn't matter. You're fired."

Kerri was shaken, but Jon was steaming, his face red with anger. He leapt out of his chair.

"It was an accident, okay?" he said, confronting the director. "And she's the reason you even have a job. She's the writer. We're the writers. We met you at the script meeting." And under his breath he muttered, "Idiot."

"We're also the consulting producers," Kerri added.

Before things escalated, Amari appeared in a robe and flip-flops. Lukas morphed from Hyde to Jekyll, throwing compliments at Amari as he added, "I was just telling our wonderful writers how much I admire their work."

Kerri hated the bullshit. They settled back into their chairs and watched the crew set up the first shot of the production. The scene they were filming was not the opening of the movie. It happened around seventeen minutes into the film when Amari's character, Tiffany Brooks, a rich party girl who always seemed to be getting into some sort of tabloid or *TMZ* trouble, was about to be cut off by her parents, who wanted her to settle down, as her antics embarrassed them. In true rebel fashion, Tiffany throws a blowout twenty-fifth birthday party on the rooftop of a hotel, which of course gets out of control. A fire breaks out, and the diamond heiress is saved by the blue-collar firefighter. It was the perfect meet-cute.

Evan came over. He had calmed Lukas down and was back on the set. Evan explained how the smoke would be piped in and how they would add some fire in post with computer graphics.

"How's their chemistry?" Kerri was less worried about the special effects and more concerned about Amari and Cage Riley.

"Not sure. Lukas doesn't want them to meet each other until they're in character and filming that scene," Evan explained.

The set got quiet, the extras were positioned, and Amari removed her robe, revealing a sexy diamond bikini. The assistant director held out the clapboard, calling out: "*Fire and Ice*. Scene twenty-two. Take one." Lukas called "Action."

The music kicked in, and the extras started dancing as if it was a rooftop rave. The special effects team had the smoke machines positioned just out of the camera's view.

"More smoke. More smoke," Lukas yelled. He quickly got

more smoke than he ever imagined, as one of the extras had accidentally tossed their robe on the smoke machine. There was so much fake smoke that no one could see the real smoke…

…The robe had caught fire. And that inflamed the cabana cloth wall, causing the cabana to catch on fire. The extras screamed. A fire alarm went off. A real fire alarm. Evan realized something was wrong.

Cage Riley, dressed as a firefighter, climbed on to the roof from a scaffold, but he, too, was lost in the smoke, as another cabana had caught fire. The real firefighters jumped into the scene with hoses and fire extinguishers, saving the day. The cameras were still rolling as Cage Riley emerged from the smoke, carrying bikini-clad Amari in his arms.

Lukas yelled, "Cut!" But it would take a few more minutes for things to calm down. The real firefighters were not happy. Cage was shaken, and Amari was confused. The extras were filing down the stairs to safety as the sounds of fire alarms blared out.

The only person who was happy was Lukas Wright. "Perfect!"

Jon and Kerri sat frozen in their chairs, realizing that this wasn't supposed to happen. They looked at each other. "The movie might be a lot tougher than I thought," Jon said.

"Production is never easy, but this is going to be a whole new level," Kerri added.

Then they heard Evan's voice. In the bedlam, he had fallen and had somehow landed on his back. He was now in massive pain.

CHAPTER 11

December 2

KERRI WOKE UP SMILING TO the sun streaming through the window and breathed in deeply, enjoying the light on her face. It was great to have another sunny day. Then she remembered she was still in LA. Of course, it was sunny. Her lips turned down as she remembered her movie had started filming and the first day had been awful! Her good mood dissipated.

Her phone dinged with a text. It was a selfie of Beau looking tired in Mohali, India, in front of a large nondescript building with the message:

Arrived in India. Not sure if it's day or night.

Kerri texted back. Wow!

Kerri watched as bubbles formed on her phone. Then another message appeared form Beau.

How's the movie going?

Kerri texted back, Not so wow.

Gotta run. Meeting starting. Talk later.

She desperately needed some caffeine but didn't want Jon to

see her in pajamas. The phone read 6:00 a.m., and she hoped he might still be asleep as she slipped into the kitchen hoping for the best. But of course, he was already up and sitting at his laptop! She had forgotten how he liked to get up at the crack of dawn to read the papers. He used to joke that sleeping was overrated, while she always needed at least eight hours.

He looked up and smiled when she entered. "Nice pajamas." Kerri was wearing her Christmas pajamas with pink flamingos in Santa hats.

"Haha. Coffee?"

"Already made. And I got the peppermint mocha creamer you like."

"For Christmas. Thanks." Kerri poured herself coffee and inhaled. "You do make the best coffee."

"Going to need it today."

"Was yesterday as bad as I thought it was?" Kerri wondered.

Jon nodded his head. "It was worse. The script supervisor texted me this morning. She overheard Lukas talking to the cinematographer." Jon read the text: The director is making a story about a fireman hooked on opioids who falls for a rich socialite so that he can access her medicine cabinet.

"That's a joke, right?"

"I hope so," Jon said.

"What's the call time?" Kerri wondered.

"Nine a.m. At the tar pits. They changed the location overnight."

"No! Let me see." Kerri leaned over Jon's laptop to read the day's call sheet, which listed what scenes they'd film that day along with all the actors who were needed. And on top was the location with the address. Jon was right. It said LA BREA TAR PITS.

"This was supposed to be a romantic scene at Griffith Observatory, and now he's setting it against the backdrop of a baby elephant drowning in tar with his mother crying nearby?" Kerri wondered out loud.

———————

Jon and Kerri rushed onto the set at La Brea Tar Pits. They passed the large pit of tar where a life-size model of a mother elephant from ten thousand years ago watched her baby elephant sinking into the tar. Jon and Kerri made a beeline for Amari's actor's trailer in the parking lot. They arrived out of breath. They both stood in front of the door, hesitating. "I'm not going in," Jon said. "This is your idea."

"Typical." Kerri rolled her eyes at him. She walked up the three steps and knocked on the door of the trailer.

"Come in," Amari sang out.

Kerri opened the door cautiously, worried Amari might be getting dressed. But Amari was sitting in front of the mirror while a makeup artist sprayed on foundation and a hair stylist teased her blond locks. "Good morning," Amari said. "Say hi to Evan."

Amari's tablet was open. On the screen was Evan lying in a hospital bed, one leg suspended in the air and his right arm in a full cast. "Hi, guys, how's it going?" he said with a surprisingly cheerful tone.

"Oh no," Kerri said.

"When the fire started, I was caught in the stampede, and someone knocked me to the ground. I broke my leg and arm," Evan said.

"How are you going to be on the set?" Jon wondered.

"I'll have my assistant carrying me around. I'll see

everything…" he said as the streaming signal deteriorated and he cut out.

"Kerri! Good to see you again. Wasn't yesterday crazy?" Amari laughed. "But I'm not worried. Better to get that one bad day of filming out of the way. Going to be smooth sailing from here on out. Want some celery juice? It's the perfect cleanser."

Kerri took a deep breath. "I was hoping to talk to you about something."

"Sure. Anything. And aren't you glowing this morning!" Amari winked at Kerri, who was still flushed from her sprint around the tar pits. "Looks like someone got laid last night." Kerri blushed. She started to protest, but Amari stopped her. "At least someone is having sex. I can't believe I don't have a boyfriend and it's almost Christmas. I hate that." Amari pouted.

Kerri nodded her head, unsure how to reply to Amari's declaration. Amari continued.

"Can I tell you a secret?"

"Sure," Kerri said, finally finding her voice.

"Sometimes I hook up with my co-star, but this guy, Cage, he's such a bore. He's sexy, but he's got nothing going on upstairs. Not like Lukas."

"Isn't Lukas married?"

"Separated."

"I kind of wanted to talk to you about him…" Kerri hesitated.

"Of course. I can understand why you want to bring him up."

Kerri felt her body relax. "He's not at all what I expected in a director. I think we should make some changes."

"I totally agree. I love that we're on the same page."

Kerri's face brightened. This was going to be easier than she thought. Maybe they could even get him fired today. However, she didn't want Amari to feel bad. "But I can understand why you hired him. He is such an..." Kerri looked for a word to describe Lukas that wouldn't insult him. Then she found it: "An artist."

"I agree. And so talented. A true genius. Your script is in such good hands with Lukas."

"What?" Kerri was stunned. She'd completely misunderstood Amari.

"Which is why I think we should allow him to rewrite a scene or two, if that's okay. It won't mess up the integrity of your story."

Kerri felt her temperature rising. She was boiling with anger inside.

The hair stylist spritzed hair spray on Amari. "All done," she said as she handed Amari a mirror so she could look at the back of her head.

"Thanks, Vicky." Amari stood up. She grabbed a jacket and walked toward the door. "Good talk, Kerri." Then she blew out the door, leaving Kerri stunned.

———

Kerri sat in her director's chair next to Jon. She was still fuming, and now Jon gripped the sides of his chair, annoyed. "I am not okay with Lukas rewriting our scenes."

"I'm not either."

"So why didn't you tell Amari that?"

"Come on, you wouldn't have said anything either."

Now they were glaring at each other.

The assistant director called, "Action," and then, "Roll camera." Amari and Cage were in their places. Kerri and Jon watched as the firefighter and the diamond princess had a heartfelt scene, sitting on the bench in front of the tar pits. The dialogue was correct, but the location added nothing.

The director called, "Cut!" He hustled over to Cage and gave him the following note: "You're in pain, man. Don't look so happy."

Jon turned to Kerri with a "see?" look.

Kerri turned to Jon and whispered, "Look at the staging of this scene. We had them taking a romantic hike in the hills. He has them sitting on a bench. Sitting, Jon. Just sitting. That's so boring. He needs to add some movement in this scene. Even a tiny bit of motion. Movies are motion pictures. Not static pictures," Kerri ranted.

"Wow. Tell me how you really feel," Jon said, impressed. "You sound more like a director than he does." Jon and Kerri didn't agree on much, but they were united in their worry about the director.

Ten takes later, the actors looked exhausted, but the director was beaming. He'd gotten what he wanted. An addicted firefighter and a washed-up rich girl. Not the feel-good rom-com Kerri and Jon had written.

The assistant director announced they had a lunch break followed by a camera move, which meant that it would be three hours before the next shot was taken.

Jon turned to Kerri. "Sounds like we have a little break now. Want to go somewhere?"

"No, I promised I'd call Beau."

"Why? It's like 1 a.m. in India. You'll wake him up."

"He's thirty-five, not geriatric. The man can stay up past midnight."

They both left, going in separate directions. Kerri fumed, hating the instability. She felt she was standing in the wrong time zone, away from her fiancé, and had no idea what was going to happen next. She listened as the phone rang and rang. Finally, Beau picked up; his groggy voice answered. "I'm sleeping. Let's talk tomorrow," he said and hung up. Kerri hated that Jon was right.

———

And so, it was a great surprise when, thirty minutes later, they ran into each other at Tom Bergin's, a popular Irish tavern in the vicinity. Kerri was at the bar drinking a beer when Jon arrived.

"Never thought I'd see you day drinking," Jon said.

"Only under duress."

Jon sat down next to her and signaled to the bartender. "I'll have what she's having."

"And I'll have another one," Kerri said.

"How was Beau?"

"Sleeping. You were right."

"I bet that was hard for you to say."

Kerri rolled her eyes at Jon and sighed. "To the bone."

The bartender served them their draft beers.

Jon sipped his and looked around the bar. "I forgot how nice this place was."

"Me too." Kerri looked over at a wall crammed with paper shamrocks that were taped to the wall. Bergin's had a tradition of putting up shamrocks for all their regular customers. "I wonder if they still have our shamrocks."

Jon got up to look at the wall of shamrocks, and his face lit up with a smile. There they were…one paper shamrock with KERRI written on it and one with JON. He took out his phone and snapped a shot of their two shamrocks, side by side. He posted it to his Instagram.

"Come here." Kerri took out her phone. "Let's get a selfie

with our shamrocks for Amari. We need to keep reminding her that we're a couple."

"Great idea," Jon said.

Kerri held up her phone, and she and Jon squeezed together for the shot. She noticed that he smelled good. *What is that scent? Is he wearing cologne for me?* This made her smile. They both looked at the photo. They did look good together.

"I've been thinking..." Kerri said.

"Me too."

"And...I'm done whining. Going to focus on the fact that I'm out in the sunshine in December and we have a movie shooting! To hell with the crazy director!" She held up her beer. They clinked their pints.

"And we're drinking in Bergin's!" Jon agreed.

"The movie will be fine," Kerri said as she chugged more beer and started to feel warm inside.

"You're right. Let's focus on the good stuff. Like we just got paid. First day of production money."

Kerri finished her beer and signaled the waiter for another draft. She turned to Jon. "You're right. Now I have down payment money for a place in Brooklyn Heights. Beau's going to love it."

Jon froze up slightly at the mention of Beau. But he put on a good face and said, "We just have to trust this director. The movie gods brought him to us."

"Who are these movie gods you always speak of, Jon?"

"Comedy and drama. Always at war. Fighting."

"Who wins?"

"I'll let you know at the end."

CHAPTER 12

December 3

AMARI SAT NEXT TO LUKAS in her director's chair, tapping her foot and biting her nails, while all around her the crew wrapped up for the day, coiling cables, collapsing lights, and hanging up wardrobes. Lukas was going over his shot list for the next day with the assistant director.

"Lukas, I really want to see the dailies," Amari finally blurted out.

"Please trust me. This will be your best performance ever," he said without looking at her.

"I trust you, but I don't trust me. Please…just a peek," Amari pleaded.

Amari was always highly critical of her own acting. Maybe it was because she hadn't been to any of the fancy acting schools in New York, like Stella Adler or Julliard. Her theater training consisted of a few semesters at the University of Wisconsin in Madison. She turned to Lukas.

"I'd like to talk to you about the next couple of scenes. I

don't think I'm getting a feel for my character. Do you have any time tonight? I was hoping we could talk about it some more."

Lukas sighed. "Sure. Can you meet me later at the Chateau? But I don't want that to sound icky. We can meet in the bar area," Lukas said.

An hour later, Amari was in the famed Chateau Marmont bar. The storied Hollywood hotel was no longer open to the public, and it had been turned into a private club–style residence. Lukas was one of the lucky ones who had a membership to the club, but it wasn't because Lukas was such a renowned director. Rather Lukas was part of that elite "old Hollywood" group, the guys whose fathers and grandfathers had been the pillars of the movie industry in the early years. Lukas's grandfather was a director in the 1940s at RKO. His father had produced movies at Paramount in the '70s. Lukas was born to his father's fourth wife when his father was almost seventy years old. He had been hoping to avoid that fate of four wives, but alas, he was already separated from his second wife. Monogamy was a challenge for the Wright men. Lukas realized that he had checked out for a moment and had missed what Amari was saying.

"What did you say?" he asked.

"I was worried you thought I wasn't doing a good job."

"Oh, of course not. You're doing a fine job."

"I just don't think I'm getting a feel for my character."

And there it was, thought Lukas. Amari was just as insecure as every other actress. He had thought that she might be different, as she was also producing the movie. He sighed, but he knew what he had to do.

"Look. You're a very intuitive actress. Don't think so much. Allow your emotions to guide you, and everything else will follow."

Amari took out a small pad and scribbled down every word that Lukas said. "I didn't have much time to research this character. And I've never been a diamond heiress. So I don't know what that would be like."

"That's why it's called acting. You just have to pretend to be that character." He sighed again and wondered why he'd signed on to direct the film. Then he remembered: it was because he needed to start paying alimony for wife number two, and besides, Amari wasn't bad on the eyes. He was a leg man, and Amari's went on for miles; they were exquisite.

It was getting late, and the bartender was closing for the night, but Amari wanted to keep talking with Lukas and suggested that they go to his bungalow. He looked hesitant.

"Don't worry. I'm not going to bite you," Amari laughed.

"Ok, but I want you to know that I'm going to be a perfect gentleman."

Lukas put the bill on his tab and gave the bartender a tip before they left. Amari followed him through the gardens to his bungalow, and they stepped inside.

"I've always wanted to see the inside of a bungalow."

"This hotel has quite a history."

"I remember that John Belushi overdosed here."

"Yes. But before that, this place had a long-storied history for bad celebrity behavior."

Amari nodded, eager to hear more. Lukas continued, "At sixteen years old, Natalie Wood slept with a much older Nicholas Ray because she wanted to shed her goody-two-shoes persona. Then she crashed a car up into one of the windows of the hotel and asked Nicolas Ray if she was enough of a juvenile delinquent to be in *Rebel without a Cause.*" Lukas handed Amari a drink and made himself another one. "Hell, there's no *Rebel without a Cause* without the Chateau. The script was written here. And in the thirties, one of my favorite directors lived here. Billy Wilder. He made the lighthearted *Sabrina*, but he also made the much darker *Sunset Boulevard* and *The Apartment*." Lukas gulped his drink and poured another.

Amari loved listening to Lukas talk about old movie history, because he was so smart and nobody had ever talked to her about this before. Growing up in Wisconsin, everyone loved talking about cheese and microbrews, not about the grand old movies. She wanted to be like the classic stars from the studio era. Her second drink was loosening her up, and she giggled to herself because she couldn't believe that she was actually in a bungalow at the Chateau and started to imagine she was an old-fashioned studio star. Lukas looked so hot, but it was his brain that captured her heart. Listening to Lukas was intoxicating, and before she knew it, she pulled him into an embrace. Her lips were all over him. He reciprocated, and she quickly learned what she had expected: he was a great kisser. She wrapped her arms around him and guided him over to the bed, falling on top of him, her luscious locks falling in her face, which she quickly flipped back as her lips turned into a huge smile. She knew they were about to have sex, and that was exactly what she wanted. But out of the blue, he stopped caressing her and pulled away.

"Are you sure this is a good idea?"

"I'm sure."

"I just don't want to take advantage of you. I am your director."

"I know."

"And directors shouldn't use their power over their actors."

"I'm also the producer. Wouldn't you like to sleep with the producer?"

Lukas paused to consider it. "As long as you're okay." Then he was all over her, and their hands fumbled to pull off each other's clothes. Soon they were naked in each other's arms. Amari felt sexy. Lukas took in her beauty and seemed deeply appreciative. Maybe it was a combination of his vision of her or maybe it was because she hadn't been laid in a while or maybe because she was having sex with an up-and-coming director, but it was the best sex she'd had in months. She let out a huge sigh of pleasure. They collapsed in each other's arms.

"I feel like I should light up a cigarette, except I don't smoke," Amari joked.

"I'm starving. Let's order up some room service."

Amari smiled. "Great idea." And it was, because when the food arrived it was perfect. Oysters. Oxtail bruschetta. Garlicky shrimp toast. Smoked trout in crispy potatoes. Taleggio mac 'n cheese. It was a veritable feast. Amari realized she was ravenous. The two of them practically licked the plates.

"We should keep this professional," Lukas said, looking suddenly worried.

"I agree," Amari said. "I don't want the crew to know."

An hour later, Amari and Lukas slipped out of the Chateau Marmont and discovered that their affair was not going to be their secret. Paparazzi happened to be waiting outside the hotel for an A-list actor who was nowhere in sight. In truth, the Paparazzi had been about to leave when they'd been pleasantly surprised by the sight of rising star Amari Rivers hand in hand with her director, the film festival darling, Lukas Wright. Light bulbs snapped away as Amari tried to shield her eyes. But it was too late. The photos were already in the proverbial "can."

CHAPTER 13

December 4

RICHARD BRYANT WOULD CHECK HIS phone each morning at 5:30 a.m. when he woke up, scrolling through the usual sites: *Deadline, Variety, IndieWire*. He also had Google Alerts set up so any time one of his clients appeared in an article or on a website, it would pop up in his email box. Amari Rivers was his most popular client and had been since the first day he signed her. Every morning, he would have "breakfast with Amari" as he read the new stories about her while eating his Honey Nut Cheerios with almond milk. It was during these "breakfasts" with Amari that he realized he was falling in love with her. Every alert about her gave him an excuse to call her, and she usually answered. He lived for the alerts and calls, but the alert that popped up this morning had almost killed him.

TMZ, the gossip bastion with a high percentage of accuracy, had pictures of Amari dining last night with the director at the Chateau, and they were reporting that Amari and Lukas had spent the night together. Richard tossed his cereal bowl half-finished toward the sink and missed. He called his assistant. There was no "Good morning." No "I'm sorry to wake you so early." Richard was in full agent mode: "Where is Amari shooting today?"

Richard had sharklike tendencies, which he didn't like to use as he was known as one of the nicer agents in the business. *Yeah, nice guys finish last*, he thought from time to time, *and don't get the girl.* Maybe he needed to be the angry agent. He sure was angry now, but he wasn't sure why. Was he angry at the gossip site with what might be false conjecture, or was he angry because Amari had spent the night with the director he despised? Was his anger masking his jealousy? It was a combination of all three.

"They're shooting at a firehouse downtown. Amari's call time is 9:00 a.m.," the assistant told him.

Richard arrived at the firehouse to put out this fire. *Another fire*, he thought. Wasn't the fire from the first day of shooting enough? He learned that Amari was running late. That's when he noticed that no one was filming. The crew was just sitting around chatting. He found a pair of familiar faces in Kerri and Jon, who were perched in their chairs, sipping coffee and on their cell phones.

"Where's everyone? The call time was 9:00 a.m. What aren't they shooting?"

"The director didn't like the scene," Kerri said, getting back to her Wordle game.

"Are you rewriting it for him?" Richard said, looking around for Amari.

"You can't rewrite a sunset." Jon offered. Kerri nodded. They were in sync and calmly accepted the absurdity of what was happening, or not happening, on the set.

Richard borrowed the pocket-size script that was hanging from Jon's chair. On set, a small-sized paperback version of the script was given to each department. Richard quickly found the scene they were scheduled to shoot. "I remember this scene," Richard said. "It was funny. And smart. Amari visits the firefighter at the station. He shows her the fire truck. They wind up on top. They start making out. Things get hot. The fire truck is called into action. As the fire truck pulls away, their clothes fly into the air. Cut to the next scene where they walk into the Lakers store at the Crypto.com Arena and have to buy clothes."

"We gave it a Lubitsch touch, right, Jon?" Kerri said, referring to Ernst Lubitsch, the inspirational director from Germany who emigrated to America in 1921 and directed some of the great classic comedies.

"Lubitsch is a comedy god," Jon remarked.

"Why didn't we get this Lubitsch guy to direct this movie?" Richard wondered.

"Because he's dead," Kerri said calmly.

"I wish Lukas Wright was dead," Jon said.

Richard agreed with Jon.

"Now, now, Jon," Kerri said soothingly, "Lukas has a vision. He wanted the scene to be at sunset. In the rain. With lightning. And full nudity."

"Cage Riley has a nudity clause in his contract," Richard said. "He won't wear the codpiece. Said something about not being exploited for his body."

Kerri and Jon were handling this rather well. They bonded over their success, and now misery. Whatever emotional distractions they were having were put aside as they watched their movie going off the rails.

"Where's Amari?" he asked. They both shrugged, and Richard walked away.

"Why didn't you tell him?" Kerri asked.

"He'll find out soon enough," Jon said. His phone beeped, indicating a text, and he rolled his eyes.

"What's wrong?" Kerri wondered.

"Madison texted me what she wants for Christmas," Jon said. He attempted to hide the screen, but Kerri leaned over to see a pic of Maddy holding up a risqué negligee.

"Frederick's of Hollywood. Classy," Kerri noted. "I think that's more of a present for you."

Jon's phone texted again. "Now she's asking about her part."

"She texts you a lot," Kerri noted.

"I'm sure Beau is the same way."

"Beau's busy putting out his own fires in India."

"How's that working out for you?"

"He's attentive when he can be."

"How attentive can he be when he's twelve hours away?"

"I still call him. Even though when I try to reach him, it usually goes straight to voicemail."

"So," Jon probed, "you never have to say, 'I love you.'"

Quickly changing the subject, Kerri jumped up. "I'm going to get some coffee. There's a place a few blocks from here."

"No one walks in LA," Jon said, already joining her. As they walked away from the set, they could hear Richard knocking on Amari's trailer door. They didn't stop to watch.

"I know you're in there."

He banged on the door again, but when it opened, it was Lukas, who glared at Richard.

"Do you mind? We're rehearsing."

"You should be shooting!"

Lukas closed the door, and a moment later, Amari emerged. She greeted Richard with a hug. "Richard! Good to see you!"

"Amari, what is happening? You're the producer on this, Amari."

"I know I am. And Lukas has a great vision for this movie. I trust him. We'll film later today. He says we don't need all the dialogue leading up to the fire truck fuck."

Richard was hoping that was the only fuck she was talking about.

"Ok, fine. I hope he's right," Richard said. Then pivoting, "I was going to ask you if you want to review a statement before I send it."

"What statement?"

"A rebuttal to *TMZ* that states you and Lukas are not having an on-set fling."

"We're not having a fling..." Amari said. Richard relaxed for a second. "It's much deeper than that. He's a genius. He blew my mind."

Amari went back into the trailer, and a very unhappy Richard returned to his office. Meanwhile, the crew waited, unperturbed, as they were getting paid regardless.

CHAPTER 14

December 4

A FEW BLOCKS AWAY, KERRI and Jon were drinking their lattes when they both got the update: Call time is now 3:00 pm.

"He's waiting for magic hour, when the sun sets," Kerri surmised.

"Great. Now a vampire is directing our movie," Jon said snidely.

Instead of returning to the set, Kerri and Jon continued their walk. They passed the ice skaters at Pershing Square and paused to watch an older couple holding hands as they skated.

"That's so sweet," Kerri said.

"One bad fall and it's over for both of them."

"Jon!" Kerri tapped him on the arm playfully. "I wonder how long they've been together. How they met. If it was special."

"Not everyone can meet in an elevator."

"We did have a pretty great meet-cute."

"We did." They watched the skaters wistfully.

Kerri was the first to break the moment. "Come on, isn't Grand Central Market around here?"

"Yeah. We can get lunch there."

"And shop for Christmas treats! I promised Beau I'd bring back some chocolates for him."

"That's sweet. He sounds like a good guy, Kerri."

"He is."

They left the ice rink and started the walk toward Grand Central Market.

"You never did tell me how you met."

"We were both looking for a one-bedroom apartment in Prospect Park. That's in Brooklyn."

"I know that. I was born in Brooklyn!"

"So, the rental market was tight—"

"Of course. It is Brooklyn. Did I mention I grew up there?"

"Ha ha—never! Now do you want to hear my story or not?"

"Of course. Please continue."

"Any time a new place became available, I'd leave work to check it out. But I was in the middle of rehearsing the Christmas show at school, and I was late to meet the Realtor at the apartment."

"Uh, sounds like a plot twist is coming."

"I got to the apartment and absolutely loved it. The light was perfect, it faced west, the kitchen was redone, but then I stepped into the bedroom and—"

"Big turning point coming here…"

"Beau was standing in the bedroom, talking with his real estate agent! My first thought was that he was an evil villain."

"That's good. Let's continue that thought."

"But then I realized he was really hot. I mean cute. Sorry. And he was so nice. When he heard I was a teacher, he offered to let me take the apartment! His mom is a teacher."

"What? This guy sounds like an idiot. Forget what I said before about him being nice," Jon joked.

Kerri tapped him playfully on the arm. "What would you have done in that situation?"

"I would have signed a contract ASAP and invited you to move in with me. That way, if we dated and you dumped me, I would still have the apartment."

"You still have our apartment," Kerri said.

Jon shrugged, not sure what to say.

Kerri looked at Jon, but he turned away, unsure, and they were both suddenly quiet. Grand Central Market came into view, and Kerri warmed up at the sight of its neon signs beckoning her. She practically skipped into the Bazaar, delighted to discover new shops. Kerri and Jon playfully primped as they tried on vintage sunglasses at Plainsugar.

"I feel like Lauren Bacall in these sunglasses." She turned to Jon, "If you want me, just whistle. You just put your lips together and blow."

"Here's looking at you, kid."

"That's the wrong movie!"

"I know, it's *Casablanca*, and you were quoting *To Have and Have Not*."

"Good. I was getting worried about you, Romano—worried that you were slipping in your movie references."

Kerri purchased the sunglasses and walked over to the next vendor, perusing jewelry and clothing.

"Hey, Kerri!" Jon was standing outside a photo booth, aptly called Photomatica. "Remember this?"

"I do. It was our first date. The San Gennaro Feast. And together we found enough coins in our pocket to take one round of pics."

"Come on, let's do it now."

"That booth is tiny. For kids. No way I am sitting on your lap."

"What's wrong with sitting on my lap?"

"We're not on set, Jon. We can act like a couple when we're on set. Besides, if those pictures were posted online, I don't think Beau or Lexington would like it."

"You mean Madison."

"Yeah, that's what I said." She walked away in the direction of a Christmas store.

Twenty minutes and two shopping bags later, they were seated at a small table, eating freshly made pupusas from Sarita's.

"This is fun, hanging out with you again. I missed this," Jon said.

"Everything is dreamy here," Kerri retorted.

"That's why it's called the dream factory."

"Very funny. But I can see why you stayed."

"I wasn't ready to leave when you did. And I hate to admit this, but I had to borrow money from my dad."

"Did that suck?"

"It didn't feel great. But he wanted to help, so I let him. He didn't want me to give up on my dream."

"Where's your dad living now?"

"He's in a retirement home out in Riverside."

"I always liked your dad. Please thank him for me. We wouldn't be here if you hadn't stayed. If you hadn't been driving Evan Byrnes to the studio."

Jon nodded in agreement. "I know."

Kerri touched Jon on the arm softly and looked into his eyes, "And I should have thanked you sooner. But thank you for getting our script green lighted." Her hand lingered on his sleeve.

"You're welcome."

"Are we friends?" she dared to ask.

"I think we are now," Jon smiled.

Their phones beeped, signaling it was time to return to the set. They had walked five miles, so they Ubered back. They sat close together in the back seat, as Kerri put her packages next to the window. Their shoulders touched but neither one pulled away.

The sun was setting, and the fire truck was now on the street. Giant rain trucks had been brought in. Lukas was up on the camera crane. He called, "Action."

"Oh no, he's shooting right into the sun," Kerri told Jon.

"That's not good, right?"

"Only if you want it to look like the apocalypse."

"Maybe we should change the title to *Hellfire and Ice*, because that man is the devil."

The camera rolled and the rain trucks made it pour even though the sun was out. The shot was beautiful, Kerri remarked, but it wasn't right for this movie. It was like Stanley Kubrick directing a romantic comedy.

The actors ripped each other's clothes off. Cage Riley was not wearing his codpiece. Jon gaped. "Look at the size of that..."

"Well, he is a firefighter. He should have a pretty big hose."

CHAPTER 15

December 5

THE NEXT DAY ON THE set, the crew was gossiping about Cage's large endowment, and they weren't referring to his money. The men were in awe, and the women were in lust. Kerri was in the middle of talking about Cage with the hair and makeup team when she had a surprise of her own. Her parents, Diane and Troy Williams, walked onto the set, pulling suitcases on wheels. They called out to her.

"Kerri! We're here!"

Diane and Troy rushed over to Kerri and wrapped their arms around her in a huge embrace.

Kerri was stunned. She had never expected to see her parents in LA on her movie set, as she had assumed that they were busy with all their Christmas parties and their choir rehearsals for their church in Pittsburgh.

"Mom? Dad? What are you doing here?"

"Since you weren't coming home for Christmas, we decided to bring Christmas to you," Diane said. She was middle-aged but in certain light looked like Kerri's older sister. She had discovered marathon running when she turned forty, and before that she'd always done yoga. She kept her mind sharp by running a successful preschool that was sought after by all the affluent moms in Pittsburgh, but there was nothing that she loved more than her three children, especially Kerri, who was her only daughter.

"It's also kind of cold in Pittsburgh," Troy added with a smile. He and Diane had met in their freshman year at Carnegie Mellon and had just celebrated their thirty-fifth wedding anniversary with a cruise. He was a partner in a family law practice; his specialty was divorce. It was a financially rewarding career but had become tedious and sad, and he privately wanted to quit his job but was waiting until their youngest son finished college. After that, he wanted to try his hand at something more creative. He knew it sounded silly, and he had not even told Diane yet, but he secretly wanted to start a podcast about the movie business.

Her father looked around at the set, at the cameras and the crew. A small tear came to his eye.

"Dad, are you crying?"

"I'm so happy for you, Kerri. This is everything you dreamed about. All the times we were on your sets in film school, and now this. You did it."

Troy saw Jon approaching with a confused look on his face, "Troy?"

Troy now hugged Jon. "Congratulations!"

"Troy, what are you doing here?" Jon said, confused. He looked over at Kerri, who gestured that she had no idea what was happening.

"We came to celebrate Christmas with Kerri and visit the

set of her movie," Diane snarked at Jon. She was not happy to see him.

"Why is everyone hugging each other and not me?" Amari called out as she walked over in a tight diamond-studded dress.

"Mom, Dad, I want you to meet the star of our movie. This is Amari Rivers."

Kerri's dad was suddenly starstruck. His face flushed beet red. "I love your movies," was all he could say. But Kerri's mom still had her wits about her.

"It's nice to meet you, Amari," Diane said.

"Amari, this is my father, Troy. And my mother, Diane."

Amari hugged Diane and then Troy, whose face lit up like it was Christmas morning.

Amari smiled. "You came out to see the movie. I'm sure we can put you in as featured extras. You must be so proud of Kerri. Her movie is getting made, and she's engaged! She and Jon are the perfect couple."

"Jon??!!" Diane blurted out. "You mean Beau."

"Ah, Diane, it's so sweet that you call Jon her beau. I love that. So old-fashioned," Amari said.

Kerri stepped behind Amari and waved frantically at her parents, waving her hand in front of her neck, indicating them to be quiet.

"Show them the ring," Amari said with a big Cheshire cat smile. "Looks like Kerri wanted to surprise you."

Kerri held out her diamond ring, and her mom took a long time inspecting it. Finally, she said, "Very nice." But she didn't sound happy. "Jon gave this to you?" Diane said, knowing full well this was the ring that Beau had given to her. Why was Kerri saying Jon gave her Beau's grandmother's ring? Diane was about to say something truthful when Troy nudged her.

"Oh, Diane, you're so funny." Troy winked at Kerri, stating, *I've got it; I'm in on the con.* He even swiped his nose with his finger like out of the classic movie *The Sting.*

"Jon, why don't you take Amari through the new lines for the scene? And I'll get my parents settled in."

"Sounds great," Jon said. As he and Amari walked to her trailer, Amari said, "Your father-in-law is very nice. But I don't think Kerri's mother likes you very much."

"I've been telling Kerri that for years."

"How can she not like you? You and Kerri are perfect together."

"I know. I think it's because, one time, I cheated," Jon said. Amari stopped. "No, not like that. I wrote a script solo. A sci-fi script I was working on without telling Kerri."

"That's not cheating."

"I know."

———

Kerri had an assistant stow her parents' bags. She set them up at craft services and got them chairs.

"This is all very lovely, Kerri," Diane said, "and I am proud of you. But why are you telling people you're engaged to Jon?"

"Amari saw the ring. She assumed it was from Jon. She loves that we are this couple writing this rom-com. She has her own issues about love and thinks Jon and I are the perfect couple."

"You are," Troy said. Diane glared at him.

"I'm engaged to Beau, Dad. Don't you like Beau?"

"I mean, I'm just going along with this. I like Beau."

"So," Diane stated, "you want us to pretend that you and Jon and are engaged, because you are worried that, if the star of this movie finds out you're faking your engagement, she would kick you off the movie."

"Yes," Kerri said. "Glad you understand."

"I don't know how people live in this town," Diane said, not happy at all.

"Is that Cage Riley?!" Troy called out.

"Where?" Diane asked. Diane might not have liked Jon, but she knew who Cage Riley was and loved the way he looked. After an introduction and a photo, Diane settled in on the set.

"Maybe while I'm out here, I can help you look at wedding dresses too," Diane was suddenly beaming.

"Sounds good. What hotel are you staying in?"

"Oh, we're not in a hotel, Kerri," Troy said, his lips curling up mischievously.

"So where are you staying?" Kerri asked, hoping to hell they hadn't planned to stay with her, the person who hadn't planned to stay with Jon.

CHAPTER 16

December 5

TROY WAS DRIVING FAST IN a luxury car that he was renting for the week while Diane sat next to him, sunglasses on even though it was dark out. Troy raced up the curving roads, higher and higher into the Hollywood Hills.

"You rented an Aston Martin, Dad?" Kerri asked.

"You only live twice," Troy shouted to Kerri, who was stuffed into the faux back seat, which was more of a storage area for golf clubs, as he avoided a head-on collision with a car coming down the hill.

Kerri knew her dad was a big James Bond fan, and his expression was always *You Only Live Twice*, from the title of the 1967 Bond movie starring Sean Connery. Dad loved the Bond movies, and now he was driving like he was 007 getting away from SPECTRE.

Troy turned sharply into a driveway and screeched to a stop at what would pass for the villain's lair. It was a mansion in the sky. A Hollywood Hills villa with four stories.

"Isn't it great?" Diane said.

"Are you kidding? How expensive is this place?"

"Hey," Troy said, "it's Christmas. You are back with Jon."

"Dad! We're not really together!"

"Ok, fake back together. You're getting a movie made, so we went all out. Who cares about the price? We weren't going to miss Christmas with our Kerri."

"I agree with most of what your father said," Diane remarked.

"What part don't you like?" Troy wondered.

"The part about Jon. Fool me once…"

"Mom. I told you: it's a fake engagement."

"Yes, but only we know that. And where does Beau fit into this picture? Does he know his fiancée is fake engaged to someone else?"

Kerri gulped. She'd been hoping her parents wouldn't bring that up. "He's in India. I'll tell him later. When he gets home." Kerri closed her eyes, hoping that the answer appeased her mother.

Troy changed the subject: "We were thinking about coming out anyway. At first, we booked a Hilton. But I said, 'Let's live it up.' We have way too much to celebrate."

Kerri followed her parents into their rental haven, where they were already feeling at home. Troy went to work on a batch of margaritas. Diane had already had food and drink delivered and was snapping photos on her iPhone. They walked in on the upper level. Floor-to-ceiling views from Downtown LA to the Pacific Ocean. There was even a cat-piston elevator to go to the floors below.

"Can you afford this, Dad?"

"I can't afford *not* to."

What did that mean? What was really going on? Troy's phone rang. Kerri noticed her mother pause, concerned.

Troy hung up, smiling. "Just the Christmas lights guy. He'll be here in a few minutes with his crew to decorate the palm trees."

Kerri checked out more of the house. And there was a lot more. Four floors of Hollywood extravagance including antique folding wooden doors, encased floor-to-ceiling windows on the fourth floor, which opened to a stunning all-tile pool and spa, as well as an endless view from the city to the water. Eighteen-foot cathedral ceilings soared overhead.

Kerri and Diane were looking out over the City of Angels. Troy carried in a tray of margaritas.

"Welcome to the Hotel California," Troy toasted. "Isn't this incredible?" It was indeed incredible, as were the margaritas.

Kerri sipped her drink as she looked up the price of the house on her phone. "This place is a thousand dollars a night. This is crazy."

"What's wrong with being a little crazy?" Diane asked.

"If you and Jon want to work here, there's plenty of room. You can have the bedroom. Work. Swim in the endless pool," Troy offered.

"Well, that's silly," Diane said. "Jon can stay wherever he stays, just not here. But you can stay with us."

"Did you two win the lottery and not tell me?"

The doorbell rang. Troy and Diane went to answer it. It was a guy named Ray who was there to decorate the house for the holidays. Alone in a lounge chair by the side of the pool, Kerri quickly sent pictures of the villa to Jon. He replied immediately:

WTF? Where are you?

My parents rented this place.

NFW.

Texting you address. Bring bathing suits. In my suitcase.

A few minutes later, there was a commotion from outside, and Kerri hustled out to see what was going on. Ray and his team were already decorating a palm tree, wrapping Christmas lights around its trunk. Her mom was in a heated discussion with a middle-aged bald man, and Kerri recognized him as Val Stone, the once-famous action hero. Val Stone was complaining that the Christmas lights would shine into his bedroom next door.

"Just close the curtains," Diane said.

"I don't want to lose my view."

"Then enjoy the Christmas lights."

"I don't want to enjoy the Christmas lights. Take them down!" Val Stone insisted as he stepped closer to Diane in a threatening manner.

Jon arrived and Diane smirked, but Jon didn't even acknowledge her, rushing instead to help Troy. Jon planted himself between Diane and the action star, getting right up in his face. Val Stone was about four inches shorter than Jon.

"Who the hell are you?" Val Stone snarled.

"I'm the future son-in-law with a problem."

"What's your problem?"

"You," Jon countered. "I don't know what's going on here, but I'm sure it was something to do with the Christmas lights. You want to be a jerk to people the rest of the year, fine. But my future in-laws are here to enjoy Christmas, and maybe you should be a little more neighborly."

Val Stone realized Ray and his workers had their phones out, filming the altercation. He hammed up his apology. "Hey, no problem. I was just coming over to say welcome. Just try to keep the noise to a minimum."

Val Stone skulked away. The workers applauded, and Troy

hugged Jon. "Welcome to the party, pal!" Even Diane smiled slightly.

A few minutes later, Troy found the sound system and blasted "Hollywood Nights" by Bob Seger before he jumped into the infinity pool.

Kerri gave Jon a tour of the house, and they found a bedroom where they could change into their bathing suits.

"You brought me the string bikini. Where's my one-piece?"

"I couldn't find it."

"Yeah, right."

"Hey, you're the one who brought it to LA."

"It was an accident. Turn around while I get changed. Not that there's much to change into."

Jon turned away from Kerri, but she could see him in the mirror. She felt warm inside as she noticed he still had strong legs and a tight ass. He was also broader. *Had he been working out?*

Jon turned back around to see Kerri in a string bikini. She was stunning.

"Stop staring."

"I'm admiring."

They jumped into the pool just as Troy got out. "You kids want another margarita?"

"That would be great," Jon said, and Kerri agreed.

They swam in the pool, teasing and splashing each other.

"My dad said we can move in and work from here," Kerri told Jon.

"I love that idea!" Jon said.

"We're not doing that!" Kerri said, a little too loudly.

"Why not? You should always listen to your dad."

"You would say that. My dad always loved you. He was really upset when we broke up. Every guy after was not you. 'Call Jon.' 'What's Jon doing?' 'Go back to LA with Jon.'"

"Your dad's a smart man."

Kerri leaned against the pool and kicked her feet, splashing Jon. She dove under the water and swam across the pool briskly, hoping to clear her head. She looked at Jon, and the warm feeling came back. *Why does he have to look so good?* "Just keep swimming, just keep swimming."

"This is fun," Jon said, swimming closer to her.

"It is. Except we're pretending to be a couple so that our crazy star doesn't fire us from a movie that's being directed by a crazier director. I shouldn't be swimming in December. I should be back in Brooklyn directing the school play. Instead, I'm here with you, lying to my fiancé."

"Just tell the truth."

"Which truth?"

"That we're engaged," Jon joked as he put his arm around her.

Kerri felt his smooth skin on her body, not wanting to admit that she liked it. "What are you doing?!"

"Pretending." He lifted his arm as Troy walked out to the pool, carrying their drinks. They swam over to Troy and took their margaritas. Sipping thoughtfully, the two writers looked over the lights of LA as the classic song "I Love LA" played on Troy's LA-only playlist.

"I do love LA," Kerri said. Jon didn't say anything. She wondered how long she could keep pretending to herself. A thought found its way into her mind: *Did I give up on the dream too soon?*

CHAPTER 17

December 6

IT WAS SATURDAY. A DAY off from the film production. Kerri and her mom drove down Wilshire Boulevard, through Beverly Hills. Suspended above the wide street at the start of the high-end shopping area were a large decorative Santa Claus and his eight reindeer. All the street posts were decorated with garlands and bows. Large banners displaying holiday greetings flanked every street corner. The store windows were bursting with Christmas cheer. Silver-and-gold-wrapped presents were piled high in the windows. Kerri gripped the wheel of the Maserati while Diane ogled all the decorations.

"Never thought it would look so Christmassy in LA," Diane said.

"It's kind of over the top."

"Yeah, but you love it."

Kerri stopped at a red light and relaxed her shoulders as she gazed at Rodeo Drive, awash with colored Christmas lights. "You're right. I do." Kerri smiled.

"When you were a little girl, Christmas was your favorite holiday. You'd start decorating your bedroom the day after Thanksgiving."

"Doesn't everyone?"

"And the ornaments you created were so inventive. Remember those bottle caps?"

"Oh, I haven't thought about those in years. You almost killed me when I opened up every bottle of soda just to make the ornaments."

"There was a lot of flat soda that year."

Kerri's lips turned up in a big smile. She looked warmly at her mother, tapping her on the arm. "Thanks, Mom. For coming."

"I told your father I wasn't going to miss Christmas with you. Even if it's in LA." The light turned green, and Kerri continued down Rodeo Drive.

"Look! I've never seen red lights wrapped around palm tree trunks," Diane said with excitement.

"Only in LA. I'll park, and then we'll go to the Spanish Steps. I heard their decorations are amazing," Kerri said.

"Not before we look at wedding dresses. We've got to stay focused."

Kerri sighed, but it seemed that there would be no deterring her mother. She decided to try on lots of dresses and find a reason to reject every one so they wouldn't actually buy anything. They pulled up in front of the Pronovias bridal store, which Diane's bridge club Facebook group said was the best bridal store in LA.

They entered the store, and Diane almost swooned as she looked at the long flowing bridal gowns. Kerri knew that her mother had been waiting for this moment of wedding dress shopping with her daughter for far too long. Diane had gotten married at twenty-two, and Kerri was already twenty-eight. Diane was very open about her last few birthday wishes, as when she blew out the candles, they had all been for Kerri to get engaged.

Even Kerri started to get excited as she flipped through the racks of dresses. From puffy chiffon to sleek satin to lots of lace, it was overwhelming. There were almost too many choices. The salesperson asked Kerri what she was looking for, and Kerri quickly made up a few ideas. Soon Kerri was being shown to a dressing room and started trying on the gowns. The first dress made her look like the Stay-Puft Marshmallow Man monster from *Ghostbusters*. The second dress she put on was too plain. In quick succession, Kerri tried on five more dresses. Some with short sleeves, some with no sleeves, but none of them looked right. It was going to be easier than she thought to leave without buying anything. This was all just play acting.

Then the salesperson handed her a shimmery dress. "Try the mermaid one," she said. Kerri stepped into the long dress, and her mother zipped her up. It was a perfect fit for the curves of her body.

"You're radiant, Kerri. Like Daryl Hannah in *Splash*." Diane smiled. "Come out of the dressing room to see it in the natural light."

Kerri stepped out of the dressing room and caught a look at herself in the trifold mirror. She couldn't help but light up. The dress was perfect. She swirled from side to side and loved the way the fabric moved with her. She felt like a princess. And then she was brought out of her reverie.

"Kerri? Is that you?" asked a middle-aged woman who had just entered the store.

Kerri squinted her eyes as she tried to remember who it was. She recognized the voice but not the face.

"Looks like you're finally going to get use of that marriage tax exemption."

Then it hit Kerri in an instant, and she knew who it was. "Oh hi, Margo."

It was her old accountant; the one who used to do her taxes when she lived in LA. The accountant who knew how little money she'd actually made. Kerri had temped at her office during the tax season to make money, and Margo had been a de facto but cloying mom.

"Mazel tov! I didn't know you were getting married," Margo the accountant said. "I saw you in the window as I was walking by and just had to stop in to say hello."

Diane got up exuberantly to greet the accountant. "She just got engaged. And hi, I'm Diane. Kerri's mother."

"Nice to meet you, Mom. And Kerri, I thought you'd left LA." Kerri blushed. "I did. But now I'm back."

"She and Jon have a movie filming," Diane said proudly.

"So, he's the lucky guy."

"Actually—" Diane said, but Kerri glared at her mother when Margo wasn't looking at her.

"He is," Kerri quickly said, interrupting her mother.

"You two should get incorporated. I'll be sure to share all your good news with the office. Call me when you're ready to do your taxes." Margo left the store.

"Sorry, Mom. Margo's got a big mouth, and she's the accountant for lots of people in Hollywood. I can't risk telling her the truth."

Diane turned back to Kerri, her face pink from embarrassment. "I'm sorry." She touched the dress fabric and perked up.

"I don't think you need to look any further, Kerri," Diane said. "This is it."

Kerri rubbed her hand across the fabric. "I do love it."

"Great. I'm going to put down a deposit."

"Mom…" Kerri's eyes flashed, suddenly unsure. She felt her stomach flip as she watched her mom paying for the dress.

"Cheers," Diane said as they clinked champagne glasses. They were sitting on the sofa in the dressing room, waiting for Kerri to have her measurements taken. "I've been dreaming about this day for a long time. I bet you have too."

Kerri felt herself tearing up and wiped away a wet spot on her cheek. "Thanks, Mama." She gulped her champagne. *How has this gotten so out of hand?* she wondered. And then she remembered. It was all Jon's fault.

"Don't worry, it's going to be all right. Everyone gets nervous when they begin planning their wedding."

Kerri sniffed again, wondering how her mother was being so understanding. "You just can't let Jon see the dress," Diane continued as she took Diane's hand.

"You mean Beau."

"Isn't that what I said?"

"Sure, Mom."

But the moment was broken. Diane stiffly withdrew her hand from Kerri's hand.

"Am I upsetting you?"

"No, not at all. I just wasn't expecting to find a dress so easily. I wasn't prepared."

"When it's right, you know."

"That's what you always said about falling in love with Dad."

"When did you first know that you loved Beau?"

Kerri twirled the champagne flute stem in her hand. "When he kissed me—at the Grove Christmas Tree." Kerri sipped her champagne dreamily.

"So you and Beau came to LA?"

Kerri's face blanched as she suddenly realized she was talking about Jon. "Oh no! I meant, I meant the Christmas tree at Rockefeller Center." Kerri's face twitched as she said this, and she reddened again, knowing that her mother would realize that she was lying about the story with Beau. There had been no Christmas tree. There had been no magic. It had simply been while they were walking through Prospect Park and Beau had said, *I love you*, to which she'd replied with *I love you too*. It had been nothing like the moment when Kerri had looked up at Jon through the soapy snowflakes falling at the Grove in the moonlight and Jon had leaned in to kiss her while Dickensian carolers sang "Deck the Halls" around them. That had been magic.

"That sounds nice," Diane said in an unconvincing tone.

And then suddenly, completely out of the blue, Kerri burst into tears like Mount Vesuvius. "I just always wanted to get engaged at Christmas. But not like this! Not with a fake engagement with my ex!"

"There, there," Diane said as she patted her daughter's hand. "Have some more champagne." Diane lifted up the bottle that the salesperson had provided and filled up Kerri's glass.

Kerri gulped, unsure how to answer when her phone rang. She looked at the digital readout and saw that it was Jon. "Speak of the devil. Let me just get this." Kerri wiped her tears away and answered the phone. "Hello?"

"What time will you get home?" Jon teased. "I've been alone in the apartment all day. I miss you."

"I'm with my mom now. We spent the day looking at wedding dresses. And she put a deposit on one."

"Oh, I can't wait to see it. But I think that might be bad luck."

"It doesn't matter if you see it or not."

"Why not?"

"Because we're not getting married, Jon," Kerri said with a deep exhale. "I'll be back to your place by five to shower and change. We should leave by five thirty to beat the traffic."

"Where are we going? I thought we'd get some takeout from that Thai place you love and watch a Christmas movie. You know, for research."

"Amari texted. She wants to take us out for dinner."

"Oh no," Jon worried. "Is something wrong?"

"I have no idea. She just said to meet her at 6:00 p.m. at the Beverly Wilshire Hotel."

Kerri ended the call. Her mom was looking at her.

"What?"

"I'm just going to say this once. You have a look on your face that I have seen before. When you first brought Jon home…"

"Mom."

"Kerri, please let me finish. I understand this fake engagement and why you are doing it. But you cannot get back together with Jon after he cheated on you."

Kerri was stunned, confused. "Mom, Jon never cheated on me."

"You father said you caught him at 6:00 a.m. at a Starbucks."

Kerri started laughing. "I did. He was sneaking out each morning to work on a script he was writing by himself. Some science fiction 'end of time' thing he always wanted to do."

"He was writing with someone else?"

"No, by himself."

"And that's why you broke up with him? Because he was writing a script by himself."

"It was that and a lot of other things," Kerri stated.

"Like what?"

Kerri thought about it. "I got tired of chasing the dream."

"And yet, here you are," Diane commented.

CHAPTER 18

December 6

KERRI AND JON WALKED TOWARD the Beverly Wilshire Hotel, the site where Julia Roberts had lived in the movie *Pretty Woman*. Jon had been thrilled to find a parking spot on a side street, so they didn't have to pay for the expensive valet. Kerri admired his frugality even though she knew that the production would have picked up the cost. She looked up to see a large tree made up of all white lights. The awnings on the buildings changed from green to red.

"I remember standing outside this hotel and looking in when we couldn't afford to eat here," Kerri said, her stomach tightening at the memory.

"Let's hope everything is okay with Amari."

Kerri inhaled sharply. "It's Christmas. Everything is always fine at Christmastime." But she didn't sound very convincing. She pushed open the heavy door and Jon followed her. When she stepped into the hotel, all her anxiety released from her body like that moment before sleep comes. She was quickly enveloped by evergreens, rich with pine scent, red shiny balls that shone like Rudolph's nose, and Christmas carolers dressed up in period costume, singing "Hark the Herald Angels Sing." It was all over the top, but she loved it, and she felt her heart burst with happiness at the cacophony around her. It felt like Christmas morning when she saw silver-and-gold-wrapped gifts around the twenty-foot pine tree loaded with oversized ornaments and giant nutcracker statues. Kerri stood up straighter and smiled a big smile as she approached the hostess.

"We're meeting Jane Austen," she said.

Jon looked at Kerri oddly, clearly confused.

The hostess looked at her reservation board and grabbed two menus. "Right this way."

Kerri turned to Jon. "Amari's code name."

The hostess showed them to an out-of-the-way table. Kerri noticed that they'd have some privacy in their corner.

As Kerri and Jon sat down, Jon leaned toward Kerri conspiratorially. "Did you cash your check yet?"

"It's direct deposit, genius. Why?"

"In case they fire us."

"Why would they fire us?"

"You never know. It happens all the time."

"You are so insecure."

"Writers are always the first to go when there's a problem."

"Do you think there's a problem?"

"Have you met our director?"

"Good point." For the first time, Kerri was a little worried. But she tried to brush it off and keep her cool.

"I bet the dailies look bad and they need someone to blame."

"Look, right now, we don't have any information. Let's just

sit tight," she said. "The last time you thought we were being fired, I was told to stay longer."

"Right before prisoners die, they get one last meal. Maybe we're like that," Jon said.

"Yes, but I doubt that prisoners get a Michelin-starred meal. I forgot how paranoid you can get."

"Not paranoid. Just realistic."

"Well, if this is our last meal, then I'm getting a last drink." Kerri studied the drink menu. The "Feeling Pretty" caught her eye. Named for the *Pretty Woman* movie, it had champagne, vodka, Combier Peche de Vigne Liqueur, raspberries, aquafaba, and was topped with a rose petal. It sounded like perfection to Kerri.

Kerri signaled the waitress, who swiftly walked to their table. "Could I get a 'Feeling Pretty'?" The waitress nodded.

"I'll have one too," Jon said. The waitress nodded again and rushed off to the bar.

"I've never had such fast service. Must be because they know we're at Amari's table," Kerri said.

"Or maybe it's because they know we're about to get fired and are taking pity on us."

"Ha ha." Kerri chuckled. Jon could always make her laugh.

Twenty minutes later and four "Feeling Pretty"s later (two for Jon and two for Kerri), Amari arrived and slipped into her seat before removing her sunglasses and a hat. She sat with her back to the dining room, and Kerri observed that the people next to them were aware of who Amari was, but they didn't bother her.

Amari beamed at Kerri and Jon and noticed their cocktails. "Looks like you started the party without me." She smiled. "Have you been here before? This place is great. Order anything you want—it's on me."

"Thank you," Kerri said, feeling loose and relaxed from the two drinks.

Amari signaled the waitress, who immediately appeared. "Can I get what they're having?"

"Of course. And should I let Xavier know that you're here?"

"That would be lovely."

The waitress scurried away, and Amari turned to Jon and Kerri. "Xavier's the executive chef. We've never dated, but he has a big crush on me." Amari giggled. "Which is why I love coming here, because I never have to pay."

Classic, Kerri thought. Just another perk of celebrity. But how could she be upset when she was now reaping those benefits? She grinned to herself and studied the menu as if she was prepping for an exam.

Jon was in turmoil, as he still couldn't figure out what was going on. Why did Amari want to meet with them when she saw them all day on the set? He was on edge and unable to focus.

Amari studied Jon and Kerri. "I realize this might be awkward but…"

Jon's nerves dialed up to a ten. It was never good when the word *awkward* came out of someone's mouth. He knew what *awkward* meant, it meant that Amari was trying to let them down easy. He was in total panic mode.

Amari was gazing at Kerri and Jon. "As I was saying, this is awkward, but I just wish I could have a relationship like yours," Amari blurted out.

Jon gulped, and Kerri's head jerked up from the menu. So that's what this was all about?

"I'm already twenty-nine, and I can't seem to find love." Amari sighed. "Lukas is hot, and he's great in bed, but I just don't know if he's the one. I was hoping that you two could give me some advice, since you have an amazing relationship. I thought we could talk about it over dinner. And here we are!"

"We thought you were going to fire us," Kerri laughed.

"Ha ha, we know you'd never do that," Jon said with a forced smile.

Amari laughed. "That's what I love about you two; you can laugh at things."

The waiter arrived and took their orders. Jon ordered the loup de mer with a side of the black truffle fries, and Kerri ordered the same thing.

"I love how you two get the same dish," Amari said.

"That's because I usually can't decide what to get, and I always like what he orders," Kerri divulged.

"And I don't want her stealing my food because she ordered the wrong thing," Jon laughed.

"I sort of have menu phobia."

"Is that a real thing?" Amari asked, with a twinkle in her eye.

"It is for Kerri," Jon said. The atmosphere was light and happy.

"That's why we usually just get identical dishes," Kerri added.

"Because you trust Jon," Amari said.

"I guess I do. That's one of the things I like about him. He's trustworthy," Kerri said, touching Jon lovingly on the arm.

Jon was beaming. He was going to enjoy this dinner after all!

"So, Jon, what do you love about Kerri?" Amari asked.

Jon inhaled. "Wow. Do you have a few hours?" They all laughed. "Seriously. What I love about Kerri is her eternal optimism. When I get negative, she stays positive."

"Ok, but sometimes I do get negative, and that's when Jon

stays positive and makes me laugh. So, we're never down at the same time."

"Unless things get really bad," Jon revealed.

"What about you, Kerri? What do you love about Jon?"

"That's easy. I love how he always makes me laugh."

"I do?"

"Of course. You know that," Kerri said as she playfully punched him in the arm. "Jon makes me want to be a better person. He makes me want to work harder—especially when it comes to writing."

"You're no slouch either."

"Thanks, Jon."

"I mean it. Sometimes the last thing I want to do is write, and then you take out your laptop and start, which gets me motivated."

"That probably happened, like, once. You have the best work ethic that I know."

"Wow. I didn't know that. Thank you."

Amari watched as Kerri and Jon became engrossed with each other.

"You guys are amazing. You work so well together."

"He completes me," Kerri said as she laughed.

"Did you just rip off a line from Cameron Crowe's *Jerry Maguire*?" Jon asked.

"Professionals steal. Amateurs make it up."

"You had me at *hello*," Jon said.

Everyone laughed. Kerri realized that the dinner had taken an odd turn as she had suddenly been feeling so positive about Jon, and now she wanted to pivot the conversation.

"What about Richard? He's cute."

"Oh, he's my agent. I can't go out with him. He's like a best friend."

"Before we started dating, we were also best friends," Jon admitted.

"We were. We were in the same film school classes, and we used to go to movies together, especially the classic ones at Angelika and Theatre 80 before it closed. I thought he was never going to ask me out."

"I was afraid to ask," Jon said.

"Why?"

"I thought you'd say no."

"I never gave you that indication."

"But you sat down next to my friend at *Ninotchka*."

"That was one time. Besides, he was cute. I had no idea that he was gay."

Jon laughed. "You never did have any gaydar."

The food arrived. It smelled delicious and looked beautiful. Jon and Kerri dug into their identical meals. The dinner had turned out to be surprisingly fun after all. Nobody got fired.

"You two are the perfect couple," Amari said.

CHAPTER 19

December 8

THE WEEKEND WAS OVER. PRODUCTION had ramped back up, and it was going to be a long, busy week. Jon and Kerri were sipping coffee at the craft services table and looking through the schedule for the week. Kerri was starting to feel comfortable around Jon again. Maybe too comfortable, because she was about to ask him to go to a movie with her. She wondered how Beau would feel about that and decided it was better not to tell him.

"We have a short day on Thursday, and *Notorious* is playing at The Egyptian," Kerri said.

"I can't go," Jon said.

"You're kidding. You love *Notorious*," Kerri said.

"I promised Madison that I'd attend the Snowball Gala for the Los Angeles Boys and Girls Club. Her father is on the board. You should come," Jon insisted.

"I'm not going to be a third wheel," Kerri said.

"There are no wheels. This relationship is not going anywhere," Jon said.

"Are you going to tell her that?"

"No."

"Yeah, you should," Kerri said.

"Well, you should tell Beau," Jon said.

"Tell him what? That I'm engaged to another man?"

"Exactly."

"You know how I hate it when you say, 'Exactly,'" Kerri said.

"Which is exactly why I do it," Jon laughed.

"Ha ha."

"So, I guess we can do this. We can actually be friends," Jon said.

"We'll have to be. Because this engagement has an expiration point. Something like two weeks, two days, and a few hours. At least that's what the schedule says. We wrap on December twenty-fourth."

"Christmas Eve."

"Yes."

"And then you go back to Beau."

"And then I go back to Beau."

A few hours later, they were filming at the iconic Spago restaurant. Jon and Kerri had never been there, but they'd done their research and read about it. Now that the scene was taking place at the actual Spago, they were kicking themselves with excitement as they'd finally have the chance to eat there, or at least they hoped there would be food. They checked in with Amari to see if she needed anything, but she was busy with hair and makeup, so they found their chairs and watched as the crew worked to set up the shot. Kerri was bursting with joy when she saw the dolly wheeled in while tracks were laid, because when they wrote the scene, she didn't want it to be a static shot of a couple sitting at a table. She wanted to have the camera slowly circle the table and get closer and closer, to project the intimacy that Amari and Cage's characters were feeling. The words that she'd written with Jon were coming to life, and she felt her heart swell with pride.

The assistant director looked worried. They were short a few extras because two couples had called in sick. Then he noticed Kerri and Jon and rushed over.

"We could use you today in the background," the assistant director blurted out.

"Sure. That would be great," Jon quickly said.

"Awesome. Thanks!"

"Uh, we don't have the proper attire," Kerri interrupted.

"Not a problem. Stop by the wardrobe department and see what they can lend you. Jon, you need a jacket. Kerri, a dress would be perfect."

Twenty minutes later, Kerri and Jon were sitting almost cheek to cheek at a table, all dressed up. "It feels like I'm in high school going to the prom," Kerri said.

"I wouldn't know."

"Oh, I forgot. You didn't go to the prom."

"Nope."

"Which is dumb, because I'm sure there were lots of girls who would have loved to go with you."

"Nah."

"Come on, I've seen your high school pics. You were buff."

Lukas looked through the viewfinder, liked what he saw, then stepped over to where all the extras were sitting, including Kerri and Jon.

"I know you don't have lines, but I want you all to look like you're in love. So, pretend like you're with the man or woman of your dreams." He stepped back to the camera. "Hey, love, you ready?" he called out to Amari.

"For you, always."

Richard watched and rolled his eyes. He couldn't take it and left the set.

"I guess we need to seem like we're in love," Kerri said.

"Just look into my eyes. But don't laugh," Jon said.

"And, action," Lukas called out. The door opened, and Amari as the diamond heiress and Cage as the hunky firefighter waltzed into the restaurant.

Jon and Kerri looked into each other's eyes while he took her hand and caressed it, causing Kerri to giggle. She couldn't help herself. Jon always knew how to make her laugh.

"CUT!" Lukas screamed. "Who's laughing?"

Kerri made a sober face and Jon tilted his head down.

"This is a serious scene. Everyone's in love. Extras—do some stuff."

The scene rolled again, and this time Jon didn't take Kerri's hands. They stared into each other's eyes, and Kerri bit her lip so she didn't crack up. She had always been a terrible extra in film school and had ruined many takes in her friends' films. She watched as Amari and Cage waltzed into the restaurant and noticed Cage looked out of place. Amari took his hand and led him to a table. Kerri and Jon mouthed the lines to each other as Amari and Cage said them. The camera continued to swirl around them until the scene ended.

"CUT!" Lukas yelled. "I think we got it."

"On only one take?" Amari asked.

"Shouldn't we do another one? To get into character," Cage insisted.

"You're both fine." Lukas waved them off. "Trust me. Let's light for the close-up." Gaffers and grips scurried around as they moved the lights and adjusted the scrims.

Kerri and Jon continued to sit at their table. The Spago chef brought out a tray of appetizers to share with the extras and crew. "Enjoy," he said as he offered everyone a special treat.

Kerri jumped up and reached for the tiny crab canape with excitement. "Yes! I was hoping we'd try some of the famous Spago cuisine."

Jon bit into the tiny appetizer. "Amazing. I think I need to switch careers and become an extra. Writing is too hard."

Kerri laughed. "What are you going to wear to the charity gala, the one with your girlfriend?" Kerri emphasized the word *girlfriend*. She was having fun at Jon's expense, loving how he squirmed when she talked about Madison as his girlfriend.

"She's not my girlfriend, and I have no idea."

"Oh, she's your girlfriend," Kerri said playfully. "And you have to know. You want to look nice. Especially if her parents will be there. Have you met them before?"

"Once. When they brought Madison some groceries, we were in the apartment pool."

"Wait...she doesn't buy her groceries?"

"Not everyone is as self-sufficient as you are, Kerri. So, what do you think I should wear?"

"Not jeans. And not that old blue button-up. It's not as hip as you think."

"Guess I'll have to stay home."

"Not an option. When we wrap this location, I'll take you shopping. After all, you were just paid, and we are in Beverly Hills, where I seem to recall that there are a few clothing stores."

"So, you want to pull a Norma Desmond and take me shopping?"

"Yup. But I'm not paying."

Cage walked over to their table. "I hear you two are the writers," he said with a thick New York Italian accent. He reached out his hand, and Kerri quickly grabbed it. Then Jon shook his hand. "Nice to meet you both."

"You too, Cage. You are exactly the way we envisioned you," Kerri said.

"Thanks. But, ah, I don't think I would say it like this," Cage said as he took out a mini script page and pointed to his lines.

Jon and Kerri read over the lines.

"How would you like to say it?" Kerri asked.

"I know a lot of people think that just because I got these six-pack abs means I'm not a sensitive guy. But I am. I like to cry at the movies," Cage said.

"What? That line isn't in the script," Jon said.

"Oh, I was talking about me," Cage said.

Kerri and Jon were confused. What was happening here?

"Maybe I could say it with fewer words and just give her a kiss, and then we'd have sex?" Cage continued.

"Too soon for them to hook up in the movie. You don't want to tip your hand," Kerri said.

"Once they have sex, the movie's over," Jon said.

"Or the plot gets really complicated," Kerri said. "Which maybe isn't such a bad idea."

Both Jon and Kerri nodded thoughtfully.

"You're on to something, Kerri. Maybe they should have sex by the midpoint."

"Let's talk to Amari about it."

The crew was wrapping up at Spago. Kerri and Jon were back in their regular clothes. They knocked on Amari's honey wagon.

"Who is it?" she called out.

"Kerri and Jon," Kerri said.

The door opened and Amari's head popped out. "Come on in!"

Kerri and Jon stepped into the trailer. "We just wanted to say that we're heading out for the day."

"Great scenes today," Jon said.

"You think so?" Amari suddenly looked insecure.

It surprised Kerri to realize that Amari was unconfident. At first glance, she seemed so self-assured. A strong producer. A powerful actor.

"Yeah, it was exactly as I imagined it," Jon said.

"Awww." Amari sighed.

"We had an idea for a small change in the movie that shouldn't affect the filming. We'd just need to add a sex scene earlier," Kerri suggested.

"At the midpoint," Jon said.

"Hm... And that could create even more conflict because they've already slept together once."

"Exactly," Kerri said.

"I like it. Let me talk to Lukas about it."

"Thanks."

"Since we're done for the day, Kerri is going to take me shopping."

"Oh, a reverse *Pretty Woman*!" Amari laughed. "I love how you two do everything together. You're such a perfect couple."

Kerri and Jon smiled. If only Amari knew the truth.

———————

Jon and Kerri stepped in and out of several men's clothing stores on Rodeo Drive. Zegna. Dior Men. Brunello Cucinelli. Ralph Lauren. Kerri giggled like a schoolgirl as she watched Jon strut in front of the mirrors, like John Travolta in *Saturday Night Fever* or any Travolta movie, for that matter. Some of the pants were too loose, and some were too tight.

"And in a series of shots, we see Jon, trying on various blazers and pants," Kerri said, narrating the scene, with a giggle.

"Ha ha. It does feel like I'm in a screenplay montage."

"Go with the Cucinelli. It's more you."

Kerri held up a bow tie. "Now this could really complete the outfit."

"I haven't worn a bow tie since I was eight years old."

"I think they're back in style. At least they are in New York. Come on, try it on."

Kerri stepped over to Jon and handed him the bow tie.

"Can you help me put it on?"

"Sure." Kerri lifted the bow tie and leaned toward Jon, her nostrils inhaling a cologne. *Did he put that on for me?* she wondered. Her fingers fumbled from nervousness. She hadn't been this close to Jon for this long of a period in at least three years.

"Everything okay there?"

Kerri wanted to embrace him but pulled back as she quickly tied the bow. "Perfect." And in that moment, everything did feel perfect. They smiled at each other, unsure what to do next.

The salesperson came over, interrupting the moment. "You look marvelous."

CHAPTER 20

December 9

ON THAT MORNING RICHARD MADE it to the office before another round of paparazzi photos of Amari and Lukas ruined his day. Richard's twentysomething assistant, Brit, had followed him into his office with his coffee and iPad in hand.

Brit held out the iPad announcing, "TikTok just picked up more photos of Amari and Lukas. He was caught leaving her Malibu house."

"When?"

"This morning." *Damn*, Richard thought. He could easily have said, *What is the big deal? Who cares if Amari was having a romance with Lukas the director?* The answer was he cared. A lot. *Just ignore it*, he told himself. Maybe this time love was for real. But Richard felt that only his love for Amari was real, and he had to tell her. What if he didn't, and Amari married this guy? Then—Richard would have to wait a few years for her to divorce Lukas, as the average celebrity marriage lasted three to five years. It was Richard's backup plan, which even he didn't think was a good one. He was not thinking straight.

"And here's one from last night," Brit said, swiping to display a picture of Amari and Lukas kissing against the sunset. It was an amazing shot. There were champagne flutes on the deck railing. Why didn't they blow off from the ocean wind? Richard didn't have time to wonder about that. Brit informed Richard that Evan, the studio boss, wanted his call returned ASAP.

Richard told the assistant, "Get him on the video call."

Via the tablet, Evan, who was still in the hospital said, "The studio is not happy with the footage. Amari looks ill and tired. Her face is all puffy. Either fire the makeup people or make sure she gets some sleep. I can't afford to CGI the circles under her eyes!"

Richard wasn't about to argue with Evan, because he agreed with him. He didn't like that Amari was in photos making out and day drinking with Lukas. And now the studio did not like the footage that was directed by Lukas. Richard was convinced that Lukas was the problem here, and he was going to deal with him. He grabbed his jacket, intent on going to the set.

He was out the door when Brit called out loudly, "Spencer wants you to come to his office immediately!" Richard approached Brit, who knew she never should have yelled out that information.

Richard leaned into Brit, whispering, "You just screwed up. Badly. Most people here would fire you in a loud outburst. I'm not most people. Don't ever do that again. Now when I walk away, I want you to start crying. Okay?"

Brit nodded. Richard walked away. There was silence, except for the sobbing of the assistant. As far as the other agents were concerned, Richard was King Shark.

However, with the head of the agency, the great Spencer White, Richard was a goldfish about to be flushed down the toilet.

"We want to sign Lukas Wright," Spencer told Richard. "And that means we want you to sign Lukas Wright." Richard didn't reveal he was about to go to the set and convince Amari to dump Lukas.

"Interesting idea, Spencer. I thought about it. He's not as talented as his dad, and I don't think he's seasoned and mature enough for us to consider him."

"What's this 'us' shit? Amari hired him. Other agents are after him. You have access."

"I just find him to have character issues."

"Who cares about character? This is Hollywood. Sign the guy!"

Richard went back to the office, already ordering his assistant: "Get me Lukas Wright on the phone!"

"It's ringing," Brit said. Richard picked up.

"Hello, this is Lukas Wright's office," Amari answered with a giggle.

Things just kept getting worse.

"Amari?"

"Richard, I thought that was you. How are you?"

You are breaking my heart, Richard wanted to say. What he did say was, "Great. Is Lukas there?"

"Let me see if he's out of the shower."

Richard waited. Lukas answered, "Hey, Richard."

"Lukas, great. Listen, I wanted to set up a time for you to come into the office…"

"Are you wooing me?"

"I think you and I should have a conversation about what comes next. It doesn't have to be today—"

"Today is great. We're shooting nights the next few days. How about coffee in an hour at The Rose?"

Richard had wanted to meet someplace more secluded (so if he decided to kill this creep, nobody would be around to witness it), but he agreed to the more public site.

Richard drove over to The Rose Venice, where they had a large open seating area. Richard had arrived early to find the most private table in a corner. Richard heard Lukas before he saw him, with shouts from the paparazzi. "Where is Amari? Are you guys in love?"

Can these paparazzi read minds? They were everywhere Lukas was.

Lukas sat down and ordered two coffees for himself.

"Thanks for agreeing to meet with me so fast. Before we start, I just want to let you know that the studio is not happy with the way Amari looks in the movie."

"Fuck the studio," Lukas said.

"It just looks like she's been staying up all night," Richard offered.

"She is staying up all night. She's a party girl. Just like the character. I want to show the real Amari in this movie. Her character has a secret. I think it is better for a movie when the character has a secret that not even the writer of the movie knows."

"What is it? Do you know it?"

Lukas only smiled. "I'm the director. I know everything. Of course, I know it."

"Maybe you should tell the studio. They're worried."

"Richard, do you trust me as a director or not? If you want to fire me, I will quit."

Yes, you suck, the footage is bad. It's not funny. And you're sleeping with the woman I secretly love. So take your sorry ass and your paparazzi and get the hell out of LA was what Richard wished he could say.

"Fire you?" Richard said. "Not even close. I want to sign you as a client."

"I seem to be doing fine without you."

"Fine is good. Great is better. Whatever you want, we can make happen. What is your dream movie?"

Lukas leaned closer. Very seriously, he announced, "I want to direct *Satan's Prayer*."

Richard knew *Satan's Prayer* well. His friend Karen Loop was the manager of the writer who wrote it. It was unfilmable. A great script that no one wanted to make because it was too dark.

Lukas commented while Richard was still processing. "You get me that movie, I will sign with you."

Richard countered, "But *Fire and Ice* is a rom-com."

"*Fire and Ice* is not a romantic comedy. I don't do romantic comedies!"

Richard wanted to argue, but he stopped. Was Lukas serious—if *Fire and Ice* wasn't a rom-com, what was it? He put that thought aside and continued, "Hey, I am here to make your dreams come true. If you want *Satan's Prayer*, I will make that happen."

"You have twenty-four hours," Lukas said, walking away. "I hate the pace of Hollywood. Let's make it happen."

Richard's mind was already working. It was a genius idea. Lukas would be a great director for *Satan's Prayer* except for the fact that no one wanted to make *Satan's Prayer*. Every studio passed. Every star passed. But if Richard could set it up...he would set it up overseas. Budapest? *Yeah, they can shoot it there. No, it needs to be more remote. And cold. And Budapest is too nice a place.*

By the time Richard got to the office, he was thinking about Canada. Novia Scotia. Newfoundland was ideal, because it was remote and had no access. He had heard from another agent that it was the worst place in the world to film, which sounded perfect to him. He found a low-budget Canadian company looking to build their brand; then he called Karen Loop and told her Lukas Wright wanted to direct *Satan's Prayer*. Preproduction would start in January, when it was stormy and well below freezing, and then the filming would begin in March. And Richard would set up a deal to do the postproduction up in Newfoundland. From beginning to end, Lukas would be away for six months making *Satan's Prayer*, which meant six months away from Amari. Richard salivated at the prospect and rubbed his hands together like an evil genius.

By midnight the deal was done. It was announced in the trades the next morning because Richard leaked the info. The headline read: Lukas Wright Answers Satan's Prayer

The next day, Richard got to the *Fire and Ice* set early. He had sent a gift basket on a pentagram platter with oatcakes, dulse, and other delicacies of Nova Scotia.

Lukas was thrilled and actually smiled, showing his pearly whites for the first time. Amari congratulated him as she embraced him, causing Richard to grit his teeth. But Richard was also celebrating, as he'd not only signed a new client, but he'd also managed to get Lukas out of town and away from Amari. Richard grinned as he mentioned that Lukas would be gone for six months of filming.

"I'm going with him," Amari said, bursting Richard's bubble. "I'm going to star in *Satan's Prayer*."

Richard was confused. The script had an all-male cast where everyone played a monk who has to silently fight off the devil.

"All the monks are men," Richard stated.

"Lukas had this brilliant idea," Amari said, excited.

"Amari will play a monk," Lukas pitched. "The other monks don't know she is a woman. She is a monk in disguise and has been hiding there, because Satan has been searching for her. She is the daughter of the devil."

Lukas is the devil, Richard thought. He'd gotten what he wanted, and he'd gotten what Richard wanted, which was Amari, away with her in a cold place where they would find a way to keep warm.

For Richard, this was turning into a miserable Christmas.

CHAPTER 21

December 9

"I LOVE YOU," JON SAID.

"Please don't say that," Kerri said.

"I'm going to keep saying it until you say it back to me," Jon said.

"You and me. We don't make sense. We're from two different worlds," Kerri said.

"Last time I checked, this was all one world. Full of problems. Full of people who don't know what the hell they're doing. And screw anyone who doesn't think we should be together. Screw your dad. Your five stepmoms. Screw the paparazzi. I know what I'm doing when I say I love you."

"Love doesn't last," Kerri said. "We tried."

"I'm going to bet love does. With us."

"Why don't you shut the hell up and kiss me?" she said.

BANG! BANG! There was a knock on the door to the apartment. "Jon! Are you in there?" It was Madison.

"We're working, Madison," Jon called out. Kerri and Jon

were indeed working as they revised a love scene that would be filmed later in the production. Madison had come to knock on Jon's door when she overheard them saying the lines.

"Is that what you call it?" Madison asked from behind the door.

Jon rolled his eyes and Kerri laughed. "How long do you think she's been listening? Maybe I should have done the scene like Meg Ryan at the deli in *When Harry Met Sally*?" Kerri started moaning, louder and louder, "Oh my God, you are so hot. You are so big."

BANG! BANG! BANG! BANG! Madison was shouting, "JON!"

"Wow, Jon, you have one woman moaning and the other one screaming your name," Kerri laughed. "You're a stud!"

"You love this, don't you?" Jon said. Kerri smirked. She did. Jon opened the door and Madison almost fell inside. She had been leaning on it, listening in. Kerri waved as she pretended to be buttoning up her shirt.

"She goes, or I go," Madison said, not a yell but with a volume that Kerri couldn't help but hear.

"Go where? You live down the hall. I live here. She's my writing partner. We were working on a scene."

Madison's demeanor shifted. She went from angry and jealous to hopeful and kind: "Is it the one that I am going to be in?"

Jon lowered his voice. "I'm working on that."

"I miss you, Jon. I miss you inside of me." Well, nothing could become more direct than that. Madison was not subtle, and Kerri cringed. Jon led Madison back to her apartment. Now it was Kerri's turn to listen in as she noticed the voices had become softer. The door had been left open, and she could see Jon and Madison walking down the hall, and then Jon kissed her.

Madison latched on like a Venus flytrap and turned it into a long kiss. Kerri told herself she wasn't bothered watching (spying) on that, but oddly she was. Her phone went off. She ran back into the room and sat down on the couch.

"Were you spying on me?" Jon said as he returned, closing the door.

"No, I was moving around, looking for better cell service in this apartment. I'm not getting any bars on my phone by the couch. So, I went to the hallway and saw your moment of intimacy with Madison. I understand. Kissing her is probably the only way to get her to shut up."

Is she jealous? Jon thought. He didn't even respond.

Kerri continued, "Just asking as a friend who has some insights on your past relationships—what do you see in her, Jon?"

"She's not that bad. You know she used to be Miss Palisades."

"I have no idea what you are talking about."

Jon didn't want to explain that to be Miss Palisades, you had to live there and win a competition. One of the former winners went on to own the Lakers. Instead, he volleyed back.

"What do you see in Beau?"

"For one thing, he's not in this stupid business. Where else would you pretend to be engaged to accomplish your goal?"

"Ryan and Sandra in *The Proposal.*"

"That was a movie, Jon. I remember why I left: people are weird out here. They think everything is a movie. I miss New York."

"Please, New York is overcrowded and rude."

"Like everyone on any freeway in LA. Thank God I don't have to drive on the 405 anymore."

"And I don't miss getting stuck on a subway in the middle of the summer with no AC and people pressing up against me."

"New York is the capital of the world," Kerri said.

Jon laughed. "Yeah, right."

"It's sure not LA. Nothing to do here but hike and shop. Besides, LA goes to bed at 11:00 p.m. New York is up all night," Kerri said.

"Your weather sucks," Jon said.

"Yeah, it gets cold. And it snows. But that's life, Jon. Not everything is always the same. Like here in Hell-A."

"We have seasons out here," Jon defended.

"Yeah, pilot season, fire season, mudslide season, earthquake season," Kerri rattled off.

Jon stopped talking. Something clicked in his head. He smiled. Was he giving up on the NY/LA debate? "That's the scene, Kerri. That's the one we should write for *Fire and Ice*."

"They're not emotionally challenged," Kerri jumped in, talking about the characters in the film. "They're geographically challenged. I love it."

"Me too," they smiled. Kerri held her hand up for a high five. Jon slapped it. They got to work. They would sketch out the scene together, and then one of them (this time Jon) would take the lead and write a rough draft. Then Kerri would rewrite it, making it better. It's how they had worked all those years ago. Jon was proofing the scene when Kerri got a call from her mom. Kerri walked into the kitchen to take the call while Jon continued writing. Kerri came back into the living room.

"My mom is making all these Christmas-in-LA plans for tomorrow."

"Your mom doesn't like me," Jon said.

"She doesn't trust you. Besides, if she didn't like you, why would she ask if you could join us for the day?"

"She wants me around to remind me that she doesn't like me," Jon said, writing.

"How's the scene?" Kerri asked.

"Should be done in five minutes. I liked your notes."

"Great." Kerri sat on the couch and started writing on her tablet. "I'm going to work on the breakup scene."

"What breakup scene?"

"The one you're going to read to Madison."

Ten minutes later, Kerri was done. She read it: "This is very hard for me to say, because a part of me will always love you. But I can't do this anymore with you. It's just not working. We tried; we really tried to have it all. We both had the same dream, and it hasn't come true for either of us. Maybe it's time we stop dreaming, hug, and go our separate ways."

Jon stopped. He processed it. "I like it. It sounds uniquely familiar."

"It's what you said to me when we broke up years ago," Kerri said.

"That's why it sounded so real."

Neither said anything. Kerri went into the bedroom and came out in her workout clothes. "I'm going for a run. Want to join me?"

"Sure, that sounds good."

They drove over to Silver Lake, neither talking about their breakup. The fence was lined with Christmas tree lights as they hit the 2.5-mile trail. Kerri was in great shape, jogging ahead. Jon tried to keep up, but something else was bothering him. He stopped jogging, breathing deeply as Kerri circled back to him.

"What's wrong, Jon? Are you okay?"

"I'm sorry…"

"Sorry. For not keeping up with me?"

"For breaking us up. For writing that stupid science fiction script. For not believing in us. I was scared. I should be thrilled. We have this movie going. And I am. And I'm glad it's with you. I just had to say how sorry I am for what I did."

Kerri smiled, rubbing his back. "It's okay, Jon. We weren't doing well. No one was hiring us. We were a team that didn't work out. Let's just try to enjoy this now. Besides, if we didn't break up, you would never be with Madison."

Jon laughed. Kerri took off running. Jon was feeling better. He caught up with her and kept the pace. They would complete their run, grab takeout from a hip new Thai place, find Hitchcock's movie *Notorious* on a streaming channel, and enjoy what might have been their first night of real friendship.

Neither of them mentioned what they both remembered—that way back in film school, when they were first dating, they got some takeout and watched the same movie. It was after watching the movie that they'd made love for the first time.

CHAPTER 22

December 10

JON AND KERRI WERE HAVING breakfast at Hugo's in West Hollywood with Diane and Troy.

The check came, and Jon quickly grabbed it. "Oh no, we got this," Troy said, putting his hand out on the check.

"Nope. Let me get this," Jon said as he put his hand on the other side of the check.

Kerri smiled as she watched her dad and her pseudo fiancé jockey for the right to pay the bill.

"This is where we had our first meeting," Kerri suddenly remembered.

"Which is why I'm paying the bill," Jon said. "It's good luck."

Kerri looked at Jon, who had been growing on her over the past few days. Even though Kerri knew Beau would be a much better choice, she realized that she hadn't thought about Beau for a few days. They hadn't even communicated because of the twelve-hour time difference. And here was Jon, check wrestling with her dad. The restaurant was filled with his laughter. He had a way of making everyone around him feel better. He walked into every room like he owned it, even when he had only one hundred dollars in his bank account. Jon won the "who should pay the check" skirmish. Kerri watched as he gave the waitress a big tip. He was always generous about gratuities, something Kerri liked about him.

"Nice place," Troy said. "Did you two go here often?"

"Only when someone else was paying," Jon said. "We couldn't afford it."

"A producer had invited us to breakfast to talk about *Fire and Ice*. I really thought he was going to buy the script, but all he bought us was eggs," Kerri added.

"We were so naive," Jon chuckled.

"And look at you now," Diane piped up. She had been enjoying her coffee. "Now *Fire and Ice* is in production, and you're fake engaged." Diane was beaming.

"So, what should we do today?" Troy asked.

"We've got the day free because it's a night shoot," Kerri said.

"Great! Why don't we do some Christmassy things?" Diane said.

"That could be fun," Troy said. "I always wanted to go see what Christmas in LA was like." Kerri couldn't believe how giddy her parents were. Their enthusiasm was infectious. She quickly got into the Christmas spirit.

"What about ice skating?" Kerri said. "I remember that Pershing Square put up a terrific outdoor rink in December and January. And they have this great cinnamon hot cocoa."

Jon put away his credit card.

"Jon, why don't you join us?"

Jon broke into a smile. "Sure. You had me at *hot cocoa*."

The foursome arrived at Pershing Square, and even though

it was 80 degrees outside, the air felt chilly as the coolness from the ice wafted into the air. Blades scratched across the man-made rink as teenagers raced around the oval shape, almost knocking down skaters twirling in colorful skirts. The guards wore Santa hats, while little children put on red mittens to keep their hands warm. Christmas tunes blasted out of large speakers, and the smell of hot cocoa wafted out from the pop-up hot chocolate bar.

As Jon laced up his skates, he felt a thrill up his spine. He hadn't been skating since Kerri left. He hadn't been to any Christmas attractions since he and Kerri had broken up and she'd moved to Brooklyn. He sighed as he realized in that moment that Christmas had been kind of lonely without her.

Jon wobbled onto the ice, determined not to fall. Kerri was already swirling around on the rink, loving every minute. She noticed Jon struggling and raced over to him, making a quick turnaround to skate backward directly in front of him just before she grabbed his hand.

"Need some help?" Kerri asked.

"Always."

"I'm holding your hand, but don't get used to this."

Jon chuckled, but the hot cocoa wasn't the only thing making him feel warm inside.

Across the ice, Diane and Troy were holding hands as they skated side by side. They were beaming as they watched Jon and Kerri skate. "I'm starting to like Jon," Diane admitted. "It's too bad she's already engaged to Beau."

"He's a good kid," Troy added.

"Jon or Beau?"

"I don't really know Beau yet."

"Well, I like the way Jon looks at her. Reminds me of the way you used to look at me," Diane said.

"And still do," Troy said as he reached down to kiss Diane.

Across the rink, Kerri noticed her parents kissing and groaned to Jon, "Too much PDA."

"Hey, it's sweet. At least they're still in love. I think your parents are great," Jon said.

Kerri nodded. She knew that Jon was right. She had hit the lotto jackpot when it came to parents, as they'd provided a good road map for how to have a successful marriage. As they continued to skate, Jon improved and was able to skate on his own. Kerri twirled around him and practiced simple spins. She was exhilarated and couldn't remember the last time that she'd been on the ice. She'd meant to skate in New York City, but she'd always been too busy.

Troy skated over to Kerri. "Your mother is getting hungry."

"You mean you're getting hungry, Dad."

"Yes. Was it that obvious?"

"We could go to Olvera Street," Jon suggested.

Kerri just smiled. "Good idea. And I know the perfect place."

"Are you thinking what I'm thinking you're thinking?" Jon grinned.

Kerri nodded. "La Luz."

"Del Dia," Jon added.

One of the things that Kerri had loved about Jon was how he knew what was on her mind. At their best, they could be so in sync.

Thirty minutes later, Jon, Kerri, and her parents were eating alfresco at La Luz Del Dia, a cafeteria-style Michoacan Mexican lunch spot on Olvera Street. Kerri bit into her tamale and moaned.

"You okay, Kerri?" Troy asked.

"This tamale is amazing. Just the way I remembered it."

"I always liked how you moaned when you loved your food," Jon said with a twinkle in his eye.

Kerri took another bite. "The chicken is so moist, and the spices are perfect." As she chewed, she noticed the street was decorated lavishly with colorful wreaths and lights and pinatas hanging on stalls. Kerri felt giddy and pinched herself, not believing that she was back on Olvera Street, her favorite place to eat at Christmastime. Jon crunched on his chicharrones while Troy devoured his carnitas.

"Have you been here before?" Diane asked.

"Many times. We used to love coming here after a meeting in the valley. We'd just hop over on the 101," Kerri said, covering her mouth as she continued to eat.

"It was kind of our place," Jon said, prompting Troy and Diane to look up from their carnitas and nopales to stare at Jon. Kerri fidgeted and crossed her legs as she realized she'd brought her parents to the place where she and Jon had eaten many meals together, a place of happy memories. She tried to think of Beau and the name of their "place" but came up empty, because she and Beau hadn't established a place that was theirs. They didn't eat out much because of Beau's frugality.

Jon noticed Kerri's discomfort and quickly covered. "We love this place because it's so cheap—and it has great history."

"In 1915 there was a La Luz Del Dia grocery store a few blocks down on Main Street where the 101 freeway is today, and the restaurant started in 1959," Kerri added.

Kerri's parents nodded, their mouths full of guacamole. Kerri's shoulders relaxed as she realized her parents weren't going to ask her about Beau.

"So who's up for a movie?" Jon asked.

"We can see a movie anywhere, Jon," Diane replied.

"Not at The Egyptian you can't," Troy said. "*It's a Wonderful Life* is playing."

"The Egyptian!"

Kerri tilted her head up to see the ornately painted ceiling at the fabled Egyptian Hollywood movie palace. She munched popcorn, enjoying the salty, crunchy treat, and turned to Jon. "This was such a good idea. Thanks!" Kerri punched him.

"Ouch. You're punching me? Are we in first grade?" Jon laughed.

Kerri giggled. She was in her happy place and couldn't believe that she was having this much fun with Jon. It had been such a hard breakup that, at the time, she'd thought that they could never be friends again.

The giant velvet curtains parted as the lights dimmed and the movie began. Kerri settled into her seat. As she reached for the popcorn, she brushed Jon's hand and considered holding it until she remembered that they weren't a couple anymore. Troy and Diane sat next to them holding hands and smiling up at the screen as the credits rolled for the start of the film.

Kerri, Jon, Troy, and Diane walked slowly out of the theater. "I can't believe how that movie still holds up," Diane said.

"You're right. It never gets old," Troy added.

Jon squeezed Kerri's arm and smiled at her. "It's the kind of movie we'd love to write someday."

Kerri turned away from Jon, not replying to his offer, brushing the thought aside. As far as she was concerned, *Fire and Ice* was a one-and-done with Jon. She knew how lucky they were to have a green lighted film, and there was no way that lightning was going to strike twice.

Kerri checked her watch. "We'd better get moving if we want to arrive at the set on time. They're shooting at the Venice Canals. It's the boat parade. You can watch all the boats decorated with holiday lights."

"I'll go get the car. Why don't you all wait here?" Jon suggested.

Kerri waited with her parents, who were beaming. "We want you to know how much we've enjoyed this day with Jon," Troy said.

Diane added, "We know it's only a fake engagement, but we still want you to know that we were totally wrong about Jon."

"We see you two together, and it's magical," Troy said.

Kerri gulped. "Thanks, Mom. Thanks, Dad. I guess it's the magic of Hollywood." And she knew that Hollywood had that way of making you think something was magic, even when it was only fleeting. This thing with Jon wasn't going to last past Christmas, when the movie was done filming. And yet, in spite of that knowledge, Kerri knew it was going to be tough to dump Jon, her fake fiancé, no matter how perfect Beau might be.

CHAPTER 23

December 11

THE NEXT NIGHT, AFTER A slow day of filming, Kerri and Jon Ubered to the Santa Monica Pier, giddy with excitement. They had been invited to the land of Oz, also known as the fabled pier party that was thrown by their agent only for A-list clients, an exclusive list that now included Kerri and Jon thanks to their big studio movie now in production. When Kerri struggled to take off her warm sweater, Jon helped to pull it off. Her skin tingled at his touch. They both locked eyes for a moment and then pulled away. They arrived at the Pier where the strong Santa Ana winds made the giant blow-up Santa Claus fight to stay in place.

"Looks like the Pier is ready for its Christmas close-up," Jon joked.

"I'd heard about this event from Charlotte's assistant but never dreamed we'd get invited," Kerri said as she skipped happily toward the entrance.

The Ferris wheel lights illuminated a snowman. The lights of the roller coaster flashed red and green as it streaked past a

Christmas tree made of only lights. Snowflake decorations were interspersed with the Star of David and Hanukkah candles. Santa was riding the carousel with young kids and youthful adults. And Charlotte Adams was greeting clients.

"There they are. My favorite clients. Welcome to the party," Charlotte called out. Kerri and Jon recognized some famous actors enjoying the night out with their families. They were all eating boardwalk food, going on the rides.

"It's my favorite couple!" Amari called out as she walked toward them. She was dressed as a sexy elf. Richard, in a suit and Santa hat, walked beside her.

"Lukas couldn't make it," Amari explained, though no one had asked her.

"Ah, that's too bad." Jon asked, "Is Lukas okay?" Jon hoped he wasn't and would have to step down as the director.

"The holidays make him sad. He goes to a dark place," Amari said.

How could he go any darker? Jon thought.

"Always great to see you, Richard," Kerri said, defusing the tension.

"Thanks, Kerri. Nice to see you both," Richard smiled.

"Let's go on some rides," Amari squealed, already pulling Richard along as Kerri stayed frozen in place. Jon knew what was wrong, as he suddenly remembered it all too well.

"You know I hate rides," Kerri said like a little kid.

Jon smiled wickedly. "I know you do. But not tonight! This sham engagement can't have any plot holes." Kerri's face dropped as Jon dragged her toward the roller coaster. For Jon, who loved rides, this roller coaster at Pacific Park wasn't even a roller coaster; it was a toddler's plaything. For Kerri, it was a gargantuan snake that never ceased undulating. As they ascended, Jon looked out on the coastline up toward Malibu, grinning with ecstasy. Kerri held on tightly to the safety bars, already deep breathing in a failed self-calming kind of way.

"You know, roller coasters are a metaphor for life in the film business. Lots of ups and downs and twists and turns," Jon philosophized. Kerri clutched tighter, her knuckles turning white. "We're getting close to the top, looking at this amazing view, and then suddenly we're plummeting to our doom! Just like a normal day in Hollywood."

The coaster took its first dive. Jon had timed his delivery perfectly. Kerri let out a high-pitched scream and reached for Jon's hand. Jon laughed, loving the coaster. Kerri loved it when it was over.

"Never again," she said, her face ashen, which Jon took as an invitation to get Kerri on every ride with him, Richard, and Amari. The Sea Dragon. The Seaside Swing. The Scrambler.

Richard and Amari rushed off the Scrambler as they had to go say hello to some people. They would meet up with Jon and Kerri in a little bit. Kerri stumbled off the Scrambler, toward the handrails of the barrier at the edge of the pier. She felt as if the world was spinning.

"I don't feel well, Jon," Kerri said.

She looked back at the ocean. The waves were fine, but she felt like the pier was rocking. Someone was walking their way.

"Kerri? Jon? I thought that was you," Ross Canton said with a big smile. He greeted Kerri and Jon with hugs. "You okay?" Kerri nodded and Ross continued. "Roller coaster?" Ross chuckled. "So great to see you. I thought you guys had left the business. Then I saw the announcement in *Deadline*. So happy for you. I always loved that script."

Ross was one of the nice ones in Hollywood. Kerri and Jon met him when *Fire and Ice* made the rounds and no one bought it.

"You should come in. We should find something to work on together. I would love to hear your ideas. I got my own money these days. Partnered with a hedge fund."

"We have a light day on the set next Thursday, and we could stop in," Jon said.

"I'm sure you're booked," Kerri said, deflecting.

"For you two, I'll make the time," he said checking his phone. "I don't know how you two did it. Writing as a team and staying in a relationship. Congrats, by the way."

"We're very excited about the movie," Kerri said.

"Of course, but I was talking about the engagement ring you're wearing. My brother's in the jewelry business. What's that? Two carats? Good choice, Jon. I got to run. My kids are waiting, somewhere. I'll see you Thursday at 3:00 p.m."

When Ross was out of earshot, Kerri stared at Jon.

"I know. We don't have anything. But we will," Jon said. Kerri trusted him. She felt oddly calm, maybe because she was living the life she thought she always wanted. The question was, did she still want it? She could feel Hollywood pulling her back in. She could feel herself starting to dream once again.

They joined Amari and Richard, who were playing arcade games. Richard and Jon tried the baseball toss. Jon nailed it in with three throws, winning a large elf and giving a fist pump of triumph as he handed it to Kerri, who swelled with pride at Jon's win.

"Your first baby," Amari exclaimed. "Take a picture..." Kerri and Jon proudly posed with their stuffed elf.

"I think he looks like you, Jon," Kerri said.

"He does have my eyes."

"I never won a carnival prize," Richard said under his breath. He loosened his shoulders like a baseball pitcher at the mound with the bases loaded and two outs. Then he tried again. And again. He was determined to win something for Amari but wasn't coming close. Not even one block was knocked down.

Amari nudged Kerri and said, "Come with me to the restroom." Kerri tossed Jon their stuffed elf child, but Jon wasn't ready for it. It dropped to the ground. He pretended to look alarmed and quickly picked it up, rocking it like a baby, soothing it.

As they walked away, Amari commented, "You two are so cute together. How's the wedding planning?"

Kerri didn't have to lie about this one. "I went shopping with my mother for a wedding dress."

"Did you and Jon always know you would end up together?"

"We started dating in film school, and here we are."

"So, it was a set romance that led to more."

"Yes," Kerri said.

"I'm kind of in a set romance with Lukas. You and Jon give me so much hope for true love," Amari said.

Back at the baseball toss, Richard was twenty dollars in, and each throw was worse than the one before. Yet he was determined to win one for Amari. Richard pleaded, "Jon, before they get back, throw another one."

"You don't need to win a prize for Amari," Jon said.

"I do. You won one for Kerri."

"Wow, you like her, don't you, Richard?"

"It shows, right? Put in a good word for me..."

"I'll put in a good word for you if you convince her to tell that director that he needs to stick to the script."

"Deal," Richard said, smiling.

"Why does what I say matter to Amari?"

"All she keeps saying is, 'I want a relationship like Kerri and Jon. They're the perfect couple. They work together. Love together.' Now, you won a prize. I must win a prize. Hey, carnival kid, I'll give you a hundred bucks for the stuffed animal."

The teenage kid working there said that was unethical and informed Richard he would have to knock the three bottles off the stand and one of them would have to have to land upright to win the giant elephant. A frustrated Richard tossed his last baseball, not even caring where the ball went. The errant ball somehow knocked into the bottles, and they fell off the table. If it was a movie, it would have been slow motion, as the bottles fell and one landed right side up.

"Yes!" Richard roared as Amari and Kerri returned. He handed Amari the enormous elephant and her eyes lit up like it was Christmas morning. She clutched the stuffed toy and kissed Richard on the cheek.

The couples (neither of them a couple) made their way to the Christmas photo booth. This time, Kerri couldn't say no to the photo booth. They took a few pictures as a group of four. Then Richard and Amari took a few where she sat on his lap. And finally, Kerri and Jon were ushered into the booth by Amari.

They took some pictures of the two of them with their newly acquired baby elf. Amari was not satisfied.

"Give me the elf. I'll babysit. Get back in there. You have a movie going. Your career is exploding. You're planning your wedding. Show me how much you love each other."

Inside the booth, Jon looked at Kerri. "It's for the movie."

Kerri echoed, "For the movie."

They leaned toward each other at the same time, their heads turning the same way they had countless times. Their lips touched each other passionately as the photo booth clicked away.

As she kissed Jon, Kerri forgot that it was for the movie. She felt his soft lips on hers and remembered that Jon had always been a great kisser, much better than anyone else she had ever kissed. There was passion running through her veins...

As he kissed Kerri, Jon thought, *Oh my God, I am kissing Kerri.* And it felt great. With that one kiss, he tried to make up for all the years he had missed. The photos kept spitting out. Amari was already posting them to Instagram.

The carnival over, they Ubered back to the apartment. Jon looked at the photos of their kiss. Kerri was exhausted, and when the driver made a sharp curve, Kerri leaned into Jon and let her head roll onto Jon's shoulder. She relaxed and stayed there. Jon didn't want to move an inch.

"You don't have to sleep on the couch tonight," Kerri said softly.

"I don't..."

"We can share the bed."

That was good enough for Jon. He loved being back with Kerri, even if he wasn't back with Kerri. He would take what he could get.

CHAPTER 24

December 12

IT WAS FRIDAY, AND KERRI was prepacking her suitcase for the quick weekend trip she was taking to Brooklyn the next day. The school show was being performed tomorrow, and Beau would be returning from India. Amari and everyone involved in the production had no idea she was flying home for the school holiday show. Her stomach clenched as she thought about seeing Beau again. It was going to be a whirlwind two days, and Kerri should have been excited, but she was surprisingly more amped up about the pitch meeting that she had with Jon in two hours.

Jon was deciding which shirt to wear to the meeting. "What about this one?" Jon said.

"I remember that shirt," Kerri said. "You held on to everything."

Not everything, Jon thought as he watched Kerri packing for her trip to see Beau. He was surprised it was upsetting him as much as it was. He rationalized it as just nerves about the Ross Canton pitch. It had been a long time since he and Kerri had gone into a room together to pitch a story. When he was solo, he had worn Hawaiian shirts to meetings. He held one up.

"That's the Duke's shirt," Kerri chuckled, remembering.

"It is." Jon laughed. During their first year in LA after film school, Diane had flown out to visit the young couple for Mother's Day. She was not happy with their living arrangements, and to appease her, Jon and Kerri took her to Duke's for Mother's Day brunch. It was a Malibu institution. It had great seafood, bottomless mimosas, and was on the beach right next to the Pacific. A few drinks in, Diane was finally smiling, aided by the playful dolphins that swam by. Jon excused himself to go to the restroom, and when he returned to the table, another customer called Jon over to ask about the whereabouts of his meal. Why was he asking Jon? It turned out Jon had worn the same shirt as all the waiters. All this led to Kerri's mother thinking Jon secretly worked there, and she wanted the employee discount.

But that was in the past, as Jon's wardrobe had improved. He chose a tight T-shirt and open untucked flannel shirt along with jeans and his faithful pair of Allbirds. Kerri dressed in NY black. They checked in on the *Fire and Ice* movie set, which was shooting at the Santa Monica Airport.

"Good luck today," Amari said, hugging them. "Let me know how it goes."

"How what goes?" Kerri asked, trying to keep it private.

"Your meeting with Ross Canton. He called me to check up on you two. Funny, he thought you had broken up…" Amari wondered.

"Well, it is LA," Jon said. "The expiration date for any relationship out here is two years tops."

Amari smiled. "I'm so happy that you two have exceeded all my expirations." Kerri turned away to wince, hating that she was lying to Amari.

Jon and Kerri drove to the Sony lot. There was traffic, but they had left early enough to get there with extra time to have coffee, hit the restroom, and get to the meeting when the caffeine kicked in. Jon held up a CD as they merged on the 405 to the 10.

"Is that what I think it is? The PumpUp playlist?" Kerri said in disbelief.

"It is," Jon said as he inserted the CD. "This might be the only car in LA that still has a CD player that works." He pressed Play, but nothing came out. They fussed with it as the traffic snarled, but the CD was dead.

"It's okay," Kerri said, "Some things don't last. I'm surprised this car is still going."

They arrived at the studio, picked up their "drive ons" at the guard gate and parked. The commissary was closed for filming for the entire afternoon. No coffee and no PumpUp CD in the car. So far, this pitch meeting had bad karma. Jon didn't want to say it out loud, but he was certainly thinking it.

They went into the meeting, each having doubts. Ross was waiting for them with his creative team.

"Kerri, Jon! Thanks for coming in. And congratulations; have you set a date yet?"

"For what?" Kerri asked, truly confused.

"Ha ha, I love that you're so coy about your engagement."

Kerri covered up with a laugh. "Oh that, right!"

"We might elope," Jon said quickly, trying to save Kerri.

"Smart. Get to the good stuff," Ross said. "Where are you going on your honeymoon?"

Kerri didn't have time to think. Jon was already answering, "It depends."

"Depends on what?" Ross asked.

"How well this pitch goes. I'm hoping for Fiji," Jon said. Kerri smiled as she saw Jon lean a little closer to Ross. It was "game on" for him.

"No pressure," Ross joked. "What do you got?"

The screenwriting couple went into work mode.

"Funny you brought up the engagement," Kerri said. "Most mothers don't like anyone their sons bring home…"

"My mother hated Kerri."

Laughter. "They loved me," Kerri said. "She hated all your other girlfriends." More laughter. They had planned every joke and gesture.

Kerri delivered the hook: "So on the day of the wedding, an overprotective mom kidnaps the bride to be, only to find out that she is right, and the bride has been hiding something big…"

"We're calling it *Welcome to the Family*."

The execs had stopped writing; they were listening, engrossed in the story, loving the pitch. Enjoying Kerri and Jon who were back in partner mode. Hitting every joke, taking Ross and his development team through a summary of the movie, pausing for hilarity and heart.

The pitch took about fifteen minutes, and at the end, the execs leaned back. No one said anything. The team waited for their leader to speak. "Is Amari involved?" Ross asked.

Oh no, Kerri thought. *Do they only want us because of Amari?*

"No. She's not attached," Jon said. "We could ask…"

Ross relaxed. "Good. I think there are so many young actresses who would be perfect for this. Who do we call?"

Who do we call? Jon and Kerri both knew those were the magic words writers wanted to hear in a meeting. *Who do we contact to buy this story?*

Kerri and Jon had barely stepped out of the office bungalow

when Kerri's phone was buzzing with a call from Charlotte. "They want to make a deal. Stay close to the phone." A deal? A deal? Kerri was thrilled. She hugged Jon. They practically skipped to their car, and when it started, the CD roared to life. "Eye of the Tiger" blasted on, and it wouldn't turn off. It played over and over as they drove back to Jon's apartment.

The balloons from Amari arrived before the offer, with the note: CONGRATULATIONS TO MY FAVORITE COUPLE. *How did she find out so soon?* Kerri wondered. She felt like she was living a dream— the dream she had given up on. And now it was coming true.

"Do you still have it?" Kerri asked Jon, hopeful. "If you don't, I understand. It's been a long time."

Jon knew what she was talking about. He searched the back of his closet, throwing out baseball bats, tennis rackets, and boxes until he finally pulled out an old steamer trunk. He wiped off the rim and clicked it open to reveal a dusty bottle of Dom Perignon. Kerri rushed over, admiring the Dom. They'd bought the very expensive champagne their first night in LA, determined to open it when they sold their first script, assuming that would be in only a few months, six at the most. But the years had passed, and the bottle had become a paperweight in the kitchen until, finally, it was relegated to the old trunk. Kerri was impressed how Jon had kept the bottle for both of them, just as he had kept their dream alive.

They put the Dom on ice and waited for the offer. They were talking in detail about how well the pitch had gone and how in sync they were when Charlotte called. Kerri picked up the phone and switched it to speakerphone so that they both could hear.

"Five hundred thousand," Charlotte announced triumphantly. "Two hundred and fifty thousand applicable for the first rewrite. Another hundred thousand bonus when the movie goes.

And fifty thousand each for producing credit. I'm proud of you two for getting back together."

"Thank you so much, Charlotte." She ended the call.

Kerri dropped the phone, utterly stunned. She jumped up and down repeatedly, shrieking like a kid on a trampoline. Jon was smiling ear to ear as he popped the cork of the champagne; the bubbles flowed out as he poured two glasses.

"Congratulations, Kerri. Cheers."

"Cheers, Jon. Congrats!"

Jon and Kerri toasted each other, sipping the champagne.

"This is even better than I thought it would be," Kerri said.

"Worth the wait."

"Are you talking about the champagne or the deal?"

"Both." They stared into each other's eyes. Kerri looked away uncomfortably. She gulped her champagne, the bubbles tickling her throat. Kerri held out her empty glass to Jon.

"Please, sir, I want some more."

Jon poured more champagne for both of them. They clinked glasses again. "I still can't believe we sold the pitch in the room," Jon said.

"That never happens. At least not to us."

"Guess this means you're stuck working with me for a bit longer."

Kerri was starting to feel light-headed and giddy. Maybe it was because she hadn't eaten much, or maybe it was because the champagne was going to her head. But at that moment, she looked deeply into Jon's eyes and found them calling to her, and she leaped into his arms. They laughed and hugged. They would not remember who kissed who first. It didn't matter. No words were ever said. They kissed their way into the bedroom, and just like with the way they stuck the rhythm of the pitch, things happened.

CHAPTER 25

December 13

KERRI WOKE UP TO THE sound of her buzzing alarm and a throbbing headache. The champagne had gone straight to her head last night, but she had been ecstatically happy in a way that she hadn't been in a long time.

The rest of the night was a little hazy. She wasn't a 100 percent certain, but she thought that she and Jon had kissed. A kiss that turned into a big make-out session. She thought that she might have stripped off her clothes. *Did something else happen?* she wondered. She quickly sat up in Jon's bed. The realization washed over her. She had convinced Jon to have sex. Not once or twice. But three times. Yes, it was all coming back to Kerri. The hot and wet night. It was amazing. Sex with Jon had always been good, but it seemed to have gotten better. Maybe Madison had taught him a few tricks.

The front door opened, and Jon practically skipped into the room with a cup of coffee and two Tylenol. He looked giddy. She recognized that "I got me some" look. She sighed again, and this time there was no solace. To make matters worse, she realized that she had no pants on.

"Rise and shine, pretty," Jon said.

"I feel awful," Kerri said.

"Tylenol will help."

"No, I feel awful about what we did."

"Sure didn't seem that way last night."

"Jon, I'm engaged. And not to you. Not really."

"So we had some fun."

Kerri groaned. "Ugh, we shouldn't have done that."

Jon looked away. He didn't say anything. He sipped his coffee thoughtfully.

"What do you want to do?" he finally asked.

"I have to go back to New York this morning." Kerri struggled to pull on her pants and bra. When she lifted her head, it felt like a sledgehammer was crashing on her skull.

"Wait, why?"

"I told you. My students are putting on their Christmas show. I'm technically the director."

"So not to see Beau?"

"No. I mean yes. Of course, I have to see Beau. He's my fiancé." She sighed. "My real one. You saw me packing my suitcase yesterday."

Jon did remember that Kerri was going back to New York. On a 10:30 a.m. flight. He was only hoping that she might have changed her mind, after last night. He looked a little sad. "I'm too busy to drive you to the airport. You'll have to get an Uber. And it's not going to be me."

Kerri pulled on the only clean sweater that wasn't in her suitcase, the ugly Christmas sweater her parents had brought.

She looked ridiculous in the gingerbread top and moaned. It was going to be a long day.

———————

Kerri stepped onto the plane and fell asleep almost immediately. When she woke up five hours later, she felt surprisingly refreshed. Flying into JFK, she watched as the skyline of Manhattan drew closer and closer. She inhaled deeply and finally felt better. New York City always had that effect on her. It was a city that had given her nothing but happiness. A new life. A new career and a new man. She told herself that she was looking forward to seeing Beau.

When she arrived at JFK, she took the shuttle to the subway line to her apartment in Williamsburg. She loved the public transportation in New York City, something that Los Angeles was badly lacking. She shivered as she walked down Bedford Avenue in Williamsburg and realized that she'd left her down coat in her apartment, causing her to pick up her pace toward her building. As she trudged up the stairs, she felt her anxiety grow. She needed to see Beau.

The smell of chocolate immersed her senses as she stepped through the front door. Beau was there! And he was making her favorite chocolate chip cookies. He rushed toward her with a hug. Her heart caught in her throat when she first saw him.

"I hope you don't mind that I broke into your apartment," Beau laughed. He was of Scandinavian descent, tall and blond, and looked completely at home in one of Kerri's aprons.

"Silly, that's why I gave you a key. I'm just so glad you're here. When did your flight get in?"

"A few hours ago."

"You feel jet lagged?"

"A bit. It's like 4:00 a.m. for me. And I was up all night working."

Kerri fidgeted with her keys and realized their banter lacked any intimacy.

Hoping to rectify the situation, Kerri hugged him again. She felt his taut stomach pressed against hers. "I missed you. And I'm starving." Which was true as Kerri realized that she hadn't eaten anything all day since the Starbucks muffin that Jon had given her. "What is that delicious smell?"

Beau handed her the plate of cookies, and Kerri happily munched down three chocolate chip delights. "You look good, Kerri. Really relaxed."

"I slept for the entire plane ride."

"It's more than that. You look different. More confident."

"We sold a pitch yesterday."

"We?"

"Jon and I sold a pitch. For a lot of money."

"Wow. Can you taste the Mexican vanilla?" he asked.

"Hmmm. Yes. Thank you."

"So I guess this means you'll be working with Jon again."

"Yes." Kerri didn't mean to sound terse, but that's what it sounded like.

"And...this means you're quitting your job?"

Kerri laughed and grabbed another cookie. "Of course not. I love my job teaching."

Beau relaxed his shoulders, and his face lit up in a smile. "Ok, and just don't have too many cookies. I made these for the reception after the show."

"Oh, right. I can't believe you remembered!"

"And after your show, I made us 9:00 p.m. dinner reservations."

"That's nice," Kerri said, getting excited.

"At Nami Nori. I figured you might want some sushi after a long flight."

"You are just too good to be true," Kerri said as she quickly kissed him on the lips. And that's when she wondered, *Is Beau too good to be true?* She brushed aside those doubts and hurried to change her clothes.

———————

The middle school production of *A Christmas Carol* was ending, and the audience jumped to their feet and applauded—a standing ovation. Kerri was bursting with happiness as this was everything that she'd hoped for back when they first started rehearsals. Kerri had revised the classic tale to fit the life of a teenager so that Scrooge was turned into Susanne, a rich mean girl who refused to help anyone. When Susanne got into a skiing accident in the French Alps, she was forced to revisit her life in the past and present. Through looking at her past life, the audience gained an understanding of Susanne's meanness, as she was a lonely only child brought up by numerous nannies while her wealthy parents ignored her for globe-trotting and partying. While the audience watched the ghost of the present, they saw Susanne wielding power as the leader of the mean girl group that substituted for the real family that she lacked. Most sobering of all, Susanne watched her future, where there was a lavish funeral in St. Patrick's Cathedral on Park Avenue, and not one person attended. Only the priest was there, as her parents were too busy getting plastic surgery. And none of her so-called "mean girl" friends bothered to attend as they jostled for leadership in the power vacuum left in Susanne's wake. In iconic *Christmas Carol* fashion, Susanne learned the error of her ways and became a good person in the end.

The jubilant students brought Kerri up on stage, and the applause grew louder. Kerri was buzzing with happiness. The lavish and creative production had gone better than she'd ever dreamed, and she pinched herself. Parents circled Kerri and shook her hand with exclamations of "Genius idea," "Incredible writing," and "Our kids are so lucky." Kerri was beaming and told them that it wouldn't have been possible without their kids while Beau watched proudly from the back of the auditorium.

As everyone finally left, Beau brought her jacket. "It was great, Kerri. I never realized what a good writer you are."

I think there's a lot that you don't know about me, Kerri thought. The question was, how much did she want to tell him?

CHAPTER 26

December 13

KERRI MOANED WITH PLEASURE. *THIS is truly amazing*, she thought. *Life just can't get any better.* She closed her eyes.

"Kerri? Could you stop moaning? It's kind of annoying."

Kerri opened her eyes. She wasn't in bed with Beau, but he was by her side. They were eating at Nami Nori, her favorite restaurant in Williamsburg. "I forgot how amazing this sushi is." She held out a piece to Beau. "You have to try it."

Beau started to nod off, his eyes closing. Kerri thought she should just let him sleep. If he was asleep, he couldn't ask her about the movie or about Jon. If he did ask, what would she say? *I'm not sure about how the movie will come out. But I did have sex with Jon, and it was great. And confusing. And great.*

"Oh! Sorry!" Beau jolted awake. "I'm so jet-lagged." Beau rubbed his eyes.

"Makes sense." She held out the sushi to him.

"It's okay. I like my tempura."

Kerri shook her head. "You're missing out." She knew her

fiancé hated sushi, and yet he was still willing to take her to a restaurant where 95 percent of the menu was raw fish.

"Thanks for bringing me here, Beau." She leaned in to kiss him.

He pulled away, laughing. "Not with the fishy breath!"

"I can't believe how good the show was tonight. To be honest, I wasn't sure if the kids could pull it off."

"It was great." Beau struggled to keep his eyes open as his shoulders slumped.

"I'll get this to go. Let's get you to bed."

Kerri and Beau were lying in bed, but Kerri was the only one sleeping. It was 5:00 a.m., and Beau was on his laptop. "So we do need to set a date. We can't move forward without that. Kerri?" He nudged her awake.

"Huh?"

"A date. For our wedding."

Kerri sat up groggily, her jaw tightening at the word *wedding*. "Now?"

"Sorry. I know it's early, but I'm just so wired. It's like 5:00 p.m. for me."

"And 2:00 a.m. for me LA time."

"But since you're awake, let's talk about the wedding. We should figure out the venue first. And then see what dates are available." Beau continued to tap on his laptop. "I've been doing some research, and I found some possible venues. The first two are in Brooklyn." Beau typed into the search bar, and the images of a historic beaux arts building popped up.

Kerri struggled to sit up and collapsed against the pillow. "That place looks nice," she said matter-of-factly.

Beau launched into his architect's pitch mode. She'd seen him do this before when he was trying to win over a new client. "Nice? The place is an architectural dream." As Beau read from the website, Kerri's mind started to glaze over. She wondered what Jon was doing. Was he working on the pitch that they'd just sold, or was he taking the weekend off as he'd promised? She hated to miss out on anything, and he knew that about her.

Beau continued to drone on, "'Weylin's spectacular frescoed dome, intricate mosaics, wooden carvings, and period decor make it the perfect backdrop for a diverse array of events from weddings and galas to performances, art shows, and experiential activations.'" Beau paused. "Kerri? Kerri? Earth to Kerri."

Kerri jolted upward, "Sorry. Still on LA time." She leaned in to look at the website and clicked on the word *FILM*. "Wow, amazing. *The Irishman*. They filmed there. And *Orange Is the New Black*. Let's watch the clip." She tapped on the link, and they watched several film clips where the Weylin building was used as the setting.

"Yeah, that's great. Makes sense that it's being used for filmmaking. It was a focal point for an entire generation of beaux arts structures in the United States. The architect, George B. Post, later went on to design the New York Stock Exchange and Cornelius Vanderbilt II House, the largest residence in the country at the time."

"Uh-huh," Kerri said drowsily.

"The beaux art exterior serves as one of the earliest examples of the French-inspired Classical Revival style in America following the Civil War."

"So why is it called the Weylin?" Kerri asked.

"Weylin is named after a legendary character of

nineteenth-century Williamsburg. Weylin B. Seymour was a well-loved social leader, party host, and fruitful matchmaker. Serendipitously, he shared initials with the Williamsburg Savings Bank, thus sealing his fate as our beloved namesake."

"Oh. And I see that they also filmed the movie *Unforgettable* at the Weylin."

"Huh?" Beau was baffled by Kerri's lack of interest in the historical aspects of the building.

It was at that moment that Kerri realized how different their interests were. He loved history and architecture; she loved movies and entertainment. Why had she never intuited that before?

But Beau didn't seem to notice. He clicked open another website. "We could also have it on the water at The Liberty Warehouse."

Kerri sat up on her elbows, noticing her flannel pajamas. She suddenly had flashes of the previous night with Jon when she wasn't wearing any pajamas.

"Kerri?" Beau was looking at her.

"Oh, sorry. I'm still half asleep. I've heard of that place. I think my principal got married there."

Beau and Kerri leaned in to look at photos of The Liberty Warehouse. Beau's eyes lit up as he read about the history. "'Located on Pier 41 in the historic shipping yards of Red Hook, Brooklyn. The building was constructed in the pre-Civil War 1850s and has recently been renovated into a charming event space.'"

Kerri interrupted him. "I love how it's right on the water with views of the New York Harbor. We could get great shots for the video."

"What video?"

"Of our wedding."

"Oh, I thought we could just do black and white stills."

Kerri nodded. "Kind of old-fashioned." Beau's face dropped sadly. Kerri tried to cheer him. "Ok. Maybe we could do both."

Beau perked up. "So, we've got two good choices. I don't think we'll find better venues. How should we decide?"

"Maybe we should flip a coin," Kerri said with a laugh.

"I think we need to put a deposit down. The coordinators at both places told me that they're booking up. Ever since COVID, they're on overload." Kerri nodded, deep in thought.

"It doesn't have to be a lot. They said all we need is ten percent for the deposit," Beau added.

Kerri nodded as she realized she had to think of a way to slow Beau down with his accelerated plans, because she wasn't ready to move forward until the movie wrapped and Amari was out of her life.

Beau noticed her hesitation. "I don't mind putting down the deposit. It seems kind of old-fashioned that the girl's family pays for the wedding."

"Uh, this all sounds good. But I really should talk with my parents first. They might want to have the wedding in Pittsburgh. We have a lot of family and friends there."

"Makes sense." There he was again. Sweet and understanding Beau. It's what she loved about him.

"There's a cool funicular that overlooks the Pittsburgh. I know you'll love it."

"You had me at funicular," Beau said with a smile. "I'm open to Pittsburgh. There are some Frank Lloyd Wright houses there that I've always wanted to see in person."

"And Beau, I never wanted a big wedding. Can we keep it small?"

"That might be hard to do, because I have a big family." Beau noticed Kerri looking crestfallen. For the first time that day, Kerri was telling the truth. She'd never been one of those girls who wanted a grandiose wedding. If it were up to her, she'd prefer to elope or do something spontaneous without all the planning.

"But sure, we can hold off the planning, and I'll try to get my numbers down."

Kerri breathed a smile of relief. She felt like she'd just dodged a bullet. "I'm going to go back to sleep for another hour."

Beau looked disappointed. *If only he knew what was going on,* she thought. *Then he'd be a lot more disheartened.*

CHAPTER 27

December 14

KERRI LOOKED OUT HER APARTMENT window to see large wet snowflakes blanketing the sidewalks and rooftops. It was a pre-Christmas, one-inch coating that made everything festive and photogenic, but also stalled traffic. Kerri had checked her flight and was relieved to see it was still on time. She was excited to get back to LA to see what was happening on the movie shoot, and if she was being honest, to see what was happening with Jon after their tryst. She wasn't comfortable having two sexual partners and had been anxious about what might happen with Beau, but they'd been out of sync and hadn't found the time to make love. Jon had texted her, wanting to know how the show went. He was supportive and very happy for her but didn't follow up with any other texts saying *I miss you* or anything about what happened the night before she flew to New York. Kerri wasn't offering up any conversation-starting texts either, so she left it as it was. She knew the night with Jon had been an impulsive mistake and felt the new friendship she and Jon had developed could laugh off their one-night reunion.

On Sunday morning, Beau wanted to get brunch and walk around Brooklyn in the snow before she left. Romantic, possibly? Cold, absolutely. She told him she wasn't feeling well, and she didn't want Beau to catch anything from her, including catching her in a lie. Technically she had not lied to Beau, at least not yet. Nor had he asked her if she had fooled around with her ex-boyfriend. However, Beau was persistent about brunch, and she gave in, because after all he was her fiancé. They met at Mama Pho's on Bedford Avenue. Kerri had brought her luggage, as she planned to head straight to JFK airport after meeting with Beau. She was enjoying her lemongrass chicken soup when—

"So we never talked about Christmas," Beau said. "It's in ten days."

"I never make plans that far in advance," Kerri said in a Humphrey Bogart accent.

"I have no idea what you're talking about."

"It's only one of the most memorable lines of all times from probably the best movie ever."

"Which is…" Beau waited expectantly for her to reveal the movie title.

Kerri sighed in fake exasperation. "*Casablanca!*"

"Kerri, everything is not a movie! We made plans for Christmas. We're going to my parents' house in Connecticut for a few days, and then we'll drive to your parents' house in Pittsburgh for New Year's."

"I've actually been spending a lot of time with my parents because they're in LA right now. To visit the set."

"You didn't tell me that," Beau said, looking suddenly out of sorts.

There's a lot I haven't told you, Kerri thought. Instead, she burst out, "I'm kind of busy. I have a job. In fact, I have two jobs. I don't have time to share everything with you," immediately regretting what she said.

"We're engaged now. Maybe one day you will." All at once Beau seemed displeased, as *suddenly sullen* was his go-to emotion when he wasn't happy.

Kerri took a deep breath. "I'm sorry, Beau, it's not you—"

"You're giving me the it's not you, it's me, thing," Beau said, cutting her off.

"No," Kerri said, "I was going to say, 'It's not you, it's LA. I'll be better when I get back to Brooklyn. And when you get back from Toronto or India or wherever else you're going." And for emphasis she added, "For good."

"Ok. I'll be in Toronto this week. I hope we can talk at night."

The snow was coming down. Kerri decided it was quicker to take the train to the airport. Beau went with her, and neither talked much as the train rattled loudly. After a perfunctory kiss goodbye at the AirTrain terminal, Kerri waved farewell and breathed a deep sigh of relief.

The plane was on time, and she would arrive in LA, around 5:00 p.m. As Kerri sat waiting in the boarding area, she suddenly heard her name over the loudspeaker.

"Kerri Williams, please come to the counter," the gate agent announced. Kerri rushed over, slightly alarmed, her heart beating faster.

"Hello, I'm Kerri Williams, you paged me?"

"You got your upgrade to first class," the gate agent said as she handed Kerri her boarding pass.

Kerri's eyes grew bigger. "I'm confused. I didn't ask for an upgrade. Was I charged for this?" Even though she had more money in her bank account than she'd ever had in her life, she wasn't going to start spending it.

"Not charged to the original card. A Visa. Last four digits one eight eight zero."

Kerri relaxed, the tension releasing from her body. She knew that Jon had something to do with it. Kerri used to do their taxes and remembered that Jon always used a Visa card as his company card to track his business write-offs. The last four digits were 1880. She was surprisingly very moved by his gesture, making it even tougher for her not to think about him. She waited until she was in her seat, a glass of wine in her hand, to text Jon.

On plane. You didn't have to do that.
First class deserves first class.
Thank you
See you soon.

And that was it. Short and businesslike with no expectations. Her lips curled up into a smile as she took a sip of her chardonnay. She closed her eyes with the long-distance smile Jon had put on her face.

"I can see why you're so happy," a man's voice said, and Kerri recognized it immediately as it was the same producer she had met on her flight to LA a few weeks ago.

"Drew Fox!" Kerri said, opening her eyes and happy to see him. "What a coincidence. Are you 2B?"

"I was back in 3, but I saw you boarding, and I got that nice lady to switch so I could sit next to you. I hope that's okay."

"Absolutely."

Drew settled in.

"How did you know I'm happy?" Kerr asked.

"Well, one, most people don't keep smiling when their eyes are shut. And two, I figured you saw this," Drew explained, showing her his open tablet that displayed a headline from *Deadline*.

SONY SAYS WELCOME TO THE FAMILY. COMEDY PITCH SELLS FOR MID-SIX FIGURES. Below that was a picture of Jon and Kerri. Not an old picture but a recent picture from a few days ago of them smiling in the photo booth at the Santa Monica Pier. Drew read the article out loud to Kerri. Her favorite part was, "Written by the writing team of Kerri Williams and Jon Romano, whose movie *Fire and Ice* is currently in production."

As the plane taxied away from the terminal, Kerri called Jon. He answered right away. "Did you see *Deadline*?"

"I just did. It's so cool."

"I know. How did they get the pier photo of us?"

"The agency reached out to me yesterday. They wanted a picture of us. I didn't know what for. I figured that was a new one and you would be okay with it," Jon said.

"I love it, Jon. Thank you." She almost said the words she thought she would never say again, but the flight attendant reminded her to put her phone away.

Drew shut down his tablet. "You're having a pretty good month. How's the movie going?"

Kerri filled Drew in on everything that was going on, including the difficult director and how she was worried the movie would not come out well. Drew assured her he had been down that road and things could always work out. At the end of the flight, as they disembarked, Drew offered, "If you ever need anything, call me. I have a feeling we might work together someday. Tell Jon congrats."

Kerri said goodbye and had her phone out ready to call an Uber when she looked up to see Jon in a black suit, holding up a sign that said, BEST WRITING PARTNER: KERRI WILLIAMS. Kerri's body tingled, and she blushed, noticing how cute Jon looked in his driver's outfit with his homemade sign.

"Kerri Williams?" Jon pretended to be the driver who didn't know her.

"Right on time," Kerri said, playing along.

"Welcome home."

Their eyes sparkled as they looked at each other before they each leaned in for an awkward too-short hug. And then pressed in again for another hug that lingered a little too long.

Jon took her bag and led her into short-term parking. She was looking around for the car and wondered how he'd managed to get a spot on the first floor of the parking lot.

"Where's the car?" she said. "Did someone steal it?"

"Why would anyone steal that car?"

Jon pressed the alarm button on a key chain. Right behind her, a Jeep Cherokee beeped.

Kerri turned, stunned. "You bought a new car!"

"I did. Paid cash," Jon opened the door to the shiny black new car. "Come on in, we're late."

"Late? Where are we going?"

"You'll see," Jon said with a devilish grin.

CHAPTER 28

December 14

IT WAS AN AWKWARD CAR ride, as neither Kerri nor Jon wanted to address the proverbial elephant in the room of what had happened the night before Kerri left for Brooklyn. Instead, they'd made idle small talk about the new car and the weather in LA, which was nonexistent at that time of year. They got off the freeway at Sunset and drove toward the Hollywood Hills.

"Are you going to tell me what's going on?" Kerri asked, touching Jon on the arm and feeling a tremor run through her body.

"Nope," Jon laughed. "You'll just have to wait and see."

They pulled up to her parents' rental. It was decorated with bright-colored Christmas lights, and a huge blow-up Santa graced the front door. Kerri noticed that the front lawn was white. *That's odd*, she thought. Then she realized it was real snow! Adults and children were sliding down a mini hill on brightly colored plastic toboggans.

"I can't believe there's snow here! I thought I'd just left it behind," Kerri said with a laugh.

"Your dad missed the snow. So, I gave him the name of a rental company that carts it in," Jon said. "It's become a new thing to do at Christmastime out here."

"Wow. My dad rented snow. Hilarious. He hates snow! He was always complaining about having to shovel the driveway when I was a kid."

Two gorgeous twentysomething actresses ran past Kerri, both wearing cute knit hats and puffy pink jackets, the kind that would never work for temperatures below 60 degrees. Everyone seemed to be as good-looking as if they were in a movie—the irony wasn't lost on Kerri.

"Who are these people?"

"I think they're the neighbors."

"My parents have neighbors? They're renting an Airbnb. How do they know their neighbors already?"

Then Diane burst out of the house, a paper cup sloshing with chardonnay in her hand. "Kerri! You're back. And Jon!" She rushed towards them and gave Jon a big kiss on the cheek.

"I think my mother is drunk," Kerri said to Jon.

"And I have no problem with that," Jon said with a smile.

Troy walked out of the house and gave them a big hug. Unlike Diane, he was able to hold his liquor better. "Come on, you two. Let's go inside the house." Troy guided them into the house.

"Surprise!" everyone called out as Jon and Kerri stepped in to see a giant banner that read, ENGAGEMENT PARTY. Another banner read, CONGRATULATIONS TO KERRI & JON!

Kerri's mouth dropped. She quickly scanned the room, amazed by all the guests, especially the ones she recognized, including old friends from film school and everyone from the crew. "Your glass is empty!" Diane said as she rushed over with a bottle of champagne.

"I don't think I have a glass, Mom."

"We need to change that," Amari said with a huge smile. She handed Kerri and Jon each a plastic champagne flute. Richard, who was always by her side, flanked her, carrying more champagne.

"Amari!" Kerri hugged her. "I can't believe you're here! Wow, this is a great party!"

"It was her idea," Troy said. "When she called me up, she made me an offer I couldn't refuse," Troy said, quoting one of his favorite movies.

"I told him I'd pay for all the alcohol." Amari grinned.

Suddenly Amari got up on the table, her glass held high. "I want to toast my new friends, the best couple I've ever met. They embody what it means to have found true love."

"True love!" everyone yelled.

The crowd oohed and ahead while Kerri and Jon looked at each other a little stiffly, but nobody seemed to notice.

"Seriously, one of the reasons I wanted to do this movie was because the screenwriters were a couple. Can you tell everyone what it's like writing together?"

"It's great," Kerri blurted out.

"It is," Jon agreed. Under the table, he playfully fondled Kerri's knee. "The other night, we worked all night on a scene. And Kerri kept saying we need to do it again. Over and over. Again and again until we were both exhausted and satisfied."

"Jon always thought the first time you finish, it's done. I told him we need to wait fifteen minutes," Kerri added, now touching his leg.

"Maybe twenty. And we tackle the scene from a whole new angle. Trying things we hadn't before."

"And finally," Kerri said, "when we are both satisfied with the other's work—the scene is done."

"She puts a lot of thought into it. Deep down, I write too fast."

"I tell him to slow down. We can do this all night until we get it right," Kerri added. The party was silent, unsure what was happening.

"I think I just came," Amari say. Everyone burst out in laughter. Jon and Kerri were both blushing.

Jon whispered, "There's another scene I would like to rewrite."

"I think the scene is fine. We should leave it as it is." Kerri turned away.

"Here's to my future grandchildren!" Diane shouted as she held her cup in the air and then gulped the rest of the drink. She had clearly forgotten that Jon wasn't actually going to be her son-in-law.

Everyone chanted, "To the grandchildren!"

Kerri and Jon both smiled. This was getting embarrassing. But it wasn't going to stop there. Amari poured more champagne into Diane's cup.

"You know, I thought I would have had a grandbaby by now. But you messed that up when you broke up! But I forgive you, because now you're back together and I love you!"

Then the music cranked up, and Kerri and Jon joined the dancing. Trays of shots were poured, followed by more drinking. And before they knew it, the rented Airbnb had become the neighborhood hot spot that night. More actors, musicians, and even an LA Laker strolled through the front door.

Everyone was having a great time when a siren was heard

outside. Suddenly red lights were flashing in the driveway and there was a knock on the door. Troy stepped over to answer it and was shocked to see a policeman at his front door. He was young, probably fresh out of the academy.

"Good evening, officer. How can I help you?" Troy asked.

"I'm sorry to bother you, sir, but ah, we've got a call from one of your neighbors about the noise level of your party." The officer looked truly upset for having to be the bearer of bad news. He continued, "Seeing that it's now past 10:00 p.m., I'm going to have to ask you to shut down the party."

"Well, that's a shame, sir. This is an engagement party and—"

Then an inebriated Amari wandered over to the front door and interrupted with a "Hello, officer!"

The officer blanched. He couldn't believe that he was face-to-face with Amari Rivers, the hot actress that he'd had a severe crush on in high school. And during his time at the academy, he'd had her posters on the wall. "Um, Miss Rivers, it's a pleasure," was all he could think to say. In truth, she had given him quite a bit of solo pleasure in his bedroom, but it wasn't the kind of thing that he would ever admit.

"You're sooooo cute," Amari slurred. "Lez take a selfie." Amari struggled to hold out her phone, almost dropping it when Troy caught it midair.

"I'll take it," Troy said. He watched as the policeman stood stiffly next to Amari for the photo.

"No, zilly, put your arm around me, like dis." Amari threw her arms about the policeman.

The officer tried not to show how happy he was. He wanted to work in this Hollywood Hills neighborhood more often! Troy clicked a few photos on Amari's cell phone and handed it to her.

"If it's okay, I'd love to have a copy of that photo," the officer said a bit sheepishly.

"Is that okay, Amari?" Troy asked.

"Sure...I love a man in uniform," Amari said in a little girl voice, clearly very drunk.

"Ok, what's your number?" Troy asked the officer.

The officer shared his digits and then looked at his phone as the photo of Amari with her arm around his waist popped up on his screen. It was too good to be true. He had a close-up with Amari, and he had her phone number! All he could think was, *wait until I show the boys down at the station who I just met.* He was so happy that he had forgotten why he was there. He was four steps down the walkway when he suddenly realized that he was supposed to shut down the party because an irate neighbor, who was also a movie star and big supporter of the police pension fund, had yelled at the officer to do exactly that.

"Uh, why don't you just keep it down and maybe lower the music?" he said to Troy.

"Yes, sir, will do," Troy said as he closed the door and escorted Amari back into the party.

Kerri and Jon had been watching the confrontation play out. "Everything okay, Dad?" Kerri asked with a worried frown.

"It is now. It's amazing how much power a movie star has to change people's minds."

"That's why they're called stars. They shine brightly," Jon said.

CHAPTER 29

December 15

KERRI WAS UP EARLY THE next morning. She hadn't planned to spend the night at her parents' rental, and she had not expected the out-of-control engagement party thrown in her and Jon's honor. She woke up in a guest room in bed next to Jon. He had been too wasted to drive home that night and also, hopefully, to do anything else. She held her breath and peeked under the sheets, then let out a sigh of relief to see he'd slept in his boxers, which she took as a good sign that they hadn't fooled around again. *Whew*, she thought.

Her FaceTime rang, and she picked it up quickly, thinking it was Amari. All at once, Beau's face flashed on the screen. Kerri flinched, swiftly moving away from the slumbering Jon, and making sure that the camera angle didn't reveal her sleeping partner. She stepped into the bathroom.

"Hi," Kerri whispered.

"Why are you whispering? It's 10:00 a.m."

"Kind of a late night. We were celebrating."

"Celebrating what?"

"It was a Christmas party for the crew."

"Wish I could have been there."

"Yeah, me too."

"There's a beautiful Christmas market here in Toronto. I think you'd love it. Have you started shopping yet? I remember that was your thing."

"Not exactly. Not yet."

Then there was a banging on the door. "I gotta pee!" Jon yelled.

"Who's that?" Beau wondered.

"It's my, uh, dad."

"I thought you had a big place. Doesn't he have his own bathroom?"

"Maybe my mom's in it. I don't know."

"Ok, I better go anyway. I've got a client lunch. Love you."

"Love you too." Kerri hung up and opened the door.

Jon was smiling on the other side. "That's so sweet."

"Shut up," Kerri said.

Jon passed her and went into the bathroom.

Kerri needed coffee. She walked out of her bedroom in her red sweatpants, into the living room, passing the party dregs— beer cans, Solo cups, plates. Someone had spilled red wine on a chair, and she thought, *There goes the security deposit.* She found her father in the kitchen searching through cabinets.

"Good morning, Daddy," Kerri said.

"Hey, you're awake. I didn't expect to see you till noon. I'm looking for coffee," Troy said.

"You too, huh? I know where it is. Down the street. There's a place called Groundwork. I was going to walk down there. Want to join me?" Kerri asked.

"Some party, huh?" Troy said as they descended the street.

Kerri thought maybe she shouldn't have gone with her dad. He seemed to be in an inquisitive mood. She deflected. "I never saw Mom drink that much. She was crazy."

"Yeah, I know. It was fun." Troy smiled, slightly embarrassed.

Kerri laughed; she didn't want to know anything about her mom and dad's after-party activities. They trudged down Oporto Road, and suddenly the iconic Hollywood Bowl came into view, and Kerri lit up.

Troy admired it. "The Hollywood Bowl. I remember you took us there when you first moved here…"

"The John Williams concert," they said at the same time.

"That was so great. The first part was old Hollywood music and they showed clips. And the second half was all John Williams music. *E.T. Raiders of the Lost Ark. Star Wars.* And the lightsabers!" Troy said.

"It's a tradition. You can't go to the John Williams concert without bringing a lightsaber."

They both smiled at the memory.

"I think he closed with the theme song from the *NBC Nightly News*," Troy said.

"He did. Everyone put away their lightsabers and headed for the cars." Kerri laughed.

"That was fun," Kerri remembered. "The Hollywood Bowl might be the only thing in LA that is unique. There's nothing like this in Brooklyn, or anywhere near it. I miss going there."

"Maybe your mom and I can get you a subscription as your engagement gift."

"Ha ha, Dad. You know it's a fake engagement, and you know I'm not moving back."

"Ok, so how are you going to write the pitch you just sold? Is Jon moving to Brooklyn?"

Kerri shuddered at the thought. The truth was that they'd sold the pitch faster than she ever imagined, faster than she had time to think about the practicalities of how they'd write it. Of course, they could do it over Zoom or via email, but that would be cumbersome. That was a January problem, she decided.

They arrived at Ovation, the new Hollywood town center that was a tourist spot and pseudo-downtown Hollywood. On one side was the famous TCL Chinese Theatre, and the other side was the Dolby Theater, where the Academy Awards ceremony was held. They got their coffees in a new place between the two locations. Troy wanted to see the famous cement footprints and handprints in front of the Chinese Theater. He loved the fact that his feet were way bigger than Sylvester Stallone's. They even found the annoying neighbor Val Stone's footprints.

As they were walking back, Troy asked, "So how did Beau take the news of your fake engagement with Jon?"

Still tired, coffee not yet kicking in, Kerri blurted out, "I didn't tell him." If her life was a DVR, she would have been able to jump back thirty seconds and not say that. But that wasn't going to be possible.

"As a divorce lawyer, I'm obliged to tell you that you always want to be honest with your spouse-to-be."

"I know, I know."

"I'm also a pretty good judge of character."

"How does this apply to me? I'm not married yet."

"But you do have two engagements."

"So, you think you know which guy is right for me?"

"Yes."

"Tell me."

"No. That's something you need to figure out for yourself."

"I only wish I didn't have to lie to Beau. He's such a good guy."

"I should tell you what's going on. What I've been lying about."

"You cheated on Mom? With that hot woman from work?"

"Shelly? She's my work wife."

"Why do you have a work wife?!"

"It's an expression. I am not cheating on your mother. I had to have something removed from my back. And I've been waiting for the results. That's why we came out. If I got bad news, I wanted to tell you in person. Not on the phone."

"Did you get bad news?"

"I got great news. No cancer. Hence another reason for the party." Kerri felt the tension release from her body as she hugged her dad and warm happy tears dropped onto her cheeks. He looked at her. "Years back, we were on the bluffs overlooking Santa Monica Bay…"

"I remember that day," she said.

"You told me how you and Jon had broken up and how you were planning to move to Brooklyn."

Kerri nodded. She had been looking for emotional support.

"Do you remember what I told you?"

Kerri smiled, "You said, 'Please don't. I like it here.'" They laughed.

"I did. And I still do. I still hold on to the dream that you'll be rich and famous, and your mom and I can live in your guesthouse."

"Dad!"

"I know you and Jon are faking being in love, but maybe the only people you're faking out are yourselves. What can I say? I think you can have a life here with Jon."

"Wait, I thought you weren't going to tell me who you thought I should be with. And you'll like Beau, once you get to know him better," she said a little defensively.

"I'm sure I will. But I can't help liking Jon too, because even when you didn't believe in yourself, he still believed in you. And the way he acts around you—that's love. That's all I'm going to say about it."

They walked back. Troy knew when to stay quiet, and Kerri processed it all. They stepped into the house and heard voices outside on the deck, which overlooked most of Los Angeles. Jon and Diane were both laughing when the action guy, the annoying neighbor, Val Stone, walked into the house with coffee for all of them. He sat down with Jon and Diane. *When did they become best friends?* Kerri wondered.

"Good morning," Kerri said brightly.

Jon took her hand and squeezed it. "Kerri, you remember Val Stone?"

"My Dad and I just saw your footprints on Hollywood Boulevard."

"Glory days," Val said, "Hey, I didn't know you and Jon were a writing team. I'd love to talk to you about some projects I have."

"Let's talk in a few days. We've got a night shoot now," Jon said.

"That doesn't mean we're not interested," Kerri said. "We'd love to write something for you. Find a project that elevates you from action star to actor."

Val Stone loved that. So did Jon. He was wondering who this Kerri person was, this new version. He loved this new version; he also loved the old version. He knew at that moment: he loved every version of Kerri.

CHAPTER 30

December 15

KERRI AND JON STOOD UNDER the marquee of the fabled Los Angeles Theatre, the most beautiful movie palace ever built in LA. The words FIRE AND ICE FIREFIGHTER'S BALL were up on the ornate display. Kerri felt like a lit-up Christmas tree, giddy with excitement, as she and Jon took pictures of each other in front of the theater and the sign.

"How about I get one of the two of you?" a production assistant said, walking up to help prep the location for the day's shoot.

"That's okay, we're good," Kerri said.

"She's right. We're good," Jon agreed quickly. He didn't need Madison seeing him taking a couple pic with Kerri. It was bad enough Madison was on the set, but maybe not so bad, as now she was a featured extra with one line and would be in some shots in the background, far away from Jon. And with Madison on the set, he and Kerri could avoid any conversation that had to do with their strange relationship, whatever it was.

"You're the one that I want," Kerri sang out suddenly.

Jon gulped, confused. "What?"

"From *Grease*. We saw it here, remember?" Years ago, this was where Kerri and Jon had seen one of the last movies they had watched together, a sold-out revival of *Grease*. It had been a bitter-sweet evening, as they both knew that they were breaking apart.

"You know that song wasn't in the original Broadway show. It was written for the movie."

"I don't care. I still love it." Then she broke into song again, surprising even herself, and yet she felt so happy and light as a feather. Jon grinned, feeling warm all over.

They stepped inside and were transported back in time to a grand entrance lobby that was inspired by the Palace of Versailles Hall of Mirrors. But today it was also the location where the characters in *Fire and Ice* would break up. Jon and Kerri snapped a few more photos, glowing with happiness at seeing the words of their script coming to life. But Kerri's good mood was dampened when she saw Madison, wearing a very revealing red dress, showing lots of her legs and even more cleavage, and she admitted to herself that Jon's *girl next door* was stunning. Madison sashayed past Kerri, completely ignoring her, and stopping in front of Jon.

"Hello, Jon," Madison purred.

"Madison, I didn't recognize you. That's a great dress," Jon said, putty in her hands.

Kerri watched and listened. *Maybe Jon didn't recognize her, because he didn't look at his girlfriend's face—only her boobs.* Kerri tried to shake off the negative feelings, wondering why she was feeling this way. She took a half step closer, eavesdropping.

"I know you've been too busy with the movie for us to spend any time together, but I appreciate the favor of you getting me a part in the movie. I've been out here so many years hoping for a break. Thank you," Madison said sincerely.

Damn, Kerri thought, *she's gorgeous and nice.*

"Maybe this will change your luck," Jon said.

"And thank you, Kerri," Madison said, suddenly pivoting toward a surprised Kerri.

"What line are you saying?" Kerri wondered.

"It's getting too damn hot in here," Madison said, acting as if she was a demonic temptress. "I have to get to work. And Jon, while we're on set together, we should keep our personal relationship to ourselves and act like professionals."

Madison walked away, and Jon's eyes followed her like eye candy. He noticed Kerri watching him and laughing. "She's right," Jon said embarrassed, changing the subject. "We should act like professionals. Not just me and Madison. But the two of us…"

"I agree," Kerri said quickly, realizing that the tryst they'd had before her Brooklyn trip was now in the past. She tried to change the subject. "Did you recognize that line, 'It's getting too damn hot in here'?"

"There's a lot about this movie I don't recognize," Jon said, realizing that the movie being filmed was not the movie they had written. Or at least it was coming out way different.

"I thought the tone would be more fun. That's how I saw it. Like *Moonstruck*. Or *Sleepless in Seattle*. I don't know what this is—" Kerri said.

Jon tried to stay positive. "Hey, we're about halfway through. I have a feeling that things are going to start getting better."

They did. Lukas kindly asked Kerri and Jon if they wouldn't mind being extras in the movie. They agreed, and for the second time, they went to the wardrobe department. Both emerged looking breathtaking in their newfound suit and dress. Their eyes lingered on each other as now they were each other's eye candy. They slow danced under the chandeliers hanging from the Lucullan ceiling and tried to remember that they were keeping their relationship "professional."

"They have weddings here, you know," Jon said half-jokingly.

"You should tell that to your girlfriend. She's been watching us like a hawk." Indeed, she was. Madison was near the camera, but her eyes were on Jon.

After the dance, it was time for Amari and Cage's scene. Mike the firefighter had invited Tiffany to the ball. In the scene, Mike's buddies were making fun of him for thinking he was anything more than Tiffany's boy toy.

Jon and Kerri watched the rehearsal. "She is so out of your league," was one of the lines. It was something that rang true for Jon, as it was what everyone back in film school had said to him about Kerri. Lukas called, "Cut!" and Kerri noticed that the jovial character Cage was playing disappeared, as he turned it off quickly, and that's when she noticed his face was gray. She thought it had been the lighting, but it was more than that. For some reason, the color was drained from his face. "Do you think Cage is sick?" she asked Jon.

Suddenly, there was yelling, as Cage and Lukas were screaming at each other. Cage stormed off the set, marching out of the theater, and all went silent. What was happening?

"Where is Amari?" Lukas shouted. "Where is my producer?" The first assistant director tried to calm Lukas down, but it didn't work. A production assistant was ordered to find Amari, who was in hair and makeup.

Jon walked over to the production assistant and said, "What's going on?"

"Cage has locked himself in his trailer."

Amari was rushed onto the set, and the first people she saw were Kerri and Jon. She went right to them. "I need your help. Cage refuses to come out of his trailer. I need to find out why and get him back on set."

They stood there, silent, frozen, fascinated with how Amari looked. The makeup she was wearing made her look like she died five days ago. All the colors of her skin seemed drained, except for bright red lipstick.

"Amari," Kerri said, concerned, "Are you sick?"

"Sick? No, why? Come on!"

Kerri and Jon followed Amari outside to the street where there was a row of honey wagon trailers. The larger the trailer, the bigger the star. Cage Riley's was a good-sized double-banger. In front of the door to the trailer, Amari gestured for Kerri and Jon to knock. Kerri twinged as her knuckles banged on the aluminum trailer. There was no answer, and something felt wrong about this situation. Jon rapped on the trailer again. This time the door swung open, and they stepped inside Cage's *home away from home.*

Kerri and Jon both noticed Cage's skin was made up to have the same gray pallor and bright red lipstick that Amari had. They both stared at him, their eyes bulging.

"Do you know why I look like this?" Cage said. "Neither do I. But I had a suspicion. I signed on to make a romantic comedy, not a ghost story!"

Jon gasped, "A ghost story? Cage. What are you talking about?"

Kerri chuckled nervously, a pit in her stomach. "So that's what he's been doing. That's why everything is a little dark. He's playing this as if you died in the fire. And that's why he has you and Amari in so many night scenes."

Jon slumped. "A ghost story?"

"Look," Cage said calmly, "I like you guys. I like the script. I do. If you want me to lock myself in this trailer until this lunatic starts filming the script I signed on for, I will."

Kerri and Jon knew that movie productions were always troublesome, but this kept getting worse. At that moment, Kerri's phone rang. It was Beau, trying to FaceTime with her. She answered quickly and said brusquely: "Can't talk. We're in crisis mode." Beau looked alarmed and upset, but Kerri didn't have time to explain. She hung up.

Kerri turned back to Jon and Cage. "Let's go shoot the scene," Kerri blurted out, desperate for the production to move forward. "We'll talk to Amari as soon as possible. As for the makeup, it could all be color-corrected in post. This is an important scene, and we have a great location. And you are such a talented actor, you'll only make things better. Cage, we are so fortunate to have you here."

Cage smiled, now reassured. He thanked Kerri and walked out of the trailer and back to the set. Jon stared with his mouth agape.

"What?" Kerri said, as she breathed in deeply, trying to slow her racing heart.

"That was amazing. You went all Elia Kazan on Cage. He trusts you. You sounded like a director."

"Thanks." Kerri sighed. "We can't let this movie get derailed."

Back on the set, the real director was ready for Amari's entrance—or rather Tiffany's. The extras were in place, including Kerri and Jon. The camera rolled, and Amari appeared in a torn gray dress as loud headbanger music played. Jon and Kerri had imagined this scene to be more understated, but there was nothing understated when Cage/Mike jumped up seeing that

Amari/Tiffany had arrived and pulled her onto the dance floor, lit with orange and red lights. Madison hit her mark and delivered her line, screaming, "It's getting too damn hot in here!" And then she ripped off her dress as the crowd cheered.

Amari was startled and went over to Kerri and Jon. "What was that? Did you rewrite the scene?"

"No. We're as surprised as you are," Jon said.

"This was supposed to be romantic," Amari mused, as her eyes focused on the now open-robed Madison hugging Lukas. "And who the hell is that girl?"

"I never saw her before in my life," Jon lied.

"Amari, we need to talk about the movie," Kerri said. "How does it look? How are the dailies? Is it cutting together?"

"I'm not sure," Amari admitted. "Lukas hasn't let me see dailies since the second day of production."

"You're the producer!" Jon said, disbelieving.

Amari was unsettled as she watched Madison hanging on Lukas's every word, her robe still open, revealing her naked breasts.

"I don't know what's happening," Amari said, frustrated.

"I think we do," Jon stated, taking a deep breath. As he was breathing, Kerri beat him to it.

"Lukas is not making a romantic comedy. He's making a ghost story. He's been filming it as if Tiffany and Mike died in the hotel fire at the beginning of the movie."

Before Amari could scream, Madison, of all people, called out, "It's a wrap!"

CHAPTER 31

December 15

AMARI WAS STARTING TO REGRET ever wanting to be a producer. She was waiting outside Lukas's trailer, where she was trying to get up the nerve to knock on the door and demand to watch the dailies. She sighed, wanting to be anyplace else, and realized that if she had just stuck to acting, she wouldn't be in this mess. But she wanted to be like Reese Witherspoon and Margot Robbie, who were both multi-hyphenates. Going into the project, she knew that Lukas had a strong personality and an ego as big as the Pacific Ocean, but she never imagined that it would backfire. All she'd wanted to do was to make a sweet romantic comedy that her grandma could watch. Her performance in *The Christmas Couple* had earned her praise, and now she was also trying to stay in her wheelhouse and build her brand of becoming America's Sweetheart. It had worked for Meg Ryan and Julia Roberts; why not her?

She stepped up closer to the door, ready to open it, when Madison skipped out, still half-dressed, and Amari wondered why she was in Lukas's trailer.

"Be right back, Lukas! I'll get us more drinks." Then

Madison smirked at Amari, giving her a saccharine smile. She poked her head back into the trailer and spoke louder so that Amari wouldn't miss what she was saying. "The dailies look amazing. You're such a good director," Madison purred. Then she sashayed past Amari. "You know he's a genius."

Amari was furious. Why did the actress with one line get to see the dailies before she did?! She stormed into Lukas's trailer. He looked up, surprised to see her.

"Lukas, I am not going to wait any longer. I demand to see the dailies!"

"Of course, love, calm down."

"Don't call me love. I'm your producer." Amari was insulted. She rushed into the trailer and slammed the flimsy door. "Just show me the footage."

Lukas tapped the Play button on the computer, and Amari stared at the monitors, hoping for the best. But what she saw made her realize she was going to need more than a prayer to turn around the movie. The footage was awful and nonsensical.

"What do you think?" Lukas asked eagerly.

"I think…I think…" Amari's voice trailed off. What if she was wrong? Shouldn't she trust Lukas? He was a big shot director, and she was a newbie producer. "I think that I thought it was supposed to be a rom-com."

"Yes, yes, I know. But I thought it would be so much better if it was a ghost story."

"A what?"

"A ghost story. And you're dead. So is the firefighter."

"No, no, no…"

"Let me show you the assembly cut."

Amari watched in horror as the scenes played out. It all looked gray, and the camera never moved. "I want you to burn me a copy of this." And when Amari noticed that Lukas hesitated, she became more forceful. "Now." Amari curled her fingers into two fists, as she finally found her agency and was ready to fight back.

Lukas copied the rough footage onto a flash drive and handed it to Amari. "Enjoy," he said.

Enjoy was the farthest thing from Amari's mind. She got up and ran out of the trailer. Her heart was pounding. What was she going to do? The movie was already halfway through production, and it was going to be difficult to change it back. How had she let things get so out of hand? *Why haven't I been paying attention?* she wondered. But she knew why. Because she'd let her lust for Lukas get the better of her. How was she going to solve this problem? And then her face lit up as she realized the one person she could call, the guy who was always there for her. Richard.

Amari quickly dialed Richard and expected him to answer on the second or at the latest, the third ring. That's what usually happened, but this time it didn't.

———————

What Amari didn't know was that, across town, Richard was at his Beverly Hills therapist's office, in the middle of a deep conversation about his unrequited love for Amari, when he noticed that his phone was ringing, and the digital readout said, AMARI. His instinct was to answer quickly, but his therapist chided him into not answering. "You'll only enable her to continue using you."

Richard sighed. "I know. But what if she needs me? What if she's in trouble?"

"Then she'll find somebody else to help her. She's a well-paid actress who no doubt has a long list of people who are hired to help her."

"She does. I know, because I hired most of them," Richard said as he watched his phone continue to ring.

"So don't answer the phone."

Finally after what seemed like an interminable period, the phone stopped ringing. He sighed, not sure if it was relief or guilt. "I can't believe I didn't answer it."

"I'm proud of you, Richard," the therapist said to him.

———————

But Amari wasn't proud of Richard. She couldn't believe that he didn't pick up his phone and left a long rambling message about how Lukas had screwed up the film. She used her best sad and teary voice so that he'd understand the urgency, certain that, when he did check his messages, which would probably be in the next ten minutes, he would quickly return her call.

Ten minutes passed and still no word from Richard. At that point, Amari realized that it was also odd that she still hadn't heard from him. And then for the very first time in her life, she had a moment where she actually worried about Richard instead of the other way around, because he'd never missed one of her calls.

———————

Richard was wrapping up his therapy session. His therapist gave him a new challenge: she asked him not to return Amari's calls for the next five hours.

Richard, being the great agent that he was, negotiated that five hours down to one hour. But the therapist showed her mettle and countered him for three hours. In the end, they settled on two hours, leaving both Richard and the therapist feeling that they'd successfully won the negotiation. Richard put Amari's calls on a block for two hours and went to a screening for another client. The film was awful, but it took his mind off Amari. The free drinks afterward didn't hurt either, and he felt positive about the progress he was making in his desire to stop caring about Amari so much.

Amari left several more voice messages for Richard. Then she tried texting. Still crickets from him. With no place else to go, Amari found herself pulling up to Jon's apartment, hoping to find him at home with Kerri.

Inside the apartment, Kerri was baking Mexican wedding cookies. They were delicate balls of flour and crushed pecans dusted with white confectioner's sugar. Even the thought of them—warm and fresh from the oven—made her mouth water. But she had more than cookies on her mind. She picked up her phone and FaceTimed Beau.

"Hey!" Beau answered. He could see that Kerri was upset. "You okay?"

"Why did I ever come back to LA?" Kerri said.

"Did Jon do something?"

"No. Jon didn't do anything to me. Why did you think it was Jon?"

"I don't know."

"Things are starting to fall apart on the movie. Just like they always do."

"I could try and cancel my Toronto meetings and come out there."

"Don't do that. I'm just venting."

"Ok, well, I just stepped away from the client. I should probably get back. Love you."

"You too." Kerri returned to the cookies, mixing up a second batch while the first tray of cookies baked. The door opened and Jon entered, carrying two festive holiday coffee drinks.

Kerri took the peppermint mocha from Jon. "You know it's not cutting together. What are we going to do about the movie?" Kerri said to Jon in a worried tone.

"Never mind the movie, what are we going to do about our relationship?" Jon said with a tinge of annoyance, stealing a piece of cookie dough and gobbling it quickly.

"I thought you wanted us to be"—Kerri lifted up her dough encrusted fingers into air quotes—"professional."

"I do. But after this movie wraps, we've got to write that script that we've already sold. And I guess I was hoping that you'd stay in LA for a few months."

"And not go back to Brooklyn?" Kerri said, putting her diamond ring under his nose.

"I know. You're wearing his ring."

"And I still plan on marrying him. He's a nice guy."

"Duh. Of course, I know that it's not Kerri and Jon. It's Kerri and Beau."

Then there was a knock on the door. "Hello?" Amari called out.

Jon and Kerri looked suddenly nervous. Kerri whispered, "Do you think she heard you?"

Jon shrugged. He opened the door.

"Sorry to come so late, but I need to see you guys. You're the only people I can count on right now," Amari said, looking bereft.

"Of course. Come in," Kerri said.

Amari sniffed. "Smells like something is burning."

Kerri's eyes suddenly went wide. "Darn it! My cookies!" Kerri opened the oven and pulled out the blackened cookies, the smoke alarm suddenly blaring. "I'm so bummed. These are the first Christmas cookies I've finally had time to make this year."

"Maybe you should just buy some," Jon suggested.

"I can't do that! It's Christmas."

"Hello? I have problems too. I had a big fight with Lukas. The dailies are terrible," Amari said, cutting through the tension.

Kerri gave Jon an "I told you so" look.

"Maybe you should fire him?" Kerri suggested.

"Oh no, he's a good director."

Kerri secretly disagreed.

"But he's an awful person. What makes it so bad is that he lied to me about what kind of movie he was making. I hate liars," Amari said.

"Me too," Jon said as he nodded.

"My father always lied to my mother," Amari said as she sat on the couch.

Jon and Kerri shared nervous glances.

"And I can't get a hold of Richard, which is so frustrating."

"So you saw the footage?" Kerri asked eagerly.

"Yes. And I have the assembly cut here." Amari took the flash drive out of her designer purse.

Kerri popped it into her computer, and once the footage loaded up, Kerri and Jon watched in horror, immediately seeing it was awful. Jon was crestfallen while Kerri knew the director had not been getting enough shots and coverage. This looked like a serial killer movie, not a comedy.

"I just don't know what to do. He was filming a ghost story, not a comedy. He told me I'm dead in the movie."

"You're not the only one who's dead. Our careers are all going to be dead unless we do something," Kerri said in alarm.

"We should fire him!" Jon said.

But Kerri disagreed. "Look, I know he's not the right director. But if you fire him, then what?"

CHAPTER 32

December 16

RICHARD WAS LOOKING FOR HIS lost phone. He remembered going to a preview screening last night where he had enjoyed more than a few cocktails at the after-party, all of which made the experience of lying about the client's movie a little easier. He'd taken an Uber back to his place in West Hollywood and left his phone in the car.

The next morning, he had to be at the office early to meet with Lukas Wright, but Richard needed his phone. An agent without a phone was like a eunuch at an orgy with no power to make anything happen.

Via his iPad, he had tracked his phone to an apartment in Venice. He'd also found the name of the driver, Xavier, on the receipt. Richard had tipped in cash and rated Xavier with high marks. So with a name and working tracker, Richard emailed his assistant, Brit, who answered immediately and drove Richard to Venice in search of his phone.

After a couple of wrong turns, they arrived outside a small bungalow. The Uber car was in front. Richard knocked on the door and explained to Xavier's parents that he needed his phone.

The parents awakened their son, who did have the phone.

Richard got back into Brit's car with his phone and a screenplay. Xavier, it turned out, was a struggling writer.

"Read this," Richard told Brit.

Richard checked his phone. First the photos: snaps of him and Amari. He then scrolled through emails and texts. He had lots of calls from Amari and even more texts.

WHERE ARE YOU?

I NEED TO TALK TO YOU!

HELP ME RICHARD, YOU'RE MY ONLY HOPE!

Richard called Amari's phone, but the voicemail was full. When he texted her, his phone died.

"Where's your phone charger?" Richard asked frantically, digging around in the glove compartment and front console.

"I don't have one in the car. I have one at home and at work, but I never need it in my car," the assistant told him.

"Why did I hire you?" a frustrated Richard asked.

Richard got back to the office ten minutes late for his meeting with Lukas. Richard saw him waiting in the glass conference room, inches away from an extremely attractive woman. They seemed to be flirting, giggling, and laughing. Was Lukas cheating on Amari? Lukas had called this meeting to let Richard know whether he had decided to sign with him, to which Richard hoped for a negative response. The last thing he wanted was to be representing a director who may be cheating on Amari.

"Richard! Welcome," Lukas shouted. "This is Madison."

"I'm so excited to meet you," Madison said with a squeak.

"Right, yes, nice to meet you. So sorry I am late," Richard stammered, sitting down for the meeting.

"Richard, this morning, I am bringing you a gift. And that gift is me. I've decided to allow you to represent me," Lukas announced.

Damn, Richard thought to himself. But to Lukas he said with fake enthusiasm, "That's great news."

"You proved yourself with getting *Satan's Prayer* set up. Now, I need your help again on that project."

Richard's insides were churning. He'd been so distracted that morning that he'd forgotten to take his LACTAID pill before he had his latte, and on top of it, he had to deal with this idiot.

"I want Madison to star in it."

"I thought you wanted Amari. That's how we secured the deal to make the movie," Richard said, wanting to leave the conversation so that he could call Amari back, because she needed him. For a moment he allowed himself to dream that maybe she realized he was her knight in shining armor.

Lukas dug in, like an impatient brat. "I don't want Amari. Madison will bring so much more to the part. She is an unknown. Sometimes casting can ruin a movie."

Directors can ruin a movie too, Richard thought. But in a nanosecond, he realized that, if Amari wouldn't do this movie, he would have more time to say how he felt.

"Amari would stay on as producer," Lukas said.

Richard's mind was racing. *He wants them both. Who does this guy think he is?* Before Richard could respond, an assistant walked in and announced the head of the agency was waiting for Lukas.

"Come to the set later today. I would like to talk about my production company," Lukas said.

"Looking forward to it…" *shithead*, Richard replied. He kept the *shithead* part to himself. With Lukas and Madison off to see Spencer, Richard hurried to his office.

"Get me Amari on the phone!" he yelled.

"She's in your office," the assistant said, looking afraid.

Richard rushed in to see Amari slumped on the couch, visibly upset. She looked at him with tears in her eyes. "Richard, I tried to reach you. All night. I needed you."

"I am sorry. So sorry. I misplaced my phone. I'm here now." Richard went over to her and, for some unknown reason, kneeled in front of the woman he worshiped. He held out his hands, and she took them... "What's wrong?"

"I'm a ghost!" Amari said.

"I don't understand..." Richard said quizzically.

"He made me a ghost. The movie. The dailies," Amari sobbed. "I sat with the editor. He showed me some scenes. It's not good. I thought we were making a romantic comedy; Lukas was making a different movie: a ghost story. He told me that Cage and I died in the fire scene, and in the rest of the movie, we're ghosts."

"A ghost story?" Richard felt himself wanting to explode and make an angry, screaming phone call but he also didn't want to withdraw his hand from Amari's, because it felt soft and warm. "This is my fault, Amari. I should have done a better job protecting you..."

"He lied to me," Amari sneered. "He told me it was going to look great. I hate liars."

Richard had a sense that Lukas had been the wrong choice from the beginning, which was something he never told Amari, because he was scared she wouldn't have liked to hear that. He thought to himself, his mind going back to a Shakespeare class: *My fatal flaw is I always want to please her, and that is what I must do now.*

Richard smiled. "I am going to make this right. I'll fire Lukas. I will have my assistant start drafting an announcement to prepare a statement," Richard said confidently as he strode toward the door.

"Where are you going?" Amari asked.

"To fire Lukas. He's upstairs. I'll be right back."

"Are you sure?"

"Sure as I've ever been."

"Should I come with you?"

"Let me handle this." As Richard marched down the hall, he felt like a soldier going into battle, his confidence increasing as he continued up a large spiral staircase that connected his floor to the penthouse where his boss Spencer worked. Richard hustled past Spencer's two assistants.

"He's in a meeting," the lead assistant called out, meaning *Don't go in there.*

"I know," Richard smiled as he opened the door.

Spencer was laughing with Lukas and Madison. It was a charm fest.

"Ah, there he is, my agent," Lukas called out merrily.

"Great job, Richard, not only did you sign Lukas, but you brought us the next bright star: Madison," Spencer gloated. "Sit down, we're figuring a path to Lukas's Oscar."

Richard did not sit down. He stood, looking down on all of them. "That's not going to happen. At least not with us. Lukas, I have no idea what you were doing on *Fire and Ice*. But Amari is not happy, so I'm not happy. You're fired."

Spencer interjected, "Richard, what are you doing?"

"I am telling Lukas that his services will not be needed any longer on *Fire and Ice*."

"This is crazy," Lukas said jumping up. "Where is Amari?"

Lukas went for the door, but Richard blocked it with his body. "You don't get to see her. You don't get to talk to her. You talk to me. And there's nothing for us to talk about. You are fired."

"You don't fire me. I fire you. You're not my agent anymore!" Lukas shouted.

"Forgive me if I don't cry," Richard replied.

Lukas pivoted to Spencer, who was on his feet with a solution: "Lukas, there are a lot of agents here, including me, who would love to work with you. Whatever this is, we can work it out."

Lukas fumed. "Either he goes, or I go!"

Richard sneered, "I'll save you the trouble there, Lukas. I quit."

Twenty minutes later, Amari was helping Richard pack up his office. She noticed there were more than a few photos of her. Richard felt like he was sleepwalking as they waited for the elevator, but he put on a brave face, assuring Amari, "I have a plan. We put out a statement. We'll find another project. We can take some time off. Have you ever been to Costa Rica?"

"Richard, I can't go to Costa Rica. I have to finish *Fire and Ice*. I promised Kerri and Jon. Those poor kids. We have to find a way to finish the movie."

Richard clenched his fingers, wishing she had told him that before he quit, but he was determined to do anything for Amari, as he realized it was time for Richard, the former agent, to show the world and Amari what he was capable of doing. For Amari, he would move mountains... "Ok, if that's what you want. I will make that happen."

"And you can produce it. We can work together like Kerri and Jon," Amari said excitedly. The elevator door opened, and Richard and Amari stepped inside.

Even though he projected confidence to Amari, Richard had no idea what would happen next.

CHAPTER 33

December 16

THAT SAME MORNING, JON WAS awakened by a leg cramp that shot from his hip to his toes. He stretched out his calf. After the Christmas breakup with Kerri three years ago, he had become a stress eater. He would eat away his anxiety with Trader Joe's peanut butter pretzel nuggets or chocolate Joe-Joe's, quickly adding a beer belly. His foray into a science fiction virtual reality thriller script had gone nowhere. *iFear*, as in *I fear this script is terrible.*

One morning he had noticed the amount he weighed was more than the dollar amount in his checking account, and he suddenly stopped eating peanut butter pretzel nuggets and cookies, and stopped drinking beer—not because he wanted to but because he couldn't afford his bad food habit. He needed another way to get rid of his worry and his extra ten pounds, so he started taking long walks, which turned into extended runs. He had even once thought about doing a marathon. That's how stressed he had been.

Now, he was feeling the same way. Jon had no clue what

was going on, or not going on, with his new relationships. Both of them with the same woman. He loved writing and working with Kerri, and he might just love Kerri. Or he might have never stopped loving Kerri.

He had planned to sit down with her and have an open, mature talk about what happened next. As Jon stretched out the pain in his leg, he chuckled to himself. "What happens next?" was the mantra for every writer.

Sometime in the middle of the night, Amari had slipped out of the apartment, leaving only a note with the message: WILL CALL SOON. Kerri was asleep, but Jon doubted she was sleeping well. How could she? Their movie was in trouble, and for a moment, Jon felt a little guilty for bringing her back into the craziness of the film business.

Kerri must have sensed Jon was at the bedroom door.

"Anything?"

"No, Amari left sometime in the night," Jon said softly. "It's early. Keep sleeping," Jon said. He stepped in and covered Kerri with the blanket that had fallen off her.

———————

Jon started his run. No earphones. No music. No electronic watch that measured his jog. He knew where to go. The tony west side of LA had the jogging path on the beach from Venice to Temescal Canyon. People who lived near Mid City and Hollywood had Griffith Park, a sanctuary in the city with fifty-three miles of trails. As the sweat poured out of his body, he ran even harder, but it did nothing to clear his head. He stopped at The Trails, a small rustic coffee shop nestled in the foliage of the park. When he arrived back at the apartment, he heard Kerri crying.

Jon rushed in to find Kerri sitting at the small kitchen table, a tablet open in her hand. From the look on her face, she had been crying for a while.

"Kerri, what's wrong?" Jon asked, scrambling to put down the coffees.

"The movie. It's dead. They shut it down."

Jon kneeled next to her and saw the *Deadline* headline: FIRE AND ICE EXTINGUISHED. DIRECTOR FIRED.

Jon read the article aloud: "'The romantic comedy *Fire and Ice* has been put on ice. This morning the producer/star Amari Rivers announced that Lukas Wright was fired for creative differences. The movie, which began shooting in late November, has been shut down less than halfway through the production. The producer/star and the ex-director have not commented on this shocking decision. No one knows what happens next.'"

"I can't believe this," Jon said, bewildered. "We should call Amari."

"I did. She didn't pick up."

Kerri's phone rang. It was their agent, Charlotte Adams. She put it on speaker. "Holy fuck! What the hell happened?"

"We're just seeing this," Kerri said. "We know Amari wasn't happy with the footage—"

"I'm hearing rumors that that dipshit director was shooting a horror movie."

"The whole thing is a horror show," Jon said.

"We have to get ahead of this," Charlotte said. "Maybe we can get the script back."

"The script? What happens to the movie?" Kerri challenged.

"I don't know," Charlotte said. "I'm getting another call. I'll call you back."

"'I don't know?'" Kerri said. "We're paying ten percent for 'I don't know?'"

"Oh, hell, it gets worse," Jon said, looking at the *Hollywood Reporter* website. "*Hollywood Reporter* is saying that the movie set had experienced problems since the first day of shooting. There was friction on the set between all the creatives. And there's this…"

Jon handed the tablet to Kerri. She read out loud the headline below: "Madison Everson to star in *Satan's Prayer*. Lukas Wright to direct."

Jon sat next to Kerri. All they could do was to scroll.

"Fuck this fuckin' game," Jon said, quoting from a movie.

"*Bull Durham*. That's a movie, Jon. This is real."

"I know it's real."

"Then why are you quoting a movie? This is happening, Jon!" she cried, not realizing she was quoting…

"*Rosemary's Baby*," Jon said.

"Stop quoting movies." Kerri scowled.

"You said it; I didn't," Jon argued. He went to get his coffee. "So, what do we do now?"

"This is over, Jon."

"The movie or us?"

"There is no us," Kerri said starkly.

"We should talk about the other night."

"No. This was all a mistake. We will never talk about the other night. Ever. I'm engaged."

"The only thing you were engaged with the other night was us."

"Our movie just fell apart, Jon, and you want to talk about our relationship. Fine. Let's talk about it…" Kerri started to rant.

"I was happy in Brooklyn. You brought me back here. You got me to dream again. About the movies. About us. You made me think I'd given up too soon, and I was ready to try again. But that's all it was, Jon. A dream. A dream that's turned into a nightmare. I didn't want to dream again. Jon, I hate you for that."

"You can't blame this on me."

"I wish all this had never happened."

"We're good together," Jon said.

"The movie gods don't want that for us," Kerri said softly.

"Fuck the movie gods," Jon added.

Kerri's phone buzzed. "My parents are calling. I should go."

"I'll go with you," Jon offered.

"No, I'd better tell them the movie's dead."

Jon nodded. "Take the car."

"I'll get an Uber."

"We never should have broken up. I'm sorry I cheated on you."

"With Madison?"

"No, by writing that other script."

"Oh, that...that wasn't cheating. Cheating would be if you were working with another writer, but you were writing by yourself. It's like I caught you masturbating."

Jon smiled. "That's funny." But nobody was smiling.

Kerri nodded and walked outside for the Uber.

Jon was alone. He went to his closet, opened a bag in the back, and started eating a box of Trader Joe's Joe-Joe's that happened to be way past the expiration date.

CHAPTER 34

December 16

KERRI WAS DEVASTATED. HOW HAD she let her hopes rise again only to be dashed horribly? She thought about the adage, *Fool me once, shame on you... Fool me twice, shame on me.* "It's the Most Wonderful Time of the Year" played on the car radio, which only made her sadder. She looked out the windows of the Uber as they whizzed down Sunset Boulevard. At least there was no traffic. But even that didn't make her feel any better. All the Christmas decorations hanging on the lampposts made her feel sad, as she realized that this was probably going to be the worst Christmas of her life. She hated to think that her favorite holiday was ruined, knowing it would take her months to get over it.

Her phone rang, and she looked down to see who was calling. It was Jon. She hit Decline on her cell. There was no reason to answer his call, as they'd already said everything that there was to say. A tear leaked from her eye, which she wiped away.

The Uber driver watched her from the rearview mirror. "You okay?" he asked.

Kerri sniffed. "Yes. I mean no."

"I'm sorry to hear that, miss."

The Uber driver's compassion made her feel even worse, and Kerri burst into tears. Suddenly she was baring her soul. In between sobs she blurted out, "My movie. It collapsed. Director was fired. My first script. Ever produced."

The Uber driver nodded sympathetically. "Oh, I heard about that. *Fire and Ice* with Amari Rivers."

Great, Kerri thought. *Even the Uber driver has heard about the debacle.* For some reason, that thought made her stop crying. Oddly, it legitimized her sorrows. "Yes, that's my movie. I mean was my movie."

"It was all over *Deadline* this morning."

The car pulled up to her parents' Airbnb. "Thanks for the ride," Kerri said and then added, "Since you're reading *Deadline*, I'm guessing that you want to be in the film business."

The Uber driver nodded. "Yes, I have a script."

But Kerri cut him off. "Don't. Don't go into the film business. Take my advice. It's a soulless pit of despair that you can never climb out of." She grabbed her suitcase and stepped out of the car. She watched the Uber speed away. Now she was all alone with her dread. Kerri remembered the last time she was there, when she was so happy and having a great time at her fake engagement party with Jon. She sighed and walked up the long driveway.

She knocked on the front door and heard Christmas carols wafting out. Nobody answered the door, so she pushed it open. The music got louder, and laughter sprinkled out. She walked into the large living room and saw that her parents were singing and dancing to "Jingle Bell Rock."

They noticed her and called out, "Kerri! This is a surprise," Troy said as he sipped a glass of eggnog.

"Perfect timing!" said Diane happily. "Val brought us over a nice bottle of Grey Goose, and it called out for an impromptu party."

Kerri walked in to see the movie star neighbor holding a bottle of vodka.

"There she is. My favorite writer," Val said with a huge smile.

"Add some more to my glass," Diane said as she held out her eggnog.

Kerri had never seen them so happy. Telling the truth was going to be even harder than she thought.

"But uh-oh, a plot twist. She has her suitcase…" Val said.

Already Kerri was finding him very annoying.

"What's wrong, sweetheart?" Diane asked. Clearly a little tipsy.

"Mom, are you drunk?" Kerri said as she tried to pivot.

Troy put down his glass. "Kerri, that's not a nice thing to ask your mother. And Diane, she's here because her movie fell apart."

"What?" Kerri's eyes were wide. "How did you know?"

"I read it in the trades this morning."

Kerri noticed how the word *trades* seemed to roll off his tongue. She broke down. "Daddy, they fired the director. It's over."

"I know. There, there," Troy said as he hugged her and patted her on the back.

Diane seemed to quickly sober up. "Kerri, I'm so sorry. But it's not like they cut off your hands. You can always write another script."

Her comment made Kerri cry even louder.

Val looked alarmed. "You were at the gates of Oz. That sucks," he said.

Again, Val was irritating Kerri. She glared at him. "I know that."

"You know how hard it is to get a movie made?" Val said to no one in particular.

"Yes, I do," Kerri said.

"It's a small miracle to put a film in production," Val continued as he rubbed salt into the wound.

"I understand. Mom, Dad, can you please get this guy to leave? Please?"

Troy nodded and gently escorted Val out the door.

Alone with her parents, Kerri realized it was time to rip off the proverbial Band-Aid. "There's something else I need to tell you… Jon and I broke up."

"Again?" Troy asked.

"Well, actually, we weren't a couple."

"We know that, honey," Diane said.

Kerri nodded and stepped outside onto the patio. She looked out at the sunny view. The winter sky was clear, and she could see all the way to the mountains and the sea. She checked the weather in Brooklyn on her phone. It was 30 degrees and cloudy.

Her phone buzzed, and she noticed it was Beau, trying to FaceTime her. She accepted the call, and his face popped up on the screen.

"Hi, sweetie. I set up your movie title on my Google alerts, and this morning I got like twenty messages. How bad is it?"

"It's bad. Really bad," Kerri said.

"Okay. It's a good thing you didn't quit your job."

"Why would I quit my job?"

"I thought you might have been pulled back into the dream factory with all those happy endings," Beau said.

"What's wrong with a happy ending?" Kerri said.

Beau sputtered, "Nothing. It's just that…"

Kerri's phone dinged with a new text. Her eyes grew wide as she read. Then she returned to her FaceTime call with Beau.

"Thanks for calling, Beau, but I've got to run."

Kerri hung up and reread the message from Jon:

SPOKE WITH RICHARD
HE NEEDS US TO COME SAVE THE MOVIE
SUMMONED TO AMARI'S
MEETING IS IN TWO HOURS.
I'LL PICK YOU UP.

CHAPTER 35

December 16

IT IS STARTING TO FEEL *like the longest day ever*, Kerri thought, as she sat in the passenger seat next to Jon. They were driving up the Pacific Coast Highway back to Malibu Colony to try and save the movie.

Kerri was looking out the window at the Pacific, the water churning with violent white sea-foam, looking the way Kerri's insides felt.

"Dolphins," Jon said, pointing.

"They're heading south. Probably going to San Diego. Anything to get out of this place." She wasn't going to apologize for her negative attitude, her bad mood, and her newfound exhaustion. She felt like, when the movie died, a part of her went with it. "I'm just tired, Jon. I want to go to sleep and wake up on a plane back to New York." They approached Amari's house, where even the Christmas decorations were looking tired, as the reindeer were knocked on their side by the strong winds, and the blow-up Santa had lost its air and lay flattened on the ground.

Jon tightened his grip on the steering wheel. When he pulled into Amari's driveway, a photographer was waiting in front, his car blocking the driveway.

"You've got to move your car. You can't park there." Jon called from the car window. The paparazzi didn't budge. Jon honked, but the guy looked away. Jon looked at Kerri.

"Did you know the word *paparazzi* was coined in the film *La Dolce Vita*? Paparazzo was the name of Marcello's camera-wielding buddy. 1960."

"Not in the mood for movie trivia, Jon. What are we even doing here?"

"Amari asked us to come. We're going to go inside and figure out a way to save the movie. But first I've got to take care of his guy."

Jon was seething, and he suddenly did something very out of character. He smiled at the paparazzi, opened his car trunk, and lifted the mat and found the tire iron. He walked up to the photographer, brandishing the tire iron as the guy went for his camera. But he was too slow for Jon, who swung the tire iron and knocked the camera to the ground.

"If I were you, I would take that to a camera shop and get it repaired right away," Jon asserted.

"I'm going to sue. I'll call the police."

"Go right ahead. This is a private community. You're trespassing. So, you drive home now or crawl home later." Jon had gone full Brooklyn on the guy. He put the tire iron back in the trunk and got back in the car with Kerri as the photographer drove away. His hands were shaking.

"You're feeling pretty good about yourself right now," Kerri said.

"I can't believe I just did that."

"Do you think the movie can be saved?" Kerri said, a little more pep in her voice.

Jon and Kerri knocked on the door. Richard opened it slightly, not wanting to be seen. "Where's the paparazzi?"

"He had to get his camera fixed."

Kerri and Jon were ushered inside, and Amari rushed over to greet them. "Thank you for coming."

Kerri asked, "Why wouldn't we?"

"I thought you might be blaming me for your movie falling apart. I picked Lukas. He ruined everything. It's my fault."

"It's no one's fault. There's no movie without you," Kerri reminded Amari. "If it wasn't for you, it would still be in development hell—"

"And now it's in production hell," Jon said. Kerri glared at him. "Just kidding," Jon added.

"I don't know what I would have done if you two didn't come here today."

Amari's house was the new headquarters. From here they could band together. Richard's office was out of the question, because he didn't have an office. The production studio was closed off. So, it was Malibu or bust.

"Maybe we should see the rest of the footage," Kerri stated.

Amari brought them to the screening room, a large room in the house with theater-style seats, 7.1 surround sound, and a sizeable screen. The room was art deco. Jon was giddy. "Wow. This is phenomenal. I always wanted a place like this. Kerri, there's a popcorn machine."

Jon was obsessed with home theaters, Kerri remembered. "We're not having popcorn, Jon. We're not watching the new Marvel movie."

"I have that, if you want," Amari offered.

"Everyone, concentrate. We are here to watch the footage. The bad footage. All of it. From our movie. We are not watching the new Marvel movie," Kerri stated.

They settled in as Amari pressed a button and the lights went down. The footage filled the screen. It was an assembly cut of some of the scenes. The editor had put together the different shots in an order that followed what was in the script. But no matter what the editor had done, the footage was not good. No one said a word. The rooftop fire scene looked like a scene from a horror movie.

"Everyone is underlit," Kerri said.

The footage jumped to the Firefighter's Ball. There was a temporary film score attached to this, which sounded like a mix between EDM and heavy metal.

"This music sucks," Jon said.

"Lukas wrote it," Amari added.

"Can you mute it? It's making me ill," Kerri said.

"Hey, Kerri, your parents are in that shot," Jon said.

"Where?"

"Right behind Madison's butt," Jon said, defeated. The footage was so bad it dulled his usual wit. Jon noticed Kerri was leaning forward, making mental notes. Sometimes a scene was working, and then there would be a flash cut to a fire.

"He keeps cutting out the joke," Kerri said. "He doesn't play to the punch line. We filmed it. But it's not there."

After about thirty minutes, the footage ended, and the lights came back on.

"He killed it," Jon said, coming to terms with what he had seen.

"He killed it, but it's not dead," Kerri said with a glimmer of hope in her voice. "I think there still might be a movie there."

"I don't know about that, Kerri," Jon said sadly.

"*Bogart Slept Here*, Jon," Kerri said.

"He did? I didn't know this house was that old," Amari said, confused.

Jon knew what she was talking about and explained: "*Bogart Slept Here* was a movie with Robert De Niro. It was directed by Mike Nichols."

"I never heard of that. And I'm a big De Niro fan."

"That's because it shut down," Kerri continued. "De Niro was coming off playing Travis Bickle in *Taxi Driver*…"

"He was great in that," Amari said.

Jon continued: "He was. A traumatized army vet coming back from Vietnam. It's dark. I once read that he finished playing Travis Bickle on a Friday and started on *Bogart Slept Here* on a Monday. De Niro couldn't get out of the Bickle character and switch to the comic actor they needed for the *Bogart Slept Here* rom-com. They shot a week. Shut down the movie. Recast De Niro. Rewrote it for Richard Dreyfuss. And it came out as the *Goodbye Girl*."

"I love that movie," Amari gushed.

"So do I. One of my favorites," Kerri said, brightening.

"They started that movie all over, Kerri. We can't start over like that," Jon said rationally.

They walked back into the great room. Lunch had arrived, but no one was hungry. They were all looking at Amari.

"What is it?" she asked, worried.

Richard stepped closer. "The studio called. They want their money."

"What money?"

"Amari, as the producer, you owe them two million dollars for the two weeks you shot."

Amari was stunned.

Richard was trying to console her, but things were getting worse, and Kerri was taking it hard. "Can I go lie down somewhere? I'm not feeling well."

"Of course," Amari said and led her to an upstairs bedroom.

Richard asked the concerned Jon, "Is she okay?"

"Her movie just fell apart, what do you think?" Jon sneered.

It was then that Richard said the wrong thing: "It's just a movie, Jon."

"Maybe to you. Not to me. Not to her. Not to us. I don't know if Kerri and I can emotionally survive this movie not being made," Jon admitted.

No one said anything. Jon's phone buzzed. Whatever the news was on the phone complemented his already down and dour disposition. "I'll be right there," he said, ending the call.

Amari was walking down the staircase. "She fell right asleep."

"Thank you, Amari," Jon said. "I have to run out. But please don't make any decisions until we all have had a chance to meet again, and Kerri is feeling better. We owe her that."

Amari nodded in agreement.

"When she wakes up, tell her I went to see my dad."

CHAPTER 36

December 16

JON WAS SPEEDING ALONG I-10 toward Riverside. The speed limit was sixty-five, but that seemed to be only a suggestion, as every other car on the road matched his pace. There wasn't a cop in sight. When he'd been at Amari's house, he'd gotten a text that his dad had fallen. Jon punched in his father's phone number. It rang and rang. Finally, somebody picked up.

"Hello?" The voice sounded lost.

Jon's heart dropped. He hated that he hadn't been to visit his dad in a month, but the last time he'd visited, he'd been doing so well. "I'll be there soon, Dad."

There was no answer on the other line. Only a click.

Jon pulled off the exit toward Riverside. He'd been raised by his dad, as his mother had died from pancreatic cancer when he was three years old, and he didn't really remember her. He and his dad had always had a strong bond, and when Jon moved to LA, so did his dad, who found work as an electrician on movie sets. They used to joke that Dad got into the business faster than Jon did. After Jon and Kerri broke up and she moved to Brooklyn, Jon's dad started showing signs of dementia. He was diagnosed with early-onset Alzheimer's, and he and Jon agreed that he should move into a memory care facility. The one they could afford was two hours outside of LA

Jon entered the festive-looking lobby with a decorated Christmas tree. Wreaths and large red bows flanked the hallway. Jon signed in and smiled at the receptionist. He walked down the long hallway, passing the dining room that was empty, but the tables were set for a meal. People passed him in the hallway. He recognized some of them as neighbors of his dad and nodded a hello.

Jon passed the elevators and headed toward a single door. There was a code outside. He punched in four numbers and entered. The door swung closed behind him and locked. Then there was a second door. He stepped through that door and passed a baby's crib that was filled with doll babies and stuffed animals. He was now in the memory care unit.

Jon stopped in front of the nurses' station. Luckily, Jackie, his favorite nurse, was working that day.

"Jon, so good to see you! How's the movie going?" Jackie asked.

"Uh, it's okay," Jon said as he only wanted to be the bearer of good news. "So, what happened to my dad?"

"Oh, you know your dad. He hates that wheelchair. Told me to get rid of it."

Jon and Jackie both shared a laugh. Jackie continued, "So he was walking down the hall for lunch, and he was just going too fast. Down he went."

"The man does love his food," Jon said.

"He's a little bruised up, so I got him to rest."

"Thanks for all that you do for my dad."

"I love your dad, Jon. You know that."

Jon nodded and walked toward his dad's room. He knocked softly and entered the room. The walls were covered with framed photos of Jon from many stages of his life, especially the years in film school. Since Jon had been an only child, he had been his father's world.

The man in the bed was only sixty years old but looked much older. Alzheimer's had done that to him, robbing him of at least twenty years.

"Hey, Dad."

"Hello."

"Do you know who I am?"

Jon's dad looked at him more closely. "Yes. You're...Jon."

Jon breathed a sigh of relief. At least his father still recognized him. He knew that wouldn't last forever, and he hated to even think about that day. Jon took off his jacket and sat down next to his dad.

"I heard you were running down the hall and took a fall. Does it hurt?" Jon touched his dad's forehead, and the older man winced. "Sorry."

Jon's dad closed his eyes. Then opened them again.

"My movie is kind of in trouble," Jon said. Then stopped as he realized his dad wouldn't grasp what he was saying. His father had trouble understanding present-day events. He knew that his dad could only really comprehend things from the past. He tried again with the conversation. "Remember when I was in film school, and you took the day off to push the dolly?"

The corner of his dad's lips twitched, as they attempted a smile. In the last few months, his dad had forgotten how to smile. The gerontologist had told him to expect this. But at that moment, Jon could see a tiny moment of recognition as he could tell that a part of his dad was still in there, especially the part that loved when Jon made movies.

The day that Jon had been accepted to the NYU film graduate program was as happy a moment for his dad as it was for Jon.

"Remember how you did all the catering on my student films?" Jon asked. But it was more of a statement, because he knew his dad couldn't respond. "You made those big trays of ziti and garlic bread. All my film crew friends went nuts for your food. I think it's why they agreed to crew for me. And you rented that van for me so I could transport all the equipment." Jon smiled at the memory and was silent for a few minutes. His dad flopped over on the bed, and Jon helped him to sit up again. Then Jon's cell phone rang, and seeing that it was Kerri, he quickly answered.

"Hey," Jon said. "How are you?"

"Better. Just tired. How's your dad?" Kerri asked.

"He's okay. Took a little spill, but I think he's going to be okay."

"That's good to hear."

"Thanks for calling. It's nice of you."

"You sound surprised that I'd call."

Jon paused then decided to say what he was thinking. "A little. You were pretty upset with me earlier."

"We're friends, Jon. We're always going to be friends. Even though our movie is dead, and we are never going to talk to each other again."

Jon looked over at his dad, who was becoming agitated as he tried to sit up. "Kerri," he said slowly.

"Yeah, it's Kerri, Dad. Remember her? From film school?" His dad stared at him but said nothing. Jon turned back to the phone.

Kerri continued, "They called some director to come in. But he passed. No one wants to touch it..."

"There's got to be someone they can find to direct," Jon said in a slightly panicked tone.

"Kerri," Jon's dad said louder. Then he began to repeat her name over and over. "Kerri... Kerri..."

At that moment, Jon wondered if his dad was trying to tell him something. He had one of those light-bulb epiphany moments that he knew every good script needed.

CHAPTER 37

December 17

"I THINK I'M COMING DOWN with the flu," Kerri said to Jon, talking on her cell phone as she stood outside her parents' Airbnb. Jon was driving as he talked.

"Are you sure you can't rally? You saw their email. It came flagged as important. Priority. Studio lawyers want to meet with us. I have no idea what's going on."

"No one dies with this movie. I trust you. Whatever decision you make, I support."

"Really?" Jon said. "I think you should be there."

"Help me, Obi-Wan, you're my only hope," Kerri said, with a smile in her voice, quoting a part of the infamous Princess Leia line, and hanging up before Jon remembered it.

Jon was frazzled, as yesterday had been a long twenty-four hours, beginning with the collapse of the movie to Amari's house to the visit with his dad in Riverside. Jon checked in at the Warner Brothers gate, noticing the water tower was decorated for the holidays, but he felt like the Grinch, as this year there would be no Christmas for him, not with a collapsed movie and an angry ex-girlfriend. The soundstages were promoting their new *Bugs Bunny Christmas Movie* with Bugs in a Santa hat. Last time he parked by the executive building, but today he was across the street. He parked and stepped out of his car into a gust of hot air as the Santa Ana winds were blowing. The devil winds off the desert. Forget the Christmas season—everyone was worried about the fire season.

Jon walked through the Barham gate, his head down toward the entrance when, out of the corner of his eye, he saw the oddest thing. An eight-foot inflatable Santa was rocketing toward him. Jon was not ready for it, and it knocked him to the ground. Two stagehands were running after it, yelling, "Sorry."

Santa had hit him hard. Physically and metaphorically. Jon had gotten an early Christmas gift when the movie went into production—and a special night with Kerri—but now it all seemed like coal. Jon limped to the executive office, realizing this was shaping up to be a Christmas to remember.

Jon took the elevator to the third floor and greeted the receptionist. He accepted her offer of a coffee, and he waited, wishing Kerri was with him. He remembered how, after they had broken up and Kerri had left LA, he would go to meetings, and all the execs wanted to talk about was Kerri. The female execs loved her, always wanted to be her best friend, while the male execs also loved her. And some of them asked for Kerri's phone number. No one liked Jon on his own. Jon didn't much like himself on his own. He needed Kerri.

His mind went back to his visit with his dad when he kept saying, "Kerri," as Jon was on the phone talking about potential new directors. Even his dad had only wanted to talk about Kerri.

Christmas music played softly as he waited, but he wasn't in the holiday mood. He found it hard to believe that, for a brief moment, he was on the A-list. It had been the best Christmas ever spending time on the movie set with Kerri. He had started to think that they had a chance. Now their career and relationship were about to revert to what it was before—no career. No relationship. He didn't realize how much he missed her until she wasn't there with him this morning.

"Have Yourself a Merry Little Christmas" played, with its downtrodden lyrics of muddling through the year. *Meet Me in St. Louis*, Jon remembered the movie. For him, everything was a movie. He hated movies with sad endings, which always surprised his male friends. He felt like he was living a sad, terrible ending right now.

A small tear formed in his eyes when the assistant announced it was time. Time for what? He felt like a dead man walking as he was escorted into a large conference room.

Amari and Richard were there. Evan was there on a tablet, video calling in from wherever. There were a lot of suits at the table. *Lawyers*, Jon thought. *And executives*.

"We're not happy," Mr. Gray Suit said. "Are you happy?"

Amari stared him in the eyes. "We never expected to be in this situation."

"You're the producer." Everyone listened. Mr. Gray Suit was the only one talking. The rest were head nodders. Jon watched them nod in a synchronized motion.

"So was I," Evan said from the tablet. Jon noted it was funny to see that someone had placed a glass of water next to the tablet. "But I broke my leg the first day of production."

Richard stepped in: "You called this meeting. Obviously

you have an agenda. At this point, it might be good to tell us your plan."

"We don't think this film is salvageable. Plus, you went over budget. And since Amari was the one who fired the director, not us, she is responsible for the two million dollars that have already been spent. Your ex-director went way over budget," Gray Suit said.

At that moment, Jon saw that Amari was shaking, and so was the room. He thought, maybe, it was a minor earthquake. It caused the tablet to slip off the stand and land facedown, but no one reacted to it as they were used to minor quakes. Jon felt awful because these people were blaming Amari.

"That felt like a three," Grey Suit said. *Great, now he's a seismologist*, Jon thought.

"But we have a solution," he continued. "We will pay off the debt on *Fire and Ice*. And Amari will agree to star in two movies for us at a discounted rate of half her usual fee. No one will ever see this movie, which doesn't seem like much of a movie right now."

Jon watched Richard whisper something to Amari, and she nodded. It was a good deal for Amari. She should take it. Jon didn't want her to, but it would be the right business move. But he also thought about what Kerri had said: "I think there still might be a movie there." And what if she was right? Jon was about to intervene when—

"No," Amari said, staring down Grey Suit.

"We like you, Amari, but maybe not as a producer."

"Just sign the agreement," came Evan's voice from the fallen tablet.

"No," Amari said, looking at Jon. "I promised Kerri and Jon I would make their movie. And I will."

"You can't be serious," a very perplexed Grey Suit said.

"She said no. And no means no," Richard said forcefully.

"If this fails, you could go bankrupt." Grey Suit said.

"You can't put a price on love. I love this script. I love Kerri and Jon. They love each other. And I will finish this movie."

"You have twenty-four hours to find the two million dollars to finish the movie, find a new producer, and find a director," Grey Suit informed them angrily. He got up and walked out. All the other suits followed.

Amari lifted the tablet. Evan was still there. "I think that went well. If we can pull this off, it's a Christmas miracle."

Richard offered, "I'll get you the money, Amari. I promised." She smiled, touched.

"I can call Vera. I worked with her on my other movie," Amari said.

"Hold off on that," Jon said. "I know the perfect person who should direct this movie."

CHAPTER 38

December 17

JON TEXTED KERRI.

Where are you?

Kerri heard her phone ding and saw that it was Jon. She quickly texted back.

Feeling better. Went to farmer's market.

She watched as the text bubbles formed, and almost immediately, Jon's text appeared.

Stay there. On my way.

Kerri was happy to remain in See's Candies, where she was picking up her favorite Christmas novelties, gifts for friends in Brooklyn. She stepped over to the counter for her free piece of chocolate, an oversized bag of chocolate on the ground next to her. The See's worker plopped the day's specialty in her hand, a dark chocolate truffle. Kerri closed her eyes as she put the candy in her mouth, savoring the sweet delight. For a moment, she forgot that her movie had collapsed along with all her dreams.

When the chocolate was finished, she opened her eyes and took out her phone. She hesitated for a moment and then called Beau on FaceTime. The phone rang a few times before he finally picked up. "Hi, Kerri. Everything okay?"

"Yeah. Just wanted you to know. I'm coming home."

"For Christmas or forever?" Beau asked.

"Forever."

"Good. You belong in Brooklyn."

"I'm buying some See's Candies. I got some for your nieces and nephews. And a special gift for you. Chocolate peanut butter Santas." Kerri held up a cellophane bag.

"You know I don't eat peanut butter."

"Really? Who doesn't eat peanut butter? Are you allergic?"

"No. I just don't like the smell or the texture. But it's a nice gesture. Sorry, but I gotta go. Can't wait to see you."

They hung up and Kerri stepped into the farmer's market for a chai latte.

She was sipping the latte waiting for Jon. She knew his "I'll be right there" would take at least an hour in average LA traffic. It was all right, as she had nowhere to go at that moment. She told herself to stop feeling sorry for herself. She had sold another pitch, though that might fall apart if *Fire and Ice* was extinguished. She knew that Hollywood hated failure. *But who cares?* she thought. She had two men who loved her. She had started a Jon/Beau pro/con list but had then deleted it from her phone. She realized that the worst part of the movie collapsing was she would no longer have an excuse to hang around with Jon. Jon—the man who had never given up on their dream and had never given up on her. Jon sat down next to her, catching his breath. He noticed the bag of chocolate peanut butter Santas.

"Oh, I love these. Can I have one?"

"Why not? Someone else doesn't want them."

"Lucky me. Peanut butter and chocolate is the greatest idea in the history of ideas."

Kerri smiled. She mentally added *peanut butter* to the pro Jon column in the Jon/Beau pro/con list.

As Jon munched on the chocolate, he said, "We don't have much time. The suits tried to shut down the movie completely, but Amari stood up for us. And Richard promised to find the two million we need to finish the movie."

"Do they have a director?"

"No. I mean not yet."

"Then they have a problem."

"I've got a great idea for a director."

Kerri nodded and took another sip of her latte. "This is good. Want a sip?"

Jon took a gulp and then quietly said, "You're the director, Kerri."

Kerri burst into laughter, spitting up some of the latte onto her blouse.

"I'm serious. Come on."

"Jon, I don't want to do this anymore. I'm going back to Brooklyn."

"No, no. You belong here. On a set."

"I give up. This town wins."

"I'm going to fight for this dream. Come on, you know how much you love to direct."

"I do."

"That's why you went to film school."

Kerri nodded her head, thinking. Jon was starting to get to her.

"Remember your first film? *Big Time*? It was good. You already had a director's vision. And then *Losers Anonymous*? That was such a high-concept film. You've always had good instincts. And now your latest off-Broadway show, *A Teenage Christmas Carol*."

"Off-off-off-Broadway," Kerri said with a laugh.

"Good... Now you're taking this idea seriously."

And she was. Kerri's mind was spinning. "We can keep the hellish footage and have a funny voice-over."

"That's a good idea," Jon said with encouragement.

"Or we could reshoot...that scene with the two of them in an alcove looking down on the crazy party. And that would allow us to keep some of Lukas's footage from that party scene."

Kerri's voice became more animated the more she spoke. Jon's lips curled up in a smile.

And forty-five minutes later, Kerri and Jon were back in Malibu at Amari's house. Kerri was pitching how she'd save the movie. Amari loved her ideas, and Richard seemed happy too.

Kerri wrapped it up and stopped speaking. For a moment it was all silent, and Kerri held her breath, not sure what would happen next. Then Amari broke into a big smile.

"I love it!" she said. "Your vision solves so many problems."

Richard grinned too, but he was less effusive. "It's good, Kerri. But the problem we're going to run into is that you're a first-time director and Amari's a first-time producer. We can't have both."

Kerri was suddenly crestfallen. She knew that she shouldn't have gotten her hopes up.

"What if I got a second producer? Someone more experienced," Amari suggested.

"I was thinking the same thing. You sure you're okay with that?" Richard asked.

"Of course. I'll still be a producer."

"Well, you'd have to share your fee if we bring on another producer."

Kerri found herself holding her breath for the second time that day as she waited for Amari to say something.

"No problem. I'm okay with sharing."

"So now we just need to find a producer who can jump in on short notice," Richard said.

Jon had stayed quiet while Kerri pitched her take, as he knew how important it was for the director to take the reins. But now he had to speak up. "I know the perfect producer." Everyone leaned forward, eager for his next words. "Drew Fox."

"That's a great idea, Jon!" Kerri said excitedly. "I've run into him twice in the past few weeks, and he's always asked about the movie. Plus, he read the script."

"I'll put a call in to his agent," Richard said.

"No, that's going to take too long to get a hold of him," Kerri said. "No offense, but we don't have time to drag in his agent."

"So how do you suggest we find him faster?" Richard asked.

"Knowing him, he's probably on a plane."

Richard called Drew's office. He got the flight information.

Kerri and Jon waited by the baggage claim, hoping to run into Drew Fox. They'd already been there an hour.

"Maybe this wasn't such a good idea," Kerri said.

"Patience," Jon said.

It was true that, while Kerri knew that patience was a virtue, it wasn't one of hers. They knew Drew was flying in from somewhere, because his cell was turned off. Drew was typically glued to his phone like a mouse to a trap.

"I still can't believe you convinced me to direct this movie."

"I can," Jon said with a smile. "And I also knew you'd be able to convince the suits."

"Thanks." Kerri squeezed Jon's hand warmly.

They watched as a slew of people walked into the baggage area. Another plane had just arrived, and Kerri looked around hopefully for Drew. And then the clouds seemed to part, and a light glowing atop Drew's head appeared, or at least that's what it looked like to Kerri.

In typical Drew fashion, he was talking on his cell.

"Drew!" Kerri called out.

Drew looked around. Then he noticed Kerri and smiled.

"Hello? What are you doing here?"

"Looking for you," Kerri said.

Jon held out his hand "Hi, I'm Jon."

"The fiancé."

"Uh, writing partner," Jon said.

"Sure," Drew said with a laugh.

They walked over to the carousel and waited for Drew's luggage to come out.

"My office said your people have been trying to reach me. So, what seems to be so urgent twelve days before Christmas?"

"We need you to produce our movie," Kerri blurted out.

Drew furrowed his brow. "But you're already in production. And you have a producer."

"See, that's the thing," Jon said. "The director was fired."

"Oh," Drew nodded. He understood the gravity of the situation.

"And I want to direct the movie, and Amari signed off on that—" Kerri said before Drew interrupted her.

"But you're a first-time director and Amari's a first-time producer, so the completion bonds company needs some assurance that it won't fall apart again. Which is where I come in."

"Exactly," Jon said. He had to admit, Drew Fox was slick, but he was also super savvy.

"Let me think about it. I just got back from a long week in Budapest. I need a little downtime."

"That's the thing. We need you to sign on by midnight. Or else..." Kerri said in an ominous voice.

"Or else the movie completely shuts down and the bond company swoops in. This is a tough break, kids."

"I remember you really liked the script," Kerri said hopefully. "When we first met on the plane a few weeks ago. Remember, you read it?"

Drew nodded, as he did remember it. In fact, he hadn't been able to get it out of his mind. It reminded him of the old-fashioned rom-coms that they used to make in the '80s. The kind of movie that his dad used to direct. And the type that his grandfather

244 JULIET GIGLIO & KEITH GIGLIO

used to make. If he signed on, he would be agreeing to continue a long tradition of Fox men making rom-coms. Of course, he'd already made *The Christmas Couple*, but that had been more of a Christmas movie and less of a pure rom-com.

Kerri and Jon stared at him expectantly. Hopefully. He could see in their faces how desperate they were. Drew knew from experience how hard it was to have a movie fall apart. "You said you had a feeling we'd work together. Guess it's sooner than you thought," Kerri said.

Drew wavered, thinking so hard that it looked like smoke was coming out of his head.

"Ok...let's make a movie...or save a movie," Drew said, flashing his beautiful white teeth.

CHAPTER 39

December 17

DREW FOX WAS THE FIRST to arrive at the small production office. He had received a thank-you basket from Mr. Gray Suit. He would normally give it to the woman he was dating, but right now he wasn't seeing anybody. He had been dumped by a screenwriter and by a small-town reporter in the last year. But he'd launched a successful franchise with *Captain Midnight* and had made *Forbes*'s "30 Under 30" list in the Hollywood and Entertainment category.

Drew believed in the power of the universe. He didn't align himself with any religious institution, but he believed in faith. Drew believed in "cosmic destiny" from the moment the creator of the *Captain Midnight* comic told him that most people are unhappy because they push back against what the universe brings them. His time in Upstate New York making a small but well-received Christmas movie had taught him that much.

His destiny was to work with Kerri. He had met her twice on the way to LA, and then she had found him at the airport. He could tell immediately that Kerri and Jon were a terrific couple, helping each other, a perfect partnership. Of course, he'd offered to jump in and try to save their movie. The biggest problem had been that they couldn't find Drew's suitcase. It had been pulled off the plane, and they were waiting at the carousel for it to arrive.

"Amari thinks we're getting married," Kerri had told him.

"She got confused thinking that we were a couple and our agent advised us to keep pretending," Jon said.

"You two look like a couple. Like Captain Midnight says, 'Maybe all of this is cosmic destiny.'"

"Loved that movie. Up there with *Star Wars* and *Guardians*."

"Which one?" Drew asked.

"*A New Hope* and the first *Guardians*." Drew liked Jon's answer.

"Amari was very happy to hear you're helping us produce," Kerri added, pivoting the conversation.

"Are you two hungry? Let's get something to eat, and you can fill me in."

Drew had insisted they grab dinner at Musso & Frank on Hollywood Boulevard. It was the night of the annual Christmas parade. The valet parking was closed off, and they had to walk ten blocks, which Kerri enjoyed. They saw some old-time film and TV celebrities heading past them followed by the man himself: Santa Claus.

"Ho ho Ho, Merry Christmas, Drew Fox," Santa called.

Kerri laughed for the first time in a while and said, "Santa seems to know you."

"I have no idea who that is. Probably an actor I met at an audition," Drew said, still walking when an elf ran up to him, holding Santa's headshot.

"Maybe we can put him in *Fire and Ice*," Jon laughed.

They sat down in an old-fashioned booth at Musso & Frank. Like a few of the customers, the place was dressed up for the holidays. The waiters wore festive red aprons, carolers sang, and people at a large table were exchanging Secret Santa gifts and enjoying their office Christmas party.

"Oh no, I forgot to buy Christmas presents," Jon blurted out.

"If we don't get this movie of yours back on track, you'll have plenty of time. Tell me everything."

And they did, while they ordered a few crazy Christmas drinks. Jon praised Kerri's directing skills, telling stories about Kerri in film school that even she didn't remember.

Then Kerri went into director mode and pitched. "We're not going to reshoot it. We're going to *Christmas Carol* the hell of it, using Lukas's footage."

"Some of Lukas's footage," Jon added.

"Some of Lukas's footage as Ghost of Christmas Future," Kerri said. "We haven't shot the opening scenes yet, so we can rewrite them. They meet-cute and don't like each other. He's arrogant. She's a snob. But they are both getting along. We keep the scenes as written with their parents. And on Christmas Eve… it's the fire. We add a scene like in *Heaven Can Wait*."

"Lots of heavenly fog," Drew added, getting excited.

"They missed their soulmates in real life, and now they're given a second chance," Kerri continued.

"Why?" Drew wondered.

"Because everyone deserves one," Jon said quickly.

Kerri wondered if he was referring to their relationship but brushed the thought aside.

"They meet again after the fire as if it's the first time. They have no memory of each other. So, we play it out as in the script.

We were scheduled to shoot the middle of the movie, and we do that. But at the end of act two, they break up, deciding they are not right for each other," Kerri said.

"And they find themselves in the bad dream. The hellish scenes," Jon said, jumping back into the conversation. "The Ghost of Christmas Future."

"And we can edit that a little... Jon thinks we have the footage. And all we have to do is film Christmas morning as they wake up and run around looking for each other."

Drew was engrossed. "Where do they find each other?"

"It's Christmas morning. And they both climb up to the Hollywood sign on Christmas morning. They kiss, and it begins to snow. As they kiss in front of the sign."

"That's the poster," Drew said excitedly. "I love it."

"I think we can do it," Kerri said with confidence. "We only have ten days to wrap it up. I can do this, Drew."

Drew scrutinized Kerri's face. Her earnestness coupled with her enthusiasm outweighed her experience. He believed she could do it. Drew signaled for the bill and turned to Kerri and Jon. "Here's what I want to do now. I'm going to Uber home and go over all the materials that you have. I'll need the script supervisor's book. And the footage. I'll call you later when I have a plan."

Drew Fox paid the bill and added. "It's really good you got great reviews on that off-Broadway show you directed."

"Oh, yes, *A Teenage Christmas Carol*. Always room for *A Christmas Carol*," Kerri said. And then added quickly, "I am so glad people liked it."

They waited until Drew left before bursting into laughter.

"It was a school play," Jon said, grinning ear to ear.

"He must have read the reviews in the school paper online," Kerri laughed. She was the first to see the absurdity of the situation.

CHAPTER 40

December 17

JON AND KERRI WERE DRIVING back to the apartment. The car was quiet except for the Christmas songs playing on the radio. They were each lost in their thoughts when Jon broke the silence.

"So, what did you think of Drew?" Jon asked.

"He's great. I wish he had been on the movie from the start."

"Me too. But then we might not have had Amari, and then the movie never gets green lighted."

"You're right. I guess things happen for a reason. I just never saw this happening."

Instead of turning onto their street, Jon made a left into Griffith Park.

"Where are you going?" she asked, just as the Christmas lights appeared on the road ahead. "Merry Christmas." Jon had driven to Griffith Park for the Holiday Light Festival Train Ride.

"Jon, we don't have time for this," Kerri insisted. She was surprised, because Jon had always been the one who chose work over pleasure.

"It's Christmas, Kerri. And for once, you and I are going to enjoy it." Jon got out and extended his hand, but Kerri didn't take it. She was stunned that they were there. Back when they were dating, they would skip a Christmas party if they were revising a script for a producer, a script that they then didn't even sell. Kerri shook off those old bitter feelings as they walked to the "station" where families, friends, newly romantic couples, and old romantic couples waited to board the train. Everything was festively decorated on a one-mile track.

As the train left the station, Kerri and Jon were squished tightly next to each other in a small car. She felt her body relaxing and allowed the feelings of euphoria to take over as they traveled through magical scenes, passing tens of thousands of captivating lights. The perfect train ride to put anyone in the holiday mood.

For both, the ride was over too soon. Jon stepped out, offering his hand to Kerri, and this time she took it, but she tripped. Jon reached out, grabbed both her hands, and caught her, making sure she didn't fall. Kerri noticed how warm his hands were, and she didn't want to let go.

"You make a beautiful couple," an older man said. "I can take your picture."

Kerri didn't object. Not even when Jon handed his phone to the older man.

"Just hit the camera icon," Jon said, as he tried to be helpful.

"Give me a break, kid. I shot over thirty features. I know how a camera works." Jon and Kerri both smiled as the older man moved around. "Light's not right. We need to move you over there."

"Caleb, just take the picture," the older man's wife protested. "It's cold."

"I take a picture to capture moments. Not just to post online.

Into the nothing-sphere. Move to the left. Big guy, lean back. You're blocking the light on your beautiful bride's face." *Click. Click. Click.* He was done. He handed them back the cell phone and walked away.

Kerri leaned close to look at the shot. It was astounding. A perfect photo of what should be a perfect couple. "I think that was Caleb Deschanel," Kerri whispered to Jon.

"I thought so," Jon whispered back. "He was nominated for an Academy Award six times as a cinematographer."

"Why are we whispering?" Kerri said in a louder voice with a laugh.

"I love this town," Jon said. Kerri didn't disagree.

"AirDrop me," she said, taking out her phone, suddenly seeing three messages from Beau. Her mood suddenly dampened, and she quickly put the phone away. "Battery is drained. I'll get them tomorrow. We should go."

"We should. You have to direct a movie soon. What kind of director hangs out with the writer?"

"Cowriter. And a very grateful director. Do you think I can do this, Jon?"

"I always believed in you, Kerri. Still do."

Under the pretense of the darkness, Jon took Kerri's hand and led her back to the car. Kerri didn't protest.

On the way home in the car, this time for real, Drew called. "Good news! It's a done deal. You ready to direct, Kerri?"

Kerri let out a "woo-hoo!" She couldn't believe it was happening. "Yes! Thank you, Drew!"

"Don't thank me, thank that writing partner of yours. I have a feeling it was his idea. Get some sleep. You're going to need it. Directing is like running a marathon."

Kerri smiled. That's what Roberta Hodes, their film school professor used to tell them.

"We'll have a day of preproduction tomorrow, and then we'll start filming on the following day." Drew hung up the phone. What he neglected to tell Kerri and Jon was that he didn't have the rest of the money. At least not yet.

———————

Kerri was lying in bed looking at her shot list for her first day of filming. Unable to sleep, Kerri got up and passed Jon, who was asleep on the living room futon. She stepped outside the apartment. Her FaceTime buzzed, and she quickly answered.

"I was just about to call you," Kerri said. "I have some great news."

"Me too. I'm coming to LA," Beau said.

"You don't have to do that."

"I do. Because I just watched *Casablanca*. I want to know if I'm Humphrey Bogart or the other guy."

"Beau, I can't talk about this right now. I'm directing the movie. Starting tomorrow."

"With Jon?"

"Not with Jon. Why would you think I'm directing this with Jon?"

"You seem to do everything with him these days."

"Beau, the movie wraps in a week. We'll talk then."

"No. I'm coming out now. See you soon. Have a good night."

Kerri sighed and walked back inside, sitting on the futon, waking up Jon.

"What are we going to do, Jon?"

"About the movie? Or about us?"

"There is no us, Jon."

"That's what we keep telling ourselves." Jon said.

"How's that working out?"

"Not good," Jon commented.

"I just spoke with Beau. He's coming to LA. He heard about the movie. He has already booked his flight."

"No matter what happens, I enjoyed this Christmas with you."

"Not Christmas yet. But yes, when I came out here, I dreaded thinking about our Christmas past," Kerri admitted. "Christmas past, Christmas present, Christmas future. Why didn't we do these fun things when I lived here?" Kerri wondered.

"No money," Jon said bluntly.

"That's not it. You had money to go to Amoeba Music and buy all those used Blu-ray DVDs."

"It was me. You always wanted to do things. Hike. Go skiing in Big Bear. But all I did was work. I was always worried about writing, even though I wasn't getting paid to write. I made those false deadlines. I didn't want to go anywhere. I put myself in development hell."

"Now we're in relationship hell."

"It's been hell, but it's been fun," Jon stated. They lingered, looking at each other.

While Kerri and Jon were prepping for their first day of filming, Drew was having yet another meeting at the studio. It was a last-ditch effort to get more money for the completion of the film. It was late, and he could tell that the four execs were getting restless and wanted to go home.

Once again Evan, the exec in charge of production, was on the tablet on the table. His broken leg was prominent in the video, as it was elevated.

"Ok—you're up and running, but you're still going to need to find two million to finish this thing," Evan told Drew from the tablet.

"Come on guys, the new director shouldn't be burdened by the mistakes of the director who was fired," Drew said in protest. Although he knew that his protestations weren't going to go anywhere. It was like he was just listening to himself speak.

"We're not paying for what Lukas did in going over budget," Evan insisted.

A serious-looking junior executive spoke up. "Today is December seventeenth, and we just need you to complete the film before Christmas."

Drew knew what day it was, and he also knew that filming past Christmas would put them into overtime. Nobody wanted to work the week of December 26 to New Year's Eve, least of all him. He had plans to fly to Iceland. This junior executive was stating the obvious. He figured she'd just graduated from business school.

"We're not all that happy that Amari chose a first-time director to finish the film," Evan said from the screen of the tablet as he winced from the pain in his broken leg.

"She's not a first-timer. She just directed an off-Broadway teenage *Christmas Carol* last month. And it might be heading uptown next year."

"Teenage *Christmas Carol*?" Evan mulled around the idea, as he paused for a moment. "Not a bad idea. Rachel, see if you can get the rights."

"Of course," the junior executive said quickly as she scribbled down some notes.

CHAPTER 41

December 18

THE PROBLEMS STARTED EARLY ON Kerri's first day of directing. She had decided to rehearse the first scene that they were going to film, and it was already proving difficult. It was the scene where Cage, as the firefighter, takes Amari to the firehouse. They'd already filmed the exterior for the location, but now they were getting the indoor scenes in the firehouse kitchen they'd replicated on a set at the studio lot.

Kerri called for action and watched as the two actors spoke their lines. Amari was flawless, and Kerri marveled at her acting. But Cage was dreadful. He was leaden and couldn't get out of his head.

"Ok, stop. Cage, what's going on?" Kerri asked.

"Once I found out I was dead, I went to a dark place," Cage confessed.

"You're not dead anymore—I got you out of that."

"I know. But I just can't get back into character." Cage sighed.

Amari rolled her eyes. "It's called acting, Cage."

"I'm a method actor, Amari. I trained under Judith Weston. Substitution. Everything is a substitution."

And I bet there's someone we can substitute for you, Kerri said under her breath. But to the actors, she said, "Ok, let's take a break. Cage, do what you need to do to get back into character?"

Just as Kerri thought it couldn't get worse with Cage, Drew pulled her aside.

"Cage's agent just called. Said that on the original schedule, he was finished as of tomorrow. The agent's demanding that we pay Cage fifty thousand dollars a day to continue past tomorrow."

"You're kidding!" Kerri said in a furious voice. "What can we do?"

"We can reason with him. If Cage agrees to change the original contract, there's nothing that the agent can do. The agent has to comply with the client."

"Ok. Got it. I'll see if I can talk to him."

Kerri walked toward Cage, but at that moment her parents arrived.

"Kerri!" Troy called out. "I'm ready for my close-up!"

"Dad, you already said that," Kerri said, but she was laughing. It was good to see friendly faces. She hugged her parents.

"How's it going?" Diane wanted to know.

"Oh, it's going," was all that Kerri wanted to say. "Why don't you grab a snack over at craft services and hang out with Jon?"

She hugged her parents again and then walked toward Cage, who was sitting in the chair with his name on it.

"Hey, Cage, we just got an interesting call from your agent."

Cage looked at her guiltily.

"Anything I can do to change your mind about the fifty

thousand dollars a day? You know we don't have the money for that, much less enough to even finish the film yet."

"That's not my problem."

"Is this the real reason you were unable to get into character earlier?"

"Maybe."

Kerri was seething inside but tried to keep her cool. And at that moment, a small Christmas miracle occurred because Val Stone, the action hero who lived next door to her parents' Airbnb, walked onto the set!

Kerri and Cage watched as Diane and Troy rushed to greet Val.

"You made it!" Troy said.

Jon hustled over to greet the action star. They shook hands. "Hey, dude, so good to see you again."

Drew noticed the commotion and looked over at Val. A big smile broke out on his face. He walked over confidently to greet Val, carrying the script pages.

"Val, my man. Good to see you again," Drew said.

"I didn't know you were producing this movie," Val said.

"Just started. And your timing is perfect. We might need a new leading man. A firefighter."

"I can play a firefighter," Val said as he flexed his muscles.

Cage continued to watch the interaction, suddenly very worried that he was about to be replaced. And that's when Cage sprinted over to Drew and Val and Jon.

"I cleared my schedule. I can be here for the rest of the filming. No extra charge. This is a work of love for me," Cage babbled.

Drew and Kerri gave each other a look.

"Hold on, not so fast; you said I could have the part," Val growled.

"It's my part! You can't have it," Cage insisted.

"Sorry, Val. I owe you one," Jon said. He'd been the one to ask Val to come to set to help them out. "Thanks again for coming down. Let me walk you out."

Jon and Val stepped off the set, away from Cage, and immediately burst into laughter. Jon hugged Val. "That was awesome. I love you, man. Did you see how scared Cage was? He thought you were going to take his part!"

"Exactly as we planned. I told you that I know actors. But don't think you're off the hook. You and Kerri are still writing a script for me. Maybe a big sci-fi thing. It's like *Die Hard* on a Mars colony."

"That sounds great."

When Jon walked back onto the set, the camera was rolling, and everyone was in position. He watched as Kerri seamlessly directed the scene. Cage was even back in character. All was well with the world. Jon smiled. He was confident that nothing else would go wrong that day.

CHAPTER 42

December 18

BEAU FRANKLIN STEPPED OUT OF the rented Kia Soul and walked toward the studio. He was sweating in his black cashmere sweater, not prepared for the warm California December weather. The guard at the gate had given him a pass that Kerri had left for him. *So far so good*, Beau thought.

As Beau walked through the Warner Brothers gate, he was impressed by the architecture of the old studio, at least the iconic buildings. The stages were large boxes with huge black numbers painted on them. Beau found stage twenty but noticed a red flashing light outside the stage door. He knew enough not to open the door, so he waited.

A minute later, the light clicked off, and Beau stepped through the door into the firehouse movie set. He noticed bright lights hanging from the ceiling. The crew was scattered around. Then he saw her, the love of his life. "Kerri!" he called out.

Kerri was behind the camera looking at the shot that the cinematographer had lined up. She didn't seem to hear him.

"Hi, can I help you?" asked an Italian-looking guy. Beau didn't know it, but this was Jon.

"Uh, yeah. I'm looking for Kerri."

"Are you a PA?"

Beau laughed. "Oh no."

Jon noticed that Beau was well-dressed. And attractive. So he made the next assumption. "Right. You're one of the extras. We're not ready for you until after lunch. You didn't need to get here this early."

"I'm just looking for Kerri Williams. I'm her fiancé."

Jon felt like a ton of bricks had just been thrown at him. Why hadn't Kerri told him that Beau was so good-looking?

"Oh, right."

"You're Jon Romano," Beau said as he finally figured it out.

The two men sized each other up. Beau sensed Jon was his competition. He thought, *Kerri never told me Jon was a good-looking guy.*

They both were vying for the same woman, and only one of them was going to win.

"Kerri's busy right now prepping the next scene," Jon said.

"That's fine. Is there a place I could put my stuff down?"

"Oh, sure." Jon guided Beau to where the folding chairs were set up for the extras. He watched as Beau took off his heavy sweater. Underneath was a tight black T-shirt. Jon could see that Beau was ripped. His arms bulged, and he had one of those six-pack stomachs. Jon subconsciously sucked in his stomach and tried to flatten it.

"I've never been to LA before," Beau admitted.

"City of make-believe, and you're at the epicenter right now."

"Kerri hates this place. She didn't want to come back, but I convinced her it would be good to get it out of her system. Give her some closure."

"She's here because a script she and I wrote is in production. And she's directing. So no one is closing the closure door anytime soon," Jon volleyed back. *What the hell does she see in this guy?* he wondered.

Beau continued, "Yeah, I know. Plus, the money was good. It's helping us to buy a condo in Williamsburg."

Kerri looked up from the camera. She noticed Beau for the first time, and then she saw that he was with Jon. *Uh-oh.* She hurried over to the two men in her life.

They both brightened when she approached. She smiled at them.

Jon realized that, if they were in the movie *Casablanca*, he was Bogart and Beau was Ilsa's husband. Jon sighed, wishing for the first time in his life that he and Kerri were smokers so that he could light a cigarette for her. He could have shown his dominance that way. Instead, he said, "Do you need a coffee, Kerri?"

"I'm good, thanks." Then she turned to Beau. "You made it! So good to see you, Beau!" She hugged him.

Jon noticed that she didn't kiss Beau. It was more of a friendly type of hug. *Yes!* Jon thought.

But Beau didn't mind. He was more of a hugger. He also understood that PDA wasn't good in a workplace environment.

"It's been a chaotic morning, but we're finally getting off some shots. Jon can help you get a coffee. And this is a good place to sit. But I can't talk right now, okay?" Then Kerri turned to Jon. "Can I talk to you a second about the scene?"

Jon smiled. "Absolutely." He followed Kerri to the camera to look at the shot.

Jon stepped behind the camera. "The shot looks good. I like how you lined it up. Nice thirds."

Kerri laughed. "I know it looks good. That's not why I brought you over here. I need you to watch Beau today."

"As in babysitting him?"

"Sort of. Keep him away from Amari."

"How?"

"I don't know. You'll figure it out."

Jon's mind raced, thinking quickly and not wanting to leave Kerri's side yet. Especially since Beau was watching them intently from afar. "Ok, I'll tell Beau that she doesn't like talking to nonpros."

Kerri nodded. "That's good. I like that." And then she added, "And if Amari asks me who he is, I'll tell her he's an old family friend who stopped by the set to visit."

"That's good. But with a suitcase?"

"Good point. Maybe you can hide his suitcase."

"I'm on it."

Kerri laughed. "Thanks, Jon."

"No problem. We're partners. We work well together. See what we just figured out?" Jon said, hoping to remind Kerri of his worth before she next laid eyes on her hunky Norse god.

But Kerri was already hustling away. She called out to her assistant director, "Let's do this!"

The assistant director shook his head. "Places people!" And then, "Quiet on the set!"

Beau watched as the camera rolled. Amari stepped into the scene. He noticed how gorgeous she was and turned to say something to Jon. But Jon put his finger up to his mouth, indicating they needed to be quiet.

"And cut!" Kerri called. "That was nice, but let's do another one. This one is for you, Amari. I want you to try something completely different, so we have some choices."

"Great! Love that," Amari said. "You're doing great, Kerri."

Beau turned to Jon. "I'd love to meet Amari," he said.

Jon winced. "Not a good idea."

"She seems friendly enough."

"That's because they're all pros over there. She hates nonpros. Takes her out of her process."

"All I want is just a quick selfie. All the guys at the firm will never believe this."

"Yeah, not going to happen. She needs to stay in character. The last thing you want to do is to mess things up for Kerri, right?"

"I guess so. This is a big moment for her."

"Look, if you want to go back to your hotel and wait for Kerri, that would be okay."

Beau paused, unsure. "I don't want to upset Kerri. I promised I'd be here for her."

"She'll be fine."

Beau looked around and realized there was no place for him on the set. "Ok. I could use a nap. I had such an early flight."

"Exactly. Get some rest."

"Can you tell Kerri that I'm staying at the airport Hilton?"

"Sure. I'll let her know."

But as Beau walked off the set, pulling his suitcase, Jon had already forgotten the name of Beau's hotel.

CHAPTER 43

December 18

THE MORNING HAD BEEN TOUGH, and the lunch break was tougher. The caterer did not show up. At first, Richard thought he was late. He kept checking during the morning shoot, but the caterer was not answering his calls or responding to the text and the hungry crew.

Richard sent a production assistant out to get protein bars and had coffee brought in from studio service. The crew was not happy to eat breakfast snacks for lunch. Richard's phone rang. It was the caterer.

"Where are you?" Richard growled.

"What are you talking about? The movie shut down."

"And now it's back up! And we need food."

"Nobody told me anything."

Richard wondered how this happened. Evan should have been on this, but he was still only on Zoom, physically unable to get to the set. His duties were being handled by the assistant director who was doubling as the line producer.

"Never mind. Get here as soon as you can," Richard said.

"I can't. I'm on set out in Santa Clarita. I took another gig."

"You have a contract for this movie!"

"Hey, I don't even know if you have a movie. All I know is it's Christmas. And I need the money. Which according to *Deadline*, you don't have."

The former caterer hung up. Richard ordered two production assistants to go get pizza for lunch. He told them not to bother coming come back if they couldn't get twenty pies.

"We had a problem with the caterer. We're having pizza as soon as possible."

The crew grumbled, firing off complaints: "I don't eat bread." "How about a goddamn salad?" "If we go to the commissary, do we get reimbursed?" Some stayed, most didn't.

"Back here at 1:00 p.m.," Evan called from the tablet. Not that anyone could hear him. Richard was now talking with Evan.

"Pizza? What is this, film school? Where the hell is Drew Fox?" Evan barked.

"Trying to get us money to finish the movie. We run out in two days. I sent you an email about it."

"You know how many emails I get a day!"

"Here comes Amari. I have to go." Richard clicked off the tablet.

"Richard, we are going to be all right," Amari said.

"First day back. Everyone is adjusting. Once the pizza comes, everything will be fine."

"That better be damn good pizza," Amari said, walking away to her dressing room to decompress.

The pizza was not very good. The PAs had done their best hitting up any 7-Eleven or gas station that had a mini-mart and

Ralphs grocery store. Richard thought they had been quite clever, knowing that ordering pizza would take longer. He was going to need some new assistants and maybe Pizza Boys, as he would now call them, who would be interested in the job. Richard had never known how hard it was to break in, as his mother had made one call, and he was instantly placed in the agency mailroom. He never left, and this was the first time he was on his own. His phone texted a reminder. His mother's Christmas party was that night. There was no way he could go; he had to save this movie.

Kerri retreated to the bathroom. She had felt unsettled all morning. The pressure was on her. She and Jon had storyboarded the scene the night before, so she was prepared. But still, the morning had been tough. And Beau's arrival had not helped either. She sat in a stall when two other crew members walked in. They were Olivia and Ella from hair and makeup. Kerri sat still, hoping she wouldn't have to live out a clichéd movie scene of people talking about her while she sat in a stall.

"She has no idea what she is doing," Olivia said.

Too late, Kerri thought. She could silence their conversation with a flush, but she chose not to, intent on listening.

"Total amateur hour," Ella said.

"I thought that movie we did with Amari in Upstate New York was a bad set."

"This is worse. I heard a rumor that they don't have the money to finish it," Ella added.

Kerri shuddered.

"Hope it shuts down soon. I have Christmas shopping to finish," Olivia said.

Olivia and Ella left the bathroom. Kerri stayed there until Jon texted her:

Where are you? The pizza's here.

———————

After a very short time to inhale the pizza, the shooting continued. Fiona, the cinematographer who Lukas had hired, was adjusting the light, making the scene darker and moving Amari and Cage into shadows. Kerri approached her. "Why are they in the dark, Fiona?"

"Please don't tell me how to do my job," Fiona barked, loud enough for the crew to hear.

Kerri's mind flashed to Gordon Willis, the famous cinematographer who shot *The Godfather*. He was known as the Prince of Darkness for his love of dark scenes. Kerri also knew not to battle with Fiona because an angry cinematographer could slow down the production. All eyes were on Kerri. She could go back and hide in the video village with the monitors, or she could try to control the set.

"I want the scene to be bright. No more shadows. Only the background is muted. I want Amari's diamonds to sparkle. Start with that..."

"I am shooting the film the way Lukas and I talked about shooting it."

"I am the director now," Kerri said.

Fiona didn't answer. But she begrudgingly moved the light. The actors were in place, and Kerri called, "Action," as she watched the scene play out. It was working. Jon had written new dialogue where Amari and Cage's characters were sharing the dreams that they had for each other.

Cage was playing it perfectly. "I'm embarrassed. In my

dream, I meet you at a Firefighter's Ball, which is like a raging party straight out of hell."

"That sounds like something I used to do."

"Used to do?"

"I don't want that life anymore, Mike."

"What do you want?"

"I think I want you."

Kerri loved it. She was letting the moment linger when—

"CUT!" someone cried out. Not just someone; it was Lukas Wright, crashing the set. He marched onto the soundstage, all eyes on him, which he knew and loved. Madison had walked in but stayed back, watching.

"Lukas, you're not supposed to be here," Richard yelled.

"I wanted to see how my movie was coming out," Lukas said, smiling at the laughing Fiona.

Amari went up to Lukas. "Why are you doing this?"

"You fired me," Lukas said.

Jon approached. "Lukas, this is not your set anymore. You need to leave."

"Oh, it's Jon. In love with Kerri, your director. Amazing that they have time to look at their actors, as all they seem to do is look at each other."

Kerri got into Lukas's face. "Get off my set. Or I'll call security now."

"Fine," Lukas said. "I will leave. But not without my team. Fiona, Pedro, everyone I hired—you can waste your holiday on this little film, or you can join me on *Satan's Prayer*. The production office has been set up."

Madison walked closer to Lukas. "Lukas, please. You don't have to ruin their movie."

Lukas turned on her. "Oh, Madison, the other woman, who would do anything for a part. And I mean anything…"

"Stop!" Jon said, storming up to Lukas.

"Who are you, again?"

"I'm the writer of the script you tried to destroy."

"A writer? I'm a filmmaker."

Jon rushed Lukas. Richard jumped in the way to block him. Richard and Jon tumbled to the floor. Richard told Jon, "He's not worth it."

Lukas continued his rant: "You're right. Not worth it. This film was not worth it. Everyone, listen to me. This film is about to fall apart again. They have no money to pay you. You have every right to quit, because you originally signed on to work for me. And since my production office has been set up across the lot, now you can. Come work on *Satan's Prayer*. This isn't a movie. And she is not a director."

Kerri felt all eyes on her. There was grumbling. The camera operator was the first to walk out. "Where are you going?" Kerri asked, even though she knew the answer.

More people walked off. Amari approached them and begged, "Please don't do this."

Some were nice. Most weren't.

"*It's Christmas.*"

"*This is a mess.*"

"*I didn't sign on to work for a first-time director.*"

Kerri went back and slumped in her director's chair. The set was sadly quiet. The only sound was from the tablet being held up by a PA. It was Evan, yelling at Lukas. Lukas knocked the tablet out of the frightened PA's hand, smashing it to the ground.

Lukas stopped in front of Amari and whispered in her ear: "As an actor and a lover, you're overrated."

Amari was enraged, and she was suddenly the one who now had to be restrained. Richard grabbed Amari, who tried to get free, slinging back her elbow and accidentally striking Richard in the nose.

"Ow!" he screamed. His nose was bloodied.

"I'm so sorry, Richard."

"Where did they come from? What did he say?"

"Forget it, he's a no-good liar."

The exodus was over. Drew Fox returned to the set to find Kerri and Jon sitting in their directing and producing chairs, Amari taking care of Richard's bloody nose, and a broken tablet on the floor.

"I was gone for an hour. What happened?"

"Lukas got everyone to quit. We have no crew," Kerri said, clearly devastated.

Drew Fox added to the misery: "I couldn't get the money we need to finish the film. It's over."

There was a moment of silence, each mourning the loss.

"This is not over," Jon said, getting up out of his chair. "Yeah, we don't have a crew. And we don't have any money. But we have great actors and a great script."

Richard stepped up. "I know where we can get the money. Amari, I'll need you to come with me."

Kerri had recovered, inspired by Richard. "And I know where we can get the crew."

Even Jon wondered, "Where?"

Kerri reminded him, "It's margarita night."

Jon smiled and said, "El Coyote!"

CHAPTER 44

December 18

THE FILM SCHOOL FRIENDS SAT at a large table drinking Christmas margaritas. Henry, the wannabe editor, had arranged a Secret Santa exchange. Most of the gifts were from the 99 Cents Only Store and were either candy, pens, note cards, or packing tape. Henry got the packing tape. "Thanks, Quinn. I might be using this in the near future," he admitted.

Quinn, the wannabe assistant director and line producer, asked: "Are you moving again? Where to?"

"I'm thinking about Des Moines," Henry confessed.

Rebecca, the wannabe script supervisor, remembered: "You're not moving back in with your parents."

"Until I find a job, I am. I can't wait for tomorrow for my dreams to come true."

Pascal, the wannabe film composer, busted out lyrics, singing, "There's always tomorrow for dreams to come true." Half the table sang with him, remembering the song from the classic animated *Rudolph the Red-Nosed Reindeer*.

"Tomorrow the rent's due. And I don't have the money."

Shelby, who aspired to work in development, held up the five lotto tickets she received from her Secret Santa and said: "I do."

"Those are scratch-off lotto tickets," said Linda, the wannabe cinematographer.

"Maybe. Or maybe they're the million dollars we need to make our movie and show everyone who's not giving us a job how talented and deserving we are." She handed out the tickets to four others. "Let's make a movie! Start scratching."

Using table utensils, the five quickly scratched off the tickets. They were all duds.

Nancy, the wannabe production designer, was crying, "I don't have enough money to fly home to my parents, and I don't want my parents to pay for me anymore. They can't afford it."

The party was more like a funeral. Henry raised his glass. "Here's to next year."

"To next year," they all cheered meekly, trying to find a thread of hope to hang on to. They settled into silence.

Ira, the wannabe studio executive, said sadly, "I've been living in my car. Gloria broke up with me. I owed her a few months' rent. Moving into a new place tomorrow."

"Where?"

"I have no idea," Ira said.

More drinks were poured. Stephen, the wannabe set decorator, raised a glass. "To LA, the killer of dreams. She lures us in and kills us."

"Why is LA a she?" Nancy snapped.

"Guys, not tonight, it's our holiday party. We're here to support each other," Quinn said. "Did anyone connect with Kerri and Jon?"

"I reached out, but never heard back. What a mess." Rebecca said.

"If those two can't make it, none of us can. I always thought they would be rich, successful, and married by now. They are the perfect couple," Nancy added.

"Until Hollywood crushed them," Henry said. He wanted to call it a night, when a strolling guitar player approached them singing a rendition of "Santa Claus Is Coming to Town." After the second verse, the guitar player stepped aside to reveal two people playing Santa and Mrs. Claus.

"Ho ho ho, merry Christmas," Santa called out, putting down his sack of presents.

"What do all you young filmmakers want for Christmas?" Mrs. Claus asked.

"I don't celebrate Christmas," Ira Simon said. He wanted to work on the studio side of things.

"Maybe you do for just this one day," Santa said. And it was then Quinn yelled out, "It's Kerri and Jon!"

Everyone cheered, so happy to see them. It was Henry who said, "I guess the movie shut down again, if you have the time to come over here and drink with us movie rejects."

Kerri was concerned. "Henry, what's wrong?"

Rebecca, sitting next to Henry, held up the packing tape and said, "He's going home to Des Moines."

Jon pulled up two seats, holding one out for Kerri. "No one's going anywhere. Santa's brought some presents."

"You each get one. Don't open them until everyone has one," Kerri handed out the small packages. It felt like a paperback novel was in each one.

"Mine says, SOUND DESIGN."

"I got Editor."

"I got Film Composer." Each present was addressed not to their name but their skill set.

"Open them up," Jon said. They did and they were confused. Each present was the same: a small-sized version of the script *Fire and Ice*. It had one hole and a latch that you could attach to your belt. It was the standard size that crews had when in production.

Linda Talavera was bewildered but starting to dream again. "Mine is the cinematographer."

Kerri grinned. "I need you to shoot my movie, Linda. Just like in film school."

"You're making a short film?" Henry said, equally confused.

"No," Jon said. "You are all going to work on a long film. A feature film."

"*Fire and Ice*," Kerri explained. "We have ten days to film half a movie. And I want all of you to be the crew. If you're open to the idea."

The table erupted with cheers followed by tears. The manager ran over to make sure everyone was okay.

"We're fine," Henry said. "We all just got hired to make a movie. And we get paid, right?"

"Absolutely," Jon said. "It's a real movie."

"We know it's a lot of work," Kerri said.

Quinn's script had come with a copy of the shooting schedule. "We have ten days to do twenty days of shooting."

The reality of the task was sinking in. "It's a lot, I know. Can you do it?" Kerri asked.

"Damn right we can," Quinn said.

Everyone applauded.

Jon got up. "So read the script. The green pages are what we need to shoot tomorrow. We'll have an early morning production meeting. If you know some PAs, call them in."

"I know you two are busy," Quinn said, "but if it's okay, I'd like to call for a production meeting right now. We can talk as we read the script."

The waitress came over. "More margaritas?"

"Coffee," Henry said. "Lots of coffee. Oh, and can you throw this out for me?" He handed her the packing tape. Everyone cheered and went to work.

Kerri led the meeting, explaining the problems they'd encountered, and asked for help in fixing them. The team was on fire. They had a plan for how to fix it, and the movie was already getting better.

Kerri and Linda talked about the camerawork. Linda wanted a lot of it to be off sticks and hoped they could get a second camera so she could shoot a medium shot and a close-up at the same time, all of which Kerri agreed with.

Drew Fox video called Kerri. "How's it going? Do we have a crew?"

Kerri was bursting with pride for her nascent crew and turned the phone to show the team at work, now occupying four tables at El Coyote. She called out, "Everyone, say hello to our producer, Drew Fox."

Like a second grade classroom, the crew called out, "Hello, Drew Fox," and laughed. Kerri flipped the phone back and saw Drew grinning ear to ear. "They're excited. Good job, director. I'll get in touch with Amari and let her know."

Amari, Kerri thought. She had forgotten about the lie that she and Jon were a couple. An engaged couple. It was easy to pull off when people didn't know who they were, but the film school crew knew all about them.

Kerri called out, "Can I have everyone's attention? I'm going to head out now."

Jon added, "Me too."

"I know everyone is going to do a great job and save my ass as a director. But there's one thing you all need to know about me and Jon," she said, getting everyone's attention. Especially Jon.

"About our relationship... In something that could only happen in a classic rom-com, Amari, our star, and everyone on the set believes Jon and I are engaged to be married."

The film crew leaned forward hopefully.

"It started when Amari saw my ring and assumed Jon and I were engaged, but we're not. We're a writing team. There's no relationship."

The new crew chuckled. "Seriously? You want us to believe this?" Quinn chortled.

Kerri glared at Quinn, and everyone grew silent. "Amari considers us a dream couple. We're worried that if she finds out it's all a lie, she won't be happy, and it could hurt the movie."

Jon was having a hard time listening to all this, because he knew, sometime over the last two weeks, he had fallen back in love with Kerri for real.

CHAPTER 44

December 18

OUTSIDE OF EL COYOTE, KERRI and Jon walked toward the parking attendant. Kerri searched for the valet ticket in her bag. Jon's phone dinged, and he looked down to read a text.

"The WGA holiday party is still going on. We could stop by."

"Busy day tomorrow, Jon. Besides, that sounds so depressing."

"Only depressing because we could never get in. Now we can," Jon said, showing off his new Writers Guild of America card as he searched for a few dollars to tip the valet. "Got it in the mail today."

Kerri examined the card. "Mine must have been sent to my apartment in Brooklyn."

"You can join me as my guest. No strings attached. It's at the Academy Museum. Been dying to see that place, and it might inspire you. Not that you need inspiration—you're going to direct the hell out of *Fire and Ice*."

When the car arrived, Jon tipped the valet, who opened the

door for Kerri, but she didn't get in, choosing to stand there while checking her phone.

"Hey, you are tired. Get in. We'll just go home."

"I can't."

"Why not?" Jon said, getting out of the car.

"Because I can't. I have plans. Beau's picking me up."

A Kia Soul pulled into the valet lot the wrong way, blocking the entrance. It was Beau. He looked very confused as the parking valets surrounded his car, waving their hands.

Beau called out from the car, "Kerri!"

"He's not a very good driver."

"Jon, I can't keep avoiding him," Kerri said.

"You don't need to explain anything," Jon said as he fake-smiled.

The valets were trying to get Beau to back out of the driveway onto crowded Beverly Boulevard, where cars were zipping past, but Beau was not good at backing up. Finally, a parking attendant ushered Beau out of the car, handed him a valet ticket, and drove off, clearing the small parking lot congestion. Beau walked up and hugged Kerri.

"Why are you two dressed like Mr. and Mrs. Santa Claus?" Beau wondered.

"Office party thing," Jon said. "You two have a good night. Don't keep her up too late. She has a movie to direct." Jon settled into his Jeep.

Kerri excused herself from Beau. "I have to ask Jon something about the script. Get the car."

Beau looked around. Where was his car? The valet took Beau's ticket and said, "Ten dollars."

Kerri leaned closer to Jon. "Are you okay?"

"I thought I was." And wanting to get away from Kerri and Beau as soon as possible, Jon pulled out into the traffic quickly, cutting off another driver, who leaned on the horn.

"Should he be driving?" Beau questioned.

Kerri didn't want to think about Jon. She didn't like this implication. *You two have a good night. Don't keep her up too late.* It was the jealous side of Jon that she always hated. *What does he have to be jealous of? Things are going great between us—*

"Kerri, the car's here," Beau called out.

—oh, yes, Beau. That must be it. Beau was her fiancé. Jon should have gotten used to this by now. *Well, you didn't,* Kerri thought to herself. *You had great sex with Jon and cheated on your fiancé.*

"Kerri!" Beau called again. Now their car was blocking the cars behind from leaving. Kerri walked over.

Beau asked, "Can you drive? This place scares me."

"Tip the valet."

"For what? I didn't even park. I got here. They took my car, charged me ten dollars, and now I have to tip?"

Kerri reached into her wallet and tipped the valet. "Merry Christmas," she said. The valet was very happy and even asked for a selfie with Mrs. Claus.

"Santa's a lucky man," another valet called out.

"Too bad he only comes once a year," Kerri joked. The valets roared with laughter. Kerri got into the Kia Soul, which was way too small for her.

"You didn't have to tip him," Beau said, not happy with what had transpired. "That's why I like the subway. You don't have to tip on the subway."

"Where to?" Kerri asked.

"I'm staying at the Century Hilton. By the airport."

Great, Kerri thought, calculating the extra time she would need to battle traffic to get to the production office tomorrow morning. She thought to herself, *How did I get into this mess?*

Back at the hotel, filled with tourists from around the world, Kerri walked into the suite Beau had rented. Chocolate-covered strawberries, rose petals, and champagne were waiting for her.

"You like?" Beau asked.

"It's very nice," Kerri said. "Although I won't be drinking until this movie is over. You have a drink. I need to tell you what's going on between me and Jon."

"So what's going on with you and Kerri?" Zane Marlowe, a pretentious film school classmate, asked. Zane was the one guy from film school no one wanted to talk to. He was obnoxious when they were all making short films at NYU and became even worse when he was awarded credit on a movie he had nothing to do with.

Jon had no idea how he had wound up at the bar talking with Zane. When he arrived at the WGA party, people cheered, probably only because he was still in the Santa outfit. Thinking he was an actor who had been hired for the event, guests wanted pics with Santa. When people had enough of him, he grabbed a drink at the bar, and that's when Zane showed up. The night spiraled downhill when Zane asked about his relationship with Kerri.

"Nothing's going on with me and Kerri."

"Are you sure?" Zane said.

"Kerri and I are not romantically involved. We are a writing team. And that is all."

"You used to be a couple."

"Yes, Zane, and movies used to be in black and white."

"Some still are. Did you see *The Lighthouse*? *Mank*? Del Toro's *Nightmare Alley*?"

Jon wanted to punch him. Instead, he blasted out: "Kerri and I are not a couple. She's engaged."

Zane nodded. "I think I'm going to call her."

"Didn't you hear me? She's engaged. Some guy from Brooklyn."

"Still going to take my shot, if you don't mind."

"You know what, Zane, I do mind. But I don't think that's going to stop you," Jon said as he took a shot of eggnog and rum.

Zane smiled. "You know me too well."

"Do you know, Zane, no one from film school liked you?"

"Do you think I care what those losers are doing? Probably back in some flyover state."

"Actually, a lot of them are working on my movie that's shooting."

"I thought that was shut down."

"Nope. It's going. And Kerri's directing."

"Oh, wow, that's great. I have a script that would be perfect for her. Do you think I can send it?"

"Sure, Zane. She's looking for something new." Jon knew Kerri hated Zane. They had once tried to set him up with a friend, and he had been rude and misogynistic. Afterwards, they swore never to talk to him again.

Zane had his phone out. "What's her number?"

"Three-one-zero-F-U-C-K-Y-O-U" Jon walked away. Zane

went back to trolling unproduced screenwriters and acting as if he belonged in the Academy Museum.

Jon walked past the open exhibits of the history of Hollywood, realizing he would need to come back here. There was an interactive Oscar experience where guests could enter an immersive environment that simulated the experience of accepting an Oscar on the Dolby Theatre stage. There was a long line of writers waiting to accept their Oscar.

Jon found himself on the top floor, inside the bubble, or the sphere, and looked out on the lights of LA. Somewhere out there Kerri was with Beau in a hotel room doing who knows what. He hated that he let himself go there.

"Hey, handsome," someone said softly. It was Madison. "I've been looking for you all night."

Jon was confused. *What is she doing here?* "Madison."

"I'm not stalking you. A friend invited me." As usual she looked alluring. "I saw you when you walked in. I kept an eye on you, waiting for Kerri to show up. But I can see you're solo again."

"Lukas isn't here, is he?" Jon asked, his blood starting to boil now.

"We broke up. Once he found out that I was still in love with you."

CHAPTER 45

December 18

BACK AT THE AIRPORT HILTON, the night hadn't gone the way Beau had planned. True, Kerri was in his bed, and she was wearing one of his T-shirts instead of pajamas, but she wasn't even kissing him. She was marking up a script.

"It makes sense to start with the master shot tomorrow, but that's also going to take some time to light. Psychologically we need to knock off the first shot quickly so that the crew's spirits are buoyed."

"Sure," Beau said. But he wasn't all that interested. He had hoped by now that he would be deep in a postcoital sleep. Instead, his fiancée was sitting up talking about her work.

Kerri noticed Beau was exhausted and patted him on the head. "Aww, you're so tired. Why don't you go to sleep?"

"You don't mind?"

"Let me tuck you in," Kerri said. Beau turned to his side and fell asleep.

Kerri slipped into the bathroom and closed the door. She

pulled out her phone and called Jon, and waited as the phone rang and rang. She wanted to get his advice on the order of the shots for tomorrow's shoot. Finally, he picked up—or at least someone did.

"Hello?" said a young woman's voice.

"Oh, sorry. I must have the wrong number," Kerri said quickly.

On the other end of the line was Madison. She recognized the voice. "Kerri, it's Madison."

"Oh, hi..."

"Jon's asleep. Want me to wake him?"

"No, that's okay. I'll see him tomorrow." Then Kerri quickly hung up, seething. How could he hook up with Madison again so quickly? Then she laughed to herself, as she realized that was the pot calling the kettle black.

She tiptoed back into the bedroom and was greeted by Beau's loud snores.

———————

The night was over for Kerri and Jon, but not for Amari and Richard. They were in Beverly Hills in the streets above Sunset where the houses were supersized. Richard parked his Lexus in front of a Tudor-style mansion and leaped out of the car to run around to open Amari's door. She stepped out in a stunning full-length red silk dress, perfect for a holiday party.

"You look great. My mom's going to love you," Richard said.

"The moms always do. It's the guys that I have more trouble with," Amari said.

"My mom has had her share of man trouble. She's been married five times. I was from marriage number one."

"You're the OG," Amari said with a giggle.

They approached the front door and Amari took it all in. She realized the huge house must be at least 10,000 square feet.

"How did she get so rich?" Amari asked Richard.

"She married well a few times. She had a good lawyer and invested her divorce settlements in the stock market. She's really good at it. She's always been an early adopter of new gadgets and companies. I was the first kid on the block to get those little red Netflix envelopes. And when the company split, her husband number three told her she should sell. But she ignored him and kept all her shares. A year later, she dumped him and bought this house."

"Sounds like a smart lady. I like her already."

Richard and Amari entered the lavish foyer and passed a huge twenty-foot Christmas tree decorated in silver and gold balls. Candles burned on every available surface. It was all decorated in an over-the-top way. A string quartet played Christmas carols. Waiters dressed as elves served red cosmos with a candy cane hanging on the edge of each glass. Richard grabbed one and gulped it down. He was going to need more than just one. He grabbed a second cosmo while Amari sipped hers demurely.

"Richard...slow down."

"Trust me. I need this. I'm going to see my mother."

At the mention of "mother"—she appeared. "Richard! You're here. What a pleasure."

Celeste Bryant was truly a vision in a long green velvet dress. She was in her late fifties, but her skin glowed like she was still in her twenties. Celeste air-kissed her son and was careful not to mess up her lipstick when she noticed the beautiful actress on Richard's arm.

"Celeste, this is Amari." Richard had called his mother by her first name since he was ten years old, when Celeste decided that being called "Mom" made her seem older.

"Oh, I know who she is." Celeste smiled at Amari. "I read the trades. Especially when they're about my son."

"It's so nice to meet you, Mrs. Bryant," Amari said.

"Oh, please call me Celeste. I haven't been Mrs. Bryant in at least four husbands."

"I love your Christmas decorations," Amari gushed.

"Harold thinks they're over-the-top."

"How are things going with Harold?" Richard asked.

"Not so great. At least not for him. I'll probably dump him after the holidays. I would have done it sooner, but it's so lonely to attend a holiday party solo."

Amari and Richard nodded in agreement.

"Finding true love is so hard. I thought it would get easier over the years. It hasn't," Celeste admitted sadly. "But enough sadness. You two go dance," she said with sudden excitement.

"I was hoping we could talk first," Richard said with sudden urgency. "About an investment opportunity for you."

"No, no. First, we dance."

Then the string quartet struck up an interesting rendition of "Jingle Bell Rock." Richard took Amari's hand and they started jitterbugging. Amari whooped it up as Richard twirled her. Then she started to sing along: "Jingle bell, jingle bell, jingle bell rock…" And all at once, Amari started a choreographed dance that she remembered from the third grade Christmas show at her elementary school. Richard watched her with adoration, and she grabbed his hand to join her. Soon all the guests jumped in and followed Amari's moves for an energetic line dance. Celeste was thrilled and joined them.

The song ended and everyone applauded. Amari bowed in appreciation and slipped away to the restroom.

Celeste turned to her son. "You've got a winner there."

"I know."

"I think she's more than just a client. At least for you."

"Is it that obvious?"

"To me? Yes. You need to tell her how you feel."

Richard nodded. "I will. But first I have to get the movie back on track."

Celeste listened. She knew what he wanted. What he'd come for. "How much do you need?"

"Two million. I'll pay you back. Every cent."

"Consider it done. I'll have the money wired to your account tomorrow."

"Thank you, Celeste." Richard was hugging his mother when Amari reappeared.

"There you are," Richard said. "Let's get another Christmas cosmo."

Celeste watched as Richard took Amari's hand and swept her back toward the bar area.

———————

Richard revealed to Amari that his mother had agreed to loan him the $2 million to finish their film. Amari squealed with delight and kissed Richard on the cheek.

Then Amari leaned in and kissed Richard again. This time full on the lips. It was a deep and long kiss. At that moment, Celeste passed them and smiled.

Amari whispered to Richard. "I think I'm falling in love with you."

"It's about time," Richard said happily. "I've been waiting for you my entire life."

"This is a great party, but let's get out of here."

CHAPTER 46

December 18

RICHARD AND AMARI PEELED AWAY from his mother's Beverly Hills Christmas party. As they raced down Sunset Boulevard toward the Pacific Ocean, Richard realized that he had successfully achieved one goal, but now he had a bigger goal in mind. One that he had been working toward ever since that fateful day when he first met Amari at the premiere for *The Christmas Couple*. Amari had been luminescent in that movie, and Richard had told her as much. He also insisted she needed better representation and that he was the man for the job. A week later, Amari sat in his office wearing a short mini skirt that showed off her long gorgeous legs. But any flirtation that they might have had at the movie premiere was long gone and replaced by a business relationship.

Which was why Richard was practically speeding through every light just so that they could get to Amari's Malibu Beach house before she changed her mind. He couldn't get that kiss out of his mind. And luckily, Amari kept reminding him. When they did stop at a red light at the cross-section of Sunset Boulevard and Amalfi, Amari leaned over and kissed him hungrily.

"You. Are. Amazing."

"Wow. Thank you."

"Why did it take me so long to figure that out?"

But it was a rhetorical question, and Richard didn't expect her to answer. The light turned green, and soon they were speeding through the Palisades and then making a right onto the Pacific Coast Highway.

"I have some champagne in the fridge," Amari said. "We need to toast this occasion."

"We do," Richard agreed. But he hoped to be doing more than just toasting with Amari.

They pulled into Amari's driveway and parked. Amari fumbled with the keys to the front door, and Richard helped her. The door opened, and Amari pulled Richard into the house. There was a full moon shining above.

"It's a beautiful night. Let's go in the jacuzzi."

"I think it's like fifty degrees out," Richard said and then instantly regretted it.

"I'm a Wisconsin girl, and fifty is like eighty for me."

Richard followed Amari into the kitchen. "Open the champagne, and I'll be right down."

Richard opened the fridge and found ten bottles of champagne, ranging from Dom to Veuve. He realized that he had never been this excited in his life. He'd been anticipating this moment for so long.

He popped the cork and caught it before it hit the ceiling. He found champagne flutes and was pouring the bubbly when Amari appeared in a tiny black bikini. He almost lost it when she stood so close to him. He felt like the luckiest guy in the world.

"Should we get in the jacuzzi?"

"Sure. But I don't have a suit."

"That's okay. You can go in without one. I won't look. Here's a towel."

Richard rushed to the bathroom to rip off his clothes. He emerged from the bathroom with the towel around his waist and nothing else. He followed Amari to the jacuzzi. They sat at the rim, their legs dangling in the hot bubbling water. They toasted with their champagne glasses and then sipped the expensive drink. Amari looked at her suit, disappointed.

"I'm so bummed. I couldn't find my red bikini anywhere. This black one is so not Christmassy."

"That's okay. You look great."

Amari pouted. "You sure?"

"Yes. You're amazing. Both inside and out."

"Ok, but don't ever lie to me…" Richard nodded and sipped more of the champagne. "You know that's my thing," Amari continued.

"I know it is. And I promise that I'll never lie to you."

"About anything?"

"Yes. Anything. I promise." But then Richard remembered that he'd lied to Amari about Jon and Kerri being engaged, and he suddenly felt horrible.

"What's wrong?" Amari said as she noticed he looked worried.

"Oh, I think I left something in my car." Richard got up stiffly, trying to tamp down his growing hard-on and still wearing only the towel. "I'll be right back," Richard said.

Outside, it suddenly felt freezing, far colder than 50 degrees. But Richard was determined to call Jon and tell him that he couldn't lie for him anymore.

Richard dialed Jon's number and listened to it ring. Finally, Jon answered. "Hello?" he said in a very groggy voice.

"Jon, I need you to get back together with Kerri right now. For real."

"Who is this?"

"It's Richard. I can't keep lying about you and Kerri being a couple."

"We are a couple."

"Oh, shut up, Jon. I figured it out weeks ago. You two are lying. Now it's time for you to fess up to the truth. You love Kerri, and you know it. And by the way, I got the money to finish the film."

That got Jon's attention. "Awesome!"

"Now I'm going back to make wild passionate love to Amari. Just remember what I told you." Richard clicked off his cell phone and hurried back to the front door. He was ready to make love to Amari.

But the door was locked. He couldn't believe that he hadn't bothered to check the lock! Luckily, he had his cell phone. He took it out and dialed Amari's cell, a number that he knew by heart. But the phone rang and rang and rang. He could hear the phone ringing from the upstairs bedroom. But the music by the jacuzzi was drowning it out.

Richard banged on the door loudly. He screamed out, "AMARI! AMARI! AMARI!" At that moment, bright headlights were shining on his back. He turned around to see a police car in front of the house. A policewoman got out of the car.

"Can I help you, sir?"

"Ah, yes, I was just trying to get back into Amari's house."

"At 2:00 a.m.?"

"Look, I know this looks bad."

"Your words, not mine."

"I'm her agent. I handle her deals."

"Uh-huh. Maybe you'd like to come down to the station to explain this to me."

Richard hung his head, knowing how this looked. He also knew that there was no fighting with the Malibu police. He didn't want to end up on *TMZ* like one of those drunken and disorderly people who were obsessed with a starlet. Celeste had always taught him to obey the rules. Richard got into the cop car, in the back, behind the bars. As they pulled away from Amari's house, Richard realized that in just five minutes he had gone from the greatest night of his life to the worst.

Richard sat in the cell. Not because he was in any real trouble but because it was the only available place for him to sit. He'd been there for an hour when the policewoman called out to him: "Richard Bryant. Your ride is here."

Richard walked out of the cell in a borrowed prison robe, expecting to see Celeste or someone from the agency. But it was Amari. She was no longer in her black bikini. She had on jeans and a sweatshirt. She looked at him with a rueful smile.

"Is life always going to be crazy like this with you?" Amari asked.

"I don't know… What do you think?"

Amari smiled and grabbed his hand as they exited the police station.

"I certainly hope so," Amari said with the biggest and brightest smile. She hugged him and slapped him on the butt. "Come on, let's go home."

CHAPTER 47

December 19

KERRI AND JON ARRIVED ON the set at the same time in different cars. They parked next to each other, relishing that they each had a reserved parking spot. Another something they had dreamed about. They both got out of their cars with not a smile or hello for each other. Kerri was still angry about Madison answering Jon's phone, and Jon was still miffed she didn't attend the Writers Guild Holiday Party with him. They headed toward the set together when Kerri said, "Stop. We need to talk."

She pulled Jon behind a soundstage on the Warner Brothers studio lot. "Just so you know, nothing happened with me and Beau. Well, something happened but not what you think."

"Ok, thank you for that. And just so you know, nothing happened with me and Madison. She wanted to fool around but I said no."

"Why were you with Madison?!" Kerri wanted to know.

"Because you weren't at the party with me. She showed up."

"And tried to seduce you?"

"Yes," Jon said proudly. "But I was unseducible. What happened with you and Beau? Did you break up?"

"No, we didn't break up. But I told him about the lie."

"What lie?"

"That you and I are pretending to be a couple. Because I owed that to him. I told him this morning. He promised to go along with it. He's a good guy, Jon."

"I'm sure he is."

Kerri added, "And he's coming to the set today."

"Why?"

"So he can see nothing's going on between us," Kerri said, suddenly clutching her stomach. And that's when Kerri vomited into a handy nearby trash can.

"That's inspiring," Jon said.

"Just nerves."

"Nothing to be nervous about. We've got the best damn film crew ready to go."

And Jon was right, because when they walked into the sound-stage, it was buzzing. The film school crew was moving quickly. The doom and gloom of the earlier set was gone, while this one had energy. Kerri looked up at Jon.

"Thank you," she said heartfully.

"Thank you. Now please go make our movie."

Kerri went to talk with Linda, the cinematographer. Today they were going to shoot a scene where the firefighter's parents meet the diamond heiress's parents. Drew Fox had called in some favors. They were shooting at Warner Brothers, using the set from a TV series that was in a fancy restaurant. They were on hiatus, and Drew was able to secure the location.

Richard approached them. "There's my favorite director. Good morning. Love your crew."

"Thanks," Kerri said to Richard. Then she turned to Jon. "I'm gathering..."

"I'm gathering the principals by the table so you can talk to them about the restaurant scene. Jon, can you help with the background?"

"Anything you need, boss," Jon said and hustled off.

"Jon!" Kerri called. "My parents are coming in. Put them in a good shot."

Jon smiled and went off while Kerri headed to a chair that had her name and the word DIRECTOR. She didn't take a picture, because she wanted to get to work. She looked at her script and up at the talent waiting for her at the table. "Who's that beautiful older woman chatting it up with Amari?"

"That's my mother, Celeste. Our bank. She will need a line," Richard said as he walked over to Amari.

"I'll put Jon on it."

"Hey, Kerri," Ira, her film school friend, said as he joined them. He had some paperwork for Richard to sign.

"How's it going?"

"I got a job," he said happily.

"Yes, you did," Richard said to him. "Now go do it." Ira hustled back to work.

"You hired Ira."

"Amari and I are forming a company. Ira's our new development guy."

Kerri excused herself as Quinn, the assistant director, brought out Kerri's parents to be background extras. They were dressed to the nines, and Jon held up his phone to take pictures of them while smiling at Kerri.

Linda was lighting the scene with her team. She talked as she worked. "Kerri, I was thinking we go *Untouchables* for this scene."

Kerri knew exactly what Linda intended to do. Film was the language of moviemaking, and Linda was referencing a shot in the classic *Untouchables* movie with Kevin Costner, Robert De Niro, and Sean Connery. During a dinner scene, the camera circled the table as each character spoke. It was natural and fluid.

"I might need a few extra minutes to get it right, but it will save us from needing a bunch of single shots."

Kerri loved that idea, and she let Linda know. She moved to the table. Richard's mother, Celeste, greeted her as an equal, as a professional. "I've heard so much about you from Amari. Thank you for giving me a part in your story. Oh, and by the way, I'm Celeste."

"Thank you, Celeste. Amari, can I talk to you for a moment?"

Amari walked away from the set with Kerri. "Do you want to go over the scene?"

"No, I trust you. You know this character better than I do. If I see something that I think you can do better, I'll let you know. But never in front of everyone. Our relationship—the actor/director relationship—is special."

"It is," Amari said squeezing Kerri's hand. "I think I'm falling in love with Richard. And not because his mom funded the money we needed, or she thinks I'm nice; it's because you showed me that love is right there in front of you."

And there he was—Jon with her parents. Right there in front of them. Her parents were so proud. Kerri watched as they hugged Amari. Everyone was joyous to be shooting again with Kerri as the director.

But there was one person who didn't seem happy, and that was Beau. It was Amari who noticed the sullen Beau. Kerri hadn't even noticed he had arrived. "Who's the good-looking guy? And what's his problem?"

"An old friend of the family. His name is Beau."

"Maybe Beau wants to be in the movie. Hey, Jon, see if that guy wants to be in the movie. We can use him in the background."

Jon walked up to Beau. Kerri went back to work, hoping there was no blow-up.

"Hi, Beau."

"Hello, Jon."

"They want to know if you want to be in the movie as a background extra."

"If it's okay, I don't want to be in the movie. Aren't I doing enough acting on this set to go along with the idea that you and Kerri are the couple who are engaged? And for lying about my relationship with the woman I love who everyone thinks is in love with you? And who's wearing the diamond ring that I purchased?"

"Yes, thanks for doing that by the way." Jon pivoted away. "We're good. Beau doesn't want to be in the movie. Let's shoot this thing," Jon called out. The crew cheered.

Beau watched Kerri direct, observing how everyone listened carefully to what she said. They were ready when she called, "Action," and cheered when she called, "Cut." He watched on a video monitor as Celeste and Amari had their scene. Celeste had been an actress in her twenties and thirties, and she still had it. She was a pro.

"You should never marry for money. Only for love," she told her character's granddaughter, played by Amari.

"You married for money."

"Yes, but I love money."

Cut. Cheers. And hugs. Amari hugged Celeste like laughing with a friend. Jon announced, "Moving on!" He and Kerri huddled over the script. Jon and Kerri were in perfect sync, Beau thought. They seemed like a great couple, even to Beau.

CHAPTER 48

December 19

DREW FOX WALKED ONTO THE set, worried. He asked to see Quinn, the assistant director, and Rebecca, the script supervisor, and looked over the schedules.

"How far behind are we?"

"We're not behind. We're ahead." Rebecca showed him the completed scenes that were marked up in her script book. They were indeed ahead of schedule.

"Wright was getting seven set-ups a day. You shot twenty-two set-ups already."

"Twenty-five." Quinn smiled. "Is there anything else you need? We want to get shot twenty-six off before lunch."

"Please, do your job. Keep me out of it. You are all doing great work." Quinn and Rebecca were already planning what to do next. Drew called out louder, "I said, 'You're all doing great work!'"

"Thanks, Drew," Amari called out. She was working with Cage on a scene.

Beau watched it all happen from video village. He learned that, if he put on the headphones, sometimes the person in charge of the recording the audio would leave the crew microphones on, and he could listen in. Kerri and Jon came over to Drew. Beau listened...

"Wow, your team is amazing, running around with their camera."

"We're off the sticks a lot, but Linda holds the camera for that. She's got a steady hand," Kerri said.

"We want to reshoot the scenes that didn't come out well that he-who-shall-not-be-named directed."

"That's a good idea," Drew said. "How are you holding up, Kerri?"

"It's exhausting. But it's fun."

"I don't mean to exhaust you more, but do you mind interviewing with a local reporter? The movie received so much bad press I wanted to show them we are up and running again. It will keep the completion bond people off our back and help with foreign presales. I promise only to take a few minutes of your lunch hour. I want both of you on this, okay?"

"Why not just Kerri?" Jon asked.

"You guys wrote it. Saved it. And now you're filming it. You're an engaged couple in love working together, which would play really well."

They both agreed. Right after the last shoot, the crew applauded and broke for lunch. Kerri and Jon had a quick trip to hair and makeup and were ready for their close-up.

Beau did not go to lunch. He put down the headphones and watched. The *Entertainment Tonight* reporter started right away, telling the story of how the movie had fallen apart, and how they had somehow rescued it. He added that it was an only-in-Hollywood story because the writers, one of whom was now directing the movie, have been a couple since their days at New York University film school.

"You were always a couple. Starting at NYU Grad Film."

"Not always," Jon said. "She blew me off at first."

"We started liking each other on one Valentine's Day when we were on a set. I think it was Henry's. He's editing this movie now," Kerri offered.

"And you're directing," the reporter prompted.

"And she's very good at it," Jon said.

"Jon and I wrote a great script. We have amazing talent with Amari and Cage. And Drew Fox has come on to help us finish it."

"This will be your first produced movie," the reporter continued. "And it took a while, and then it started shooting, and bam! It shut down. How did you get through it?"

Kerri and Jon looked at each other and said at the same time: "Together." They laughed.

Beau was watching all of this and was about to walk away when—

"And you're engaged. And that is a beautiful ring. Nice taste, Jon."

"Thanks."

"Where did you get it?" the reporter asked. Kerri's mind went in search of an answer. Jon, who had the gift of gab, was on it.

"We always talked about getting married. And I wanted to surprise her this Christmas. That was before this script was set up. We had no idea any of this was going to happen," Jon said, making up the story like he had told it a thousand times. Kerri was holding on for dear life. She had no idea what Jon was going to say. He smiled at her. "We didn't have any money. Or I didn't. So, I got lucky. I went to a pawn shop."

"I hope that ring's not stolen," the reporter joked.

"No, but close to it. Some guy had flown across the country to propose to his girlfriend. When she said no, he had a little too much to drink and sold it to a pawn shop. I bought it for a lot less than it's worth. Not the most romantic story…"

They all laughed. Out of the corner of her eye, Kerri saw Beau getting up from a chair and walking away angrily.

"I'm sure it is for the both of you. What's next for you two?"

"I need a vacation," Kerri said. When the interview was over, Kerri looked for Beau. She wanted to apologize about the ring story, but Jon blocked her path.

"Kerri, we have to talk," Jon said. "I can't lie anymore."

Kerri stopped, and so did Beau. Kerri found herself between the two men. She felt as if the ground was shaking—that her world was off-balance. Because it was. Not because of the emotions colliding inside her, but because of the fault lines colliding deep underneath her. It was an earthquake!

As the ground, the stage, and the world wobbled in instability, Kerri found herself tripping and falling into one man's arms.

"I got you," Jon said.

Kerri hugged Jon. The shaking on the ground stopped. But she was shaking inside.

"It was a small one. Maybe a five. You're good."

"The shaking stopped as soon as I put my arms around you," Kerri said.

"We can put that scene in our next movie," Jon said. Neither of them had stopped hugging. He moved to kiss her when the door to the soundstage slammed.

Kerri turned, suddenly remembering Beau, and realized that he had stormed out. She took a deep breath and took a step toward the door to follow him when she stopped. She smiled and noticed her anxiety had dropped to zero. She'd call Beau and apologize after he'd cooled down.

Jon had surprised the crew by getting El Coyote to cater lunch. Kerri sat with Linda and Quinn looking over the afternoon schedule. She figured she would connect with Beau later. Kerri turned her phone back on. There was a big congratulations from their agent, Charlotte. And a selfie from Beau. He was sitting on a New York City–style stoop. His message was Meet me on New York Street. Kerri wondered, *Did Beau fly home?* How did he get back to NY so quickly? Then she realized: New York Street was the name of the street on the studio lot. She checked with Quinn about what time the next shot was and figured she had about thirty minutes until she resumed filming.

That was more than enough time to find Beau. She took the tour tram to New York Street, walked up to Beau, and sat down next to him.

"I have a few minutes before I have to get back to the set," Kerri said, concerned about Beau.

"I don't know what happened to you out here, Kerri, but I think we can get past this."

"In New York?"

"The real New York," Beau emphasized.

"I'm not moving back, Beau."

Beau didn't move. He'd had a feeling in the pit of his stomach that this was what Kerri would say.

"My career is here."

"And so is Jon. Your ex-writing partner. Air quotes on the ex," Beau said.

"It's not about Jon."

"I thought we were happy."

"I thought so too," Kerri admitted. She had been thinking about this for the last few days.

"When we met, you were a schoolteacher. Drama. And I believe you still are. And you're a great teacher."

"When we met," Kerri said, "I had forgotten how to dream. This whole movie—"

"And Jon…"

"Yes, Beau, and Jon."

Kerri jumped up. "I'm going to stay in LA and try to keep doing what I love to do. I loved you, Beau. I did. But I changed back to the person I had forgotten about."

"I don't know who you are anymore, Kerri."

"That's funny. Because for the first time in a long time, I do. And I think I have something that belongs to you now, because it doesn't belong to me anymore."

Kerri put her right thumb and index finger around the diamond ring and tried to pull it off, but it wouldn't budge because her finger was swollen. "I can't get it off."

CHAPTER 49

December 19

KERRI STRUTTED BACK ON SET to find Jon was waiting for her by the door, and she almost bumped into him.

"Were you spying on me?" Kerri asked.

"No, I wasn't trying to spy on you."

Kerri called out, "Amari. Cage. I'll need you in five. I want to talk about the next scene." They responded by raising their *Fire and Ice*–themed water bottles. "Where did those bottles come from?"

"They arrived when you were outside. Cage bought them for everyone. So how did it go?"

"Go? How did what go?"

"You and Beau." Jon wanted to know desperately, but Kerri wasn't about to reveal anything.

"Jon, remember when we started this whole thing, we both said we would keep it professional." Kerri had a surprisingly stern tone. Even she wasn't sure where it was coming from. "So where is it?"

"Where's what?" Jon asked.

"The rewritten scene for Amari and Cage. You said you would get to it."

Jon handed her the pages he had in his back pocket. She grabbed them. "Really, Jon?" She read them quickly. "An engagement scene?"

"I just felt we needed something to represent what would be the end of Tiffany's party days. So, the firefighter proposes. But she doesn't answer right away. He tells her that he will wait for her and that one day her diamond heart would melt for him."

"And this transitions into the firehouse scene, which we already filmed," Kerri added with excitement. Looking through the pages, she said, "It's a little long."

"I wasn't sure what to cut."

Kerri was deep in thought. "Not going to cut anything. We can play the last two pages over memory clips from the footage we have and some shots we can grab. Then we can use all the improved dialogue from the firehouse scene. She climbs up, and they drive off into the sunset. I love it, Jon." She was looking into his eyes. "Great work."

"Did he blow up?"

"No, he took it rather well."

"Funny, I pegged him for a blow-up kind of guy."

Five minutes later, Amari and Cage were in a booth filming the scene.

"You know this is never going to work," Amari, as Tiffany, told Cage as the firefighter. "What will you do if another sex video of me emerges?"

"Hopefully, I'm in that one," Cage said. "Look, Tiffany, I don't care about your past. I care about our future."

"We're two different people. Two different worlds. We're fire and ice."

"I don't want to put out your fire, Tiffany."

"I'm sorry, Mike. We should never have let things get so far."

"So, what are you going to do? Go back and be with Beau...?"

"Cut!" Kerri called out. She looked at Jon, who was more than a little embarrassed.

"What's wrong?" Cage wanted to know. "I got the line, right?"

"Yeah," Jon said. "I meant to write Bennet. Not Beau. Change to Bennet."

"Who's Beau?"

"Don't worry about it, Cage."

"Oh, if I'm proposing, I need a ring." A PA rushed to props to get one. "I see you two laughing. Who is this Beau? Is there something my character needs to know?"

Kerri laughed. "Beau was a mistake. Let's reset. Take it again."

"A mistake. Beau was a mistake?" the real Beau shouted, enraged. For some reason, he was back on the set. He had walked in on the worst part and was seething.

"It was a mistake in the script, Beau."

Kerri couldn't believe it. Jon was right. If this was a cartoon, steam would be coming out of Beau's ears.

"My mistake was going along with all these lies!"

"What lies?" Amari said.

"I want my ring back. Now."

"We're in the middle of shooting," Kerri told him.

"I don't care. I want my engagement ring back, Kerri! You don't get to wear it, since you broke up with me. Use some soap or something to get it off!"

Amari got up, walked over to Kerri, who was struggling

to take off the ring. "Kerri, why are you taking off Jon's engagement ring?"

"Because it's not Jon's… It belongs to him. This is Beau. who used to be my fiancé."

"Oh, before you were engaged to Jon."

Beau said to Amari, "She was never engaged to Jon."

Now Kerri waited for the smoke to come out of Amari's ears. "We need to talk right now! My dressing room!" Amari marched off. Before Kerri followed, she managed to get the ring off.

"You didn't have to do that, Beau," Kerri said, crestfallen.

Beau looked around. Everyone was glaring at him.

"Get out of here, Beau," Jon said angrily.

"You don't get to tell me what to do. You stole my fiancée."

"She made her own choice. Now, I'm done talking. Get out!" Jon stepped up to Beau. Beau turned away and hurried off, only to slam into the production assistant returning with the prop ring. They collided. The rings went flying. As did Beau. He stumbled back to his feet, grabbing the engagement ring on the floor.

"I don't like you Hollywood people filling the world with stories about the rich being unhappy and how love conquers all. If you're ever in Brooklyn, don't call me!"

"Why would I call him?" Jon asked as the door slammed behind Beau. Richard picked up the other ring and handed it back to Jon, who scrutinized the ring. "This is the wrong ring. He took the prop ring."

A moment later, Beau walked back into a very quiet set and approached Jon, who was holding Beau's grandmother's ring.

"I'd like my ring back," Beau said.

"Me too," Jon said.

Jon and Beau exchanged rings.

Although Jon had gotten the cheap prop ring, he'd clearly gotten the better deal.

———————————

Amari was staring at Kerri. "I'm sorry I lied. Please let me finish the movie, and you never have to see me again."

"Why would I do that?" Amari said, surprising Kerri.

"Because I lied."

"You sure did."

"And you hate liars."

"That's right. But you know what's worse?"

Kerri gulped. "There's a worse?"

Amari continued, "You lied to yourself. You can tell me that you were pretending that you and Jon were engaged, but you couldn't hide the truth that you still love him. That was real. I saw you together. At your worst. And at your best. You were always there for each other. Your love was my light," Amari said, adding, "You can use these lines in the script if you want."

"So, you're not angry with me?" Kerri asked.

"People do crazy things for love. You should tell Jon how you feel. I think he's going to say the same thing."

"When did you become so smart about love?" Kerri wondered.

"When I hung out with you and Jon."

CHAPTER 50

December 22

THE CAST AND CREW WAITED expectantly for Kerri to call out the words they'd been waiting for her to say: "And that's a wrap, folks! Merry Christmas, everyone!"

The cast and crew erupted in applause. Everyone was hugging each other with happiness. They'd wrapped up their first professional movie. Drew clapped loudly and walked over to Kerri. He shook her hand. Jon suddenly appeared. Kerri felt herself melting at the sight of him. Now that she'd said goodbye to Beau, she was suddenly nervous that Jon might not still like her.

"Great job, Kerri."

"Thank you," Kerri purred, and then, hoping that she didn't sound too ridiculous, said, "I appreciate that," in a more serious tone. Jon's lips curved into a smile.

"Hey, before we start packing up, let's do the Secret Santa exchange!" Quinn yelled out.

"Ok, but I want to go first," Jon said loudly and then dropped down to one knee in front of Kerri. Everyone turned to watch. Kerri was in shock. What was happening?

"Kerri, will you work with me for the rest of my life?" Jon held out the prop ring.

Kerri said, "Yes!" She and Jon kissed. The cast and crew clapped even louder than before.

"Do you know what this means?" Jon said.

"I think I do…"

"It means you are never getting rid of me."

"There's no getting rid of us. I love you, Jon," Kerri said as she choked back tears of happiness.

"I love you too," Jon said. They kissed again. Their classmates, their crew, their producers, everyone on that set cheered.

Amari cued the fake snow. It was her idea. They all watched as snowflakes fell from the rafters. It truly was going to be a wonderful Christmas.

EPILOGUE

December 25

IT WAS CHRISTMAS AT AMARI'S Malibu beach house. Amari and Richard greeted all their guests in Mr. and Mrs. Santa Claus sartorial splendor. Jon and Kerri arrived, looking blissfully in love wearing matching Christmas sweaters. Troy and Diane followed wearing matching holiday sweaters. The doorbell continued to ring as all the film school friends/crew showed up, feeling like they had landed in Oz.

Jon's phone beeped. He kissed Kerri. "I'll be right back." Kerri had no idea what Jon was up to and was shocked when, a few minutes later, Jon appeared, pushing his tuxedo-dressed father in a wheelchair.

"I had to have my dad with us on Christmas."

Kerri hugged Jon's dad. His eyes were cloudy, but when he saw Kerri, he had a moment of recognition and seemed to brighten for a moment.

"Why did he get all dressed up?"

"Because..."

"Because of what, Jon?"

"Because of this," Jon said. He took Kerri's hand and led her out onto the terrace overlooking the water. Below on the beach there were chairs and a flower-covered arch.

"Is someone getting married?" Kerri wondered.

"I was hoping we would today."

By now the party had settled down, the music was lowered, and all eyes were on Kerri and Jon.

"I don't even have a dress," Kerri said.

Diane appeared with the wedding dress box. "Sure, you do. I went back the next day to pick up the altered dress."

"We went back," said Troy.

"It's Christmas, Kerri, and the best and only gift we can give each other is each other."

"You never gave up on me," Kerri said, gripping Jon's hand.

"I never gave up on us," Jon said. "I know how much you never wanted a big wedding."

"You remembered."

"We have our parents here and all our best friends."

Everyone watched Kerri as she looked from Jon to her parents to her friends, making a decision before blurting out, "Yes, yes, I will marry you today, Jon Romano." The crowded Malibu mansion erupted in cheers.

"Who's going to marry us?" Kerri asked.

"I figured it would be appropriate if it was Mrs. Claus."

Amari, dressed as Mrs. Claus, appeared perfectly on cue.

"It's your lucky day, kid; guess who just became an ordained minister!" Amari called out.

The group all cheered. Kerri hustled away to get into her dress while Jon slipped off to get into a rented tux.

A scant twenty minutes later, they were on the beach walking down the aisle to a recording of "Over the Rainbow."

And so it was that Kerri and Jon, the couple who had faked an engagement, actually did marry after falling back in love with each other. The setting couldn't have been more perfect, as they were surrounded by their families and friends, facing each other on a beach outside a movie star's Malibu Colony mansion, being married by Mrs. Claus.

Kerri noted the setting sun.

"It's magic hour, Jon."

"Every hour with you is magic," Jon said and then broke into a smile.

"That is too cheesy, but I love it!"

And when Kerri and Jon kissed, Richard cued the fireworks. They exploded in the air in a burst of Christmas red and green. No words were needed. Kerri and Jon smiled and watched—the perfect movie moment for the perfect movie couple.

Acknowledgments

This book wouldn't have happened without the tireless guidance of our editor, Deb Werksman at Sourcebooks, and our agent, Haley Heidemann at WME. You were both a joy to work with throughout the entire process.

At Sourcebooks, we're also grateful to Alyssa Garcia who promoted our first book with such gusto. And to Susie Benton, Jocelyn Travis, and Meaghan Summers who led the book through the editing process.

To everyone at WME who helped us along the way during the writing of this book: Abigail Johnson, Sabrina Taitz, Ty Anania, Tracy Fisher, Alicia Everett and Pat Polite.

For our colleagues at the Newhouse School at Syracuse University and the English & Creative Writing department at SUNY Oswego. We're forever thankful for your kindness and support.

Many thanks to the bookstores who hosted our signing events for our first novel: The Ripped Bodice in LA, P&T Knitwear in NYC, Barnes & Noble in Syracuse, Rivers End Bookstore in Oswego, and Katherine Byrnes and Laura Mostofi at the Michigan Shores Club in Chicago. And to our friends at Christmas Con, can't wait to see you again!

To our family, especially Kevin Aires for helping make the architect character authentic, and to Sabrina, Ava, Eric, and Isla, for your endless enthusiasm.

Finally, to everyone who encouraged us to keep living the dream when we had our own trouble with tinsel, especially Juliet's mother, Ginny Aires, who passed away in 2022 and always reminded us to "just keep writing."

To all the readers who enjoyed *The Summer of Christmas*, we hope you enjoy *The Trouble with Tinsel*.

About the Authors

Juliet Giglio and Keith Giglio are a husband-wife screenwriting duo who had their meet-cute in an elevator while attending NYU Grad Film school. Their first novel was *The Summer of Christmas*. Their most recent produced films include Reba McEntire's *Christmas in Tune*, *Dear Christmas*, *A Very Nutty Christmas*, and *Christmas Reservations*. Other credits include Disney's *Tarzan*, *Pizza My Heart*, *Return to Halloweentown*, *Joshua*, and *A Cinderella Story*. Juliet and Keith are both professors who teach screenwriting at SUNY Oswego and Syracuse University, respectively. They divide their time between Syracuse and Sag Harbor. To learn more, visit jkgiglio.com.